"Mom!"

The shout came from the barn.

Tucker straightened, muscles bunching to react. There were dangers on a ranch. He'd known how to face them as a child, but city kids didn't.

A light touch on his arm stopped him.

"It's all right, Tucker." Jenny smiled. All he could take in was the prickle of sensation under her fingers. "That was a two-syllable 'Mom.' That's the my-brother-is-being-mean-to-me, life-is-unfair, I-want-to-play-the-video-game-now call. Not the call-the-ambulance call."

She took her hand away, gave him a final smile and headed to the barn. Obviously she was feeling a little superior.

No need, Jenny. I forfeit. No contest when you're up against somebody who doesn't know anything about kids, anything about families. And won't ever learn.

No contest against somebody like me.

Dear Reader,

Happy New Year! May this year bring you happiness,
good health and all that you wish for. And at Silhouette
Special Edition, we're hoping to provide you with a year
full of books that are chock-full of happiness!

In January, don't miss stories by some of your favorite
authors: Curtiss Ann Matlock, Myrna Temte,
Phyllis Halldorson and Patricia McLinn. This month
also brings you *Far To Go*, by Gina Ferris—a
heartwarming addition to her FAMILY FOUND series.

The January selection of our THAT SPECIAL WOMAN!
promotion is *Hardhearted* by Bay Matthews. This is the
tender tale of a woman strong enough to turn a gruff,
lonely, hardhearted cop into a true family man. Don't
miss this moving story of love. Our THAT SPECIAL
WOMAN! series is a celebration of our heroines—and
the wonderful men they fall in love with. THAT SPECIAL
WOMAN! is friend, wife, lover—she's each one of us!

In Silhouette Special Edition, we're dedicated to
publishing the types of romances that you dream about—
stories that delight as well as bring a tear to the eye.
That's what Silhouette Special Edition is all about—
special books by special authors for special readers.

I hope that you enjoy this book and all the stories to
come.

Sincerely,

Tara Gavin
Senior Editor

Please address questions and book requests to:
Reader Service
U.S.: P.O. Box 1325, Buffalo, NY 14269
Canadian: P.O. Box 1050, Niagara Falls, Ont. L2E 7G7

PATRICIA
McLINN

NOT A FAMILY MAN

Silhouette®

SPECIAL ▼ **EDITION**®

Published by Silhouette Books
America's Publisher of Contemporary Romance

To Bill, who—
after he stopped laughing—
answered all my questions. Thanks!

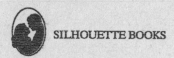 SILHOUETTE BOOKS

ISBN 0-373-09864-2

NOT A FAMILY MAN

Copyright © 1994 by Patricia McLaughlin

PATRICIA McLINN

says she has been spinning stories in her head since childhood, when her mother insisted she stop reading at the dinner table. As the time came for her to earn a living, Patricia shifted her stories from fiction to fact—she became a sportswriter and editor for newspapers in Illinois, North Carolina and the District of Columbia. Now living outside Washington, D.C., she enjoys traveling, history and sports, but is happiest indulging her passion for storytelling.

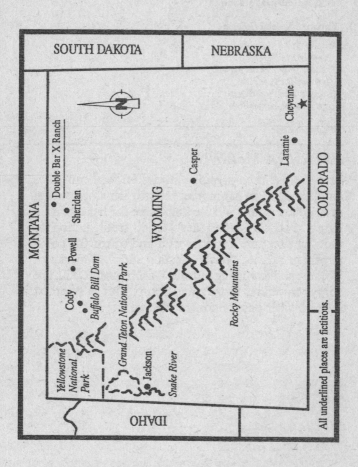

SOUTH DAKOTA

NEBRASKA

MONTANA

COLORADO

IDAHO

WYOMING

N

Double Bar X Ranch

Sheridan

Powell

Cody

Buffalo Bill Dam

Grand Teton National Park

Yellowstone National Park

Jackson

Snake River

Rocky Mountains

Casper

Laramie

Cheyenne

All underlined places are fictitious.

Chapter One

"*Guinevere* Peters. What the hell kind of name is Guinevere?"

Tucker Gates absorbed the glare that accompanied Deaver's outraged words without flinching. He'd been absorbing those glares nearly full-time for fifteen years now. They hardly nicked him these days. And this one wasn't even truly directed at him. He was just handy.

"The kind of name that belongs to someone about as likely to take an interest in the Double Bar X and Park County, Wyoming, as you are to start collecting Fabergé eggs," Tucker said calmly.

"Eggs? What'd I wanna collect eggs for? Manny gets 'em at the store these days."

"My point exactly."

"Eggs! Why're you yammerin' about eggs when we got something *serious* to discuss? Don't even keep chickens around the place anymore! Eggs?"

Tucker took a deep swallow of the thick brew that spurted caffeine directly into his tired bloodstream.

"What is there to discuss?"

"What? This Guinevere, that's what!"

"I don't see that it makes any difference if it's Guinevere Peters or Etienne de Salare who officially owns the Double Bar X. We'll have as much contact with Guinevere as we had with Etienne a few years back. Probably less."

Deaver had recovered sufficiently to give a bit of his cackling laugh. "That's right. I'd about forgot his secretary calling that time to find out if we were close enough to Aspen for the big boss to stop by between runs down the ski slopes." He cackled again. "Yeah, you gave that Frenchy a geography lesson, and we didn't hear any more from 'em."

"Only the occasional official correspondence. And that's all we'll hear from this Guinevere Peters."

"But I thought the French guy sold the Double Bar to the Ferrington bunch."

"He did. And we heard even less from Ferrington Corporation when de Salare sold them the Double Bar. Now we've been officially informed—" he held up the letter he'd been reading to Deaver "—that Ferrington Corporation has sold it to Guinevere Peters."

Actually, judging by the letter's date, they'd been informed more than a month ago, but experience had taught Tucker that letters from corporations were easily left on hold when things got busy around the Double Bar—and with cows dropping calves in bursts now, busy didn't start to describe it. Seemed to him there were a couple more Ferrington envelopes in the stack on his desk. He'd get to them eventually. If that didn't suit them, they'd call.

"We're being passed around like a hot potato," grumbled Deaver.

Tucker shrugged. "Doesn't make any difference to us who owns the Double Bar. Doesn't change when calving season comes or which fences need tending or how much rain we get."

He looked out the window into April's chill dark, almost believing he could see the familiar acres reaching toward the peaked skyline. Or the nearby buildings where he and Deaver would likely spend the night helping a couple more cows bring calves into the world. Why'd the creatures always seem to choose to be born in the middle of the night?

In reality, the window reflected back a room almost as familiar as the scene beyond it, and considerably warmer. He saw bookshelves, filing cabinets and an oversize desk from which he'd run the Double Bar X for more than a decade under three—no, this latest one made it four—absentee owners.

As far as he was concerned, having learned the lesson early and hard, those were the only kind of people to work for. The kind who stayed the hell away, and out of his life while he ran their business.

"Time to relieve Manny and Karl. Let's go."

"But, geez, Tucker, bein' owned by a *woman.*"

Tucker fought down a grin. Except that his voice hit the lower registers, old Deave sounded just like a kid horrified by the notion of playing with girls.

"It won't make any difference, Deaver. You'll see."

Jenny knew the silence from the back seat was ominous. But she was too grateful to care.

She didn't know how much longer she could have withstood the whining—terrible to call your own children whiners, but she'd finally learned to call a spade a spade. And Greg and Debbie *had* been whining. In spades.

Whining while they closed up the house. Whining while they waited at Chicago's O'Hare Airport. Whining in the air and whining on the ground during the delay in Denver. The flight to Wyoming had provided something of a respite, but only because they couldn't be heard over the commuter-plane engine without shouting. They'd more than made up for it when she'd insisted the three of them take the rental car and drive directly to the ranch instead of spending a night in the Cody Holiday Inn.

"You're going to deny us a final night in civilization?" her daughter had demanded tragically.

That remark had felt like a special betrayal. Barely a year older than Greg's nine, Debbie had always been the quieter, more observant and blessedly less critical of her children.

"Yes."

She'd had to make the decision to go on to the ranch without making a stop. She could feel her own will eroding under the tension of the trip, her children's unrelenting resistance and the cumulative effect of a year's worth of drastic changes.

Jenny hadn't even stopped to cancel the hotel reservation. She feared if she stepped into the impersonal comfort of the lobby, she'd just curl up on the floor until somebody came and took care of her.

When she realized she'd taken the wrong highway out of Cody, she didn't turn back, unwilling to get even that close to temptation. Instead, she kept going, reading the map by the overhead light found only after fumbling around the strange car with no help from her children.

At least there was little traffic on the road, so if she wove across the center line it didn't really matter. This was a strange sensation for someone who'd always kept her path carefully inside the yellow lines.

She turned onto the narrow road the map promised would carry her back toward where she wanted to go.

"This is the middle of *nowhere*," Greg wailed.

"It's not the middle of anywhere," Debbie corrected grimly. "Not even nowhere. It's gotta be the outer edge of nowhere."

Jenny didn't answer. She needed every bit of energy just to keep going through the dark, unpopulated landscape.

It was barely ten o'clock, but it had the feel of the small hours of the morning—that deserted, lonely, isolated feeling of the darkest hours. It felt familiar.

Occasionally, a light betrayed an inhabited outpost. But now she didn't feel drawn to them, no urge to stop the car, knock on the door and ask to be taken in.

She stopped keeping track of time or miles. In the quiet, she found she wanted to keep hurtling along through the dark, with the black silhouette of mountains to her left and the unknown all around her, even behind her.

"That's it, isn't it? Don't you see the sign?"

She hadn't. And she wouldn't have if Greg hadn't pointed it out. She would have kept driving until the tires stopped rolling. It had been so hard to get started, she wasn't sure what would happen when she stopped.

She turned sharply into the road, spraying gravel onto the paved surface they'd just left, and jolting the car over the ruts. All three of them let out grunts as fannies reconnected with car seats.

"Geez, Mom!"

"Sorry. I'm sor—" She bit it off. No more apologizing.

Once her tires found the ruts instead of fighting them, it wasn't too bad. Really not much worse than sections of the Edens Expressway that hadn't been repaved lately. Although, Jenny realized as she looked at the speedometer, for the same amount of suspension-jolting, she would be going sixty miles an hour there instead of the nine here.

Bare-limbed trees lined the road, creating a winding ribbon of darkness. The silence in the back seat tightened, and she felt as if she'd been driving on this dirt road for twice as long as she'd been on the highway. Despite the gloves she wore, her fingers were so cold it hurt to bend them, so she held the steering wheel mostly with her thumbs and palms.

Another curve. But at the same time, the road widened and the trees stepped back, opening for a circular road. She slowed almost to a stop.

The loop enclosed a patch of earth about a hundred feet wide. At its opposite side stood a two-story farmhouse, painted yellow and with only one first-story window lit. Behind it and to the right stood a massive barn in faded red, plus angles and slices of buildings that suggested a hodge-podge of structures of varying purposes and vintages. Floodlights atop three poles lit the scene.

She followed the road around. To the right of the farm-house it widened into an area that once might have been graveled. She tried to look at everything at once, to sort the impressions and questions. From the silence behind her, she suspected the children were doing the same.

With a city-dweller's instinct, she pulled the car into the most brightly lit area. She didn't notice it was also the wettest area until the car stopped moving forward, although the wheels kept turning.

"Oh, great! Now we're stuck!"

She gritted her teeth at Greg's too-perfect rendering of his father's tone.

"Since we aren't going anywhere else, it doesn't matter. Let's get out."

She couldn't stretch her leg quite far enough to avoid getting a swatch of mud on her polished flats, but she reached dry land and had time to look around while her children skirmished over which side to exit, what path to take and the "grossness" of the trip through the mud.

The stark lighting gave the buildings the otherworldly, faintly ominous appearance of an Edward Hopper painting. Beyond them was night so dark it seemed to have substance and weight.

"Just a barn," Jenny muttered to herself, pushing back her growing unease. A barn, a shed of some sort and a, uh, a garage, maybe, and... She had no idea what the other buildings were.

A man came out of the building to their right that Jenny had identified as the barn, and eyed them while he wiped his hands on a bandanna. He was no taller than Jenny's five foot six and wiry except for a gentle bulge over the top of his jeans. His hair was what her mother used to describe as salt-and-pepper, because Alexandra Ferrington would have considered it impolite to actually say someone was going gray. In this case, the salt had the upper hand, and the pepper had started off as cayenne.

With her best smile, Jenny started forward, but moving cautiously to avoid the generous number of mudholes. Was that ice forming a glistening skin on their tops? So much for spring.

"Tucker!"

The man's bellow made Jenny jump and stop abruptly. It even quieted the disgruntled mutterings from her children.

A door opened in a small building to their left and someone emerged, so brightly backlit that the figure appeared merely as a man's lanky silhouette.

"Visitors," the first man announced with a jerk of his head toward where Jenny stood, uncertain whether to move ahead, turn back or face this newcomer.

"Help you, ma'am?" The voice was a slightly raspy drawl, marginally polite but not patient.

Before she could form an answer, Greg gave a disgusted snort from behind her. "Yeah, she could use a lot of help."

The figure shifted slightly, apparently to take in Greg, slouching in his baggy pants and oversize Bulls T-shirt under the already abused lightweight ski jacket he'd just gotten that winter. Something in the tenor of that indiscernible look spoke of disapproval, and, as often as she'd tried to get Greg to straighten up—posture, as well as attitude—she tensed.

The figure turned back toward her.

"Need directions, ma'am?"

"No, I—"

"Yeah, which way is Chicago?"

Why couldn't Greg shut up?

This time the figure turned more fully toward Greg, and she saw the outline of a sharp chin and, when he pushed back the low brim of his cowboy hat, a strong forehead and straight nose.

Even before he spoke, his body language had her motherly instincts on alert to defend her offspring from a putdown. She opened her mouth, but nothing came out.

Maybe one putdown wouldn't be so bad. She'd been listening to Greg's snide delivery since first light and she was tired, so tired....

"Well," the figure drawled. "Right offhand, I'd say it's east of here a ways."

The first man made a derisive sound, but Greg opened his mouth for another round, too young, too full of himself to know he'd lost the last one.

"Actually," Jenny interposed, "we were looking for the Double Bar X Ranch."

The man turned to her, caution more than welcome evident in his posture and tone. "You found it."

She let out a breath she hadn't been aware of holding. "Thank heavens."

"What do you want here?" demanded the first man, older, shorter and squatter than the silhouetted figure.

"We're staying here."

"The hell you are!" the older man exclaimed.

"Mom?" Debbie sounded shaky.

Jenny felt shaky too, but forced herself to stand straight.

"We *are* staying here, Mr., uh...mister." *Strong start, weak finish.* "It was arranged through Ferrington, because..."

Because, not knowing how to go about it, she'd let her father's office take over. She'd told herself it was because she had so many other things to arrange, but here in this starkly lit oasis amid foreign darkness, she knew the truth. She squared her shoulders. She grimaced inwardly. She still had a long way to go. But that was exactly why she'd come to Wyoming.

"Owners!" The older man grumbled under his breath and turned his head toward the darkness behind him.

From the sound, Jenny suspected he'd spit, but at least she didn't see it.

The lanky silhouette moved forward into the light, resolving into a lanky man wearing jeans and a blue work shirt stained by a long day. Strong arms emerged from rolled-up sleeves, with dark hair curling below the cowboy hat whose brim shadowed his face. With those three slow steps, he'd taken command of the spotlight without even trying. Jenny realized everybody was waiting for him to speak. If she had gumption, she'd take charge, she'd...

"There's been a mix-up, ma'am. Ferrington no longer owns the Double Bar X."

He was so sure of himself, her apology came automatically. "I'm sorry if there's been a mix-up, but—"

The slightly raspy voice rode right over her explanation. "We'll straighten that out later. What we'll do now is put you folks up for the night—"

"What! Tucker—"

"Deaver." The even-toned word sounded more quelling than a shout. "It's late. It would take 'em an hour or more to get back to Cody. You want to send a woman and two children back out this time of night?"

She noticed he hadn't bothered to ask her what *she* wanted to do.

"Wouldn't bother me a bit," the older man said staunchly.

One side of the lanky man's mouth lifted. At least she thought it did. It was hard to tell amid the shadows and dark stubble on his face.

"Well, we're not going to. We're going to put them up for the night. Then we'll set this straight in the morning. In the meantime, I'm Tucker Gates, general manager of the Double Bar X. And this member of the local welcoming committee is Deaver Smith."

"You're the manager?"

Maybe he heard something more in her voice than simple relief, because his "yes" had an echo of wariness.

"Then we don't have to wait until morning to straighten this out. It's very simple. These are my children, Greg and Debbie, and I'm Jenny Peters—Guinevere Peters—and I'm the new owner of the Double Bar X."

Tucker Gates said nothing.

What Deaver Smith said had more to do with what street sweepers clean up after horse-drawn wagons come through than with the neighborhood welcoming committee.

* * *

If she'd known what was in store for her, she might have stayed in Illinois. In fact, she might have stayed in bed.

It wasn't the welcome Jenny would have hoped for. Heaven knows the kids' response hadn't been what she would have hoped for. Not even this house was what she would have hoped for.

Up close, the yellow exterior could use at least a good washing and the back porch that a still-silent Tucker Gates led them across needed a wholesale cleaning. Everything that Jenny saw testified to the need for attention—not only the clumps of mud scraped loose just short of the door and left to dry into deformed bricks, but the broken step stool, the plastic bucket with a tear in its side and a nearly bald broom that rested on similar detritus mercifully hidden in the shadows.

The inside wasn't much better, though in a different way. With one exception, the rooms she glimpsed as their ragged procession trailed Tucker Gates's long strides were clear of all extraneous decoration. In fact they were lifeless. Sheets covered large shapes that could be a sofa, a chair, a dining-room table, but in the dim light they resembled huge, wily beasts—or an overcrowded graveyard with blank headstones. The drapes were closed, the walls bare.

With no offer of help with their luggage from either Tucker Gates or Deaver Smith, they'd each grabbed the overnight case Jenny had insisted they carry on-board "in case." She'd been thinking along the lines of lost luggage, not a sojourn in the Addams Family mansion.

She didn't even reprimand Greg when he let the leather end of his bag *bump, bump, bump* against the wall as they went up the stairs.

On the shadowy second floor, the Double Bar X's manager bundled covering sheets off two single beds in one poorly lit room and off another single in a second room, stirring faint clouds of dust that drew a triplet sneeze from the travelers.

Pointing first to one hall door, then another, he said, "Bathroom. Closet." With that, he headed downstairs.

Greg and Debbie stared at her wordlessly. Reproach shouted from their nearly identical blue eyes. At least they were too tired, or too horrified, to say the words out loud.

Jenny forced a smile. "Debbie, why don't you use the bathroom first, while Greg and I start on the beds?"

Her daughter dredged up a sigh from the depths of her soul as she picked up her overnight tote. "I am not sleeping in the same room with *him*," she declared, and sailed off toward the bathroom with the dignity of a queen who'd just tossed off a law or two.

"Yeah? Well, I wouldn't let you share my room anyhow. Not even in this rat hole!"

Jenny cravenly dived into the linen closet before they could decide to turn their united discontent on her.

Cedar-chip sachets hadn't quite defeated the mustiness of disuse; it floated out as she made the beds with token help from Greg. The rooms held the same aura of desertion, and even the bracing air that flowed in when she opened a window in each room did not completely dispel it.

In fact, the only exception she'd seen to that air of desertion was the kitchen, the first room they'd come through. It had suffered from the effects of being too much used—counters were cluttered and open spaces dulled with patches of something certainly sticky, while dirty dishes littered the sink, and the floor bore testament to the fact that not all the mud had been scraped off outside the door.

Stereo sneezes followed her from the bedrooms where Debbie and Greg had begrudgingly settled as she started down the stairs in search of that kitchen. She'd longed to collapse into the remaining bed—mustiness and all—but after the reaction from Tucker Gates and Deaver Smith, she feared she'd dream all night of being packed up and dumped back in Cody before she knew it. She was too new at all this. She needed to assert her right to be here before she'd rest easy.

At the base of the stairs, she heard voices coming from the vicinity of a lighted rectangle halfway down the dark hallway that crossed the back of the house, the opposite direction from the kitchen. Without thinking about it, she kept her approach quiet as she followed the voices.

"You said this wouldn't happen," Deaver's tone reproached.

"You said that already."

"Well, how did it happen?"

"I don't know. But it's not the end of the world."

From just outside the open door of what appeared to be an office, Jenny could see Tucker Gates sitting behind a large, plain desk, clearly at home in that position of authority. Despite the hat he still wore, she could see him clearly for the first time. Between dark brows and sharp slashes of cheekbones, his eyes were black and unrevealing. Below a straight nose slightly flared at the end, curved grooves flanked a firm-lined mouth. He was not an easy man, for all the relaxed way he'd hooked an arm over the back of his chair, twisting his broad shoulders.

"Near enough for my taste." From the position of Deaver's worn boots—the only part of him visible to Jenny—he sat across the desk from Tucker. "I'd think you'd be the last person to be wanting a couple kids running around the place. The very last person on God's green earth."

Tucker said nothing, his expression remaining unchanged, yet Jenny would have sworn the tension level multiplied.

Deaver's grumbling went on unabated. "Bad enough to be bossed by a woman, but—"

"I'm the boss of the Double Bar."

Tucker Gates was very sure of himself. So sure that Jenny found herself disproportionately relieved at the appearance of twin creases between his eyebrows. At least he was human enough to show that one small sign of concern or discomfort or uncertainty.

"Yeah, but she's the owner. And she's *here*."

"Not for long."

A beat of silence followed.

"What you got in mind to do, Tucker?" Deaver voiced the question rumbling in Jenny's head.

"Not going to do anything. Not going to need to. You saw those kids. You saw her. They won't be sticking around. Just relax."

Deaver's relieved chuckle approached a cackle.

Jenny felt no inclination to laugh.

Sometimes in life you had to take a stand. She'd spent most of her life not realizing that. Placating, doing what was expected of her, pleasing others, never rocking the boats other people put her in. In fact, the only real stand she'd taken was divorcing Edward.

In the fourteen months since then, she'd started changing, remaking herself into the person she'd always wanted to be. Now she saw that what had appeared as giant leaps were merely small steps, often as not aided by her father and his wife, Liz, and all leading her to this. Would she turn tail and run before the disapproval of some stranger now?

How the second stand of her life came to be occurring in the office of a Wyoming ranch house some time after midnight on a chilly spring night, she was too tired to unravel at the moment. But a stand it was—and it wouldn't be the last one, not if the new Jenny Peters was to survive.

"Mr. Gates. Mr. Smith." Jenny breezed into the room pretending to be blind to both Deaver Smith's jolt of displeased surprise and Tucker Gates's narrow-eyed look from her to the dark doorway. Avoiding the other chair pulled up in front of the desk, she removed a shuffle of papers from a worn wing-back by the fireplace and sat down, consciously aligning her forearms on the leather arms in a position of at-ease authority.

"Mr. Gates, please make yourself comfortable by removing your hat."

She'd been wrong about his black eyes being unrevealing. They revealed in quick succession irritation, begrudging amusement and then the confidence that allowed him to acknowledge an opponent's hit.

Without a word, he removed the hat, running his free hand straight back through black hair in an automatic gesture. The hair, well-cut at some point in the not-too-recent past and not trimmed since, curled slightly around his fingers and over the collar of his blue work shirt.

"Thought you'd gone to bed, Mrs. Peters."

"Yes, I imagine you did." Surprised at her own temerity, she met his look steadily. Let him wonder if she'd been listening, and what she might have heard. This uprooting your life, going a thousand miles west, being exhausted and encountering someone who expected you to be weak could be incredibly bracing. "But I've managed temporarily to resist the lure of these . . . accommodations."

He didn't look the least abashed by the state of the house.

His black eyes surveyed her. Not in a sexual way, but like an art critic viewing the latest work by an artist he didn't like. She was abruptly aware that this was probably the first time he could see her clearly. She wished she'd taken time to wash up. Her face was probably pale, her eyes shadowed and her hair ruffled. Not an appearance likely to instill employees with respect for the new owner.

A doubt hit her full force. "You were informed by the Ferrington corporate office, weren't you?"

"They wrote and told us the Double Bar'd been sold off again, yes."

Maybe the excessive blandness of his voice prompted her to pursue it. "But about our coming?"

"No."

The merest flicker of his eyes toward the desk wouldn't have been noticed by most. But she wasn't a mother for nothing. Her gaze fell on the jumbled pile of envelopes on his desk, and her confidence rebounded.

Raising one eyebrow, she looked from the unopened envelopes to his face and back. "Perhaps you *were* notified. How could you possibly know?"

"They call if it's something important."

Just that easily he dismissed her arrival—dismissed *her*—as unimportant. No apology. No defensiveness for not checking his letters.

An inane urge to apologize herself, the result of a lifetime of training first by her mother and then by Edward, trembled on her lips. No! That was the old Jenny. The new Jenny would take control...but how? No answer came. Her mind scrambled for an idea. What would a forceful person do? Her father...her father was forceful. What would he do?

"If you'd called, Mrs. Peters, and asked me about coming out here—"

"I own the Double Bar X, Mr. Gates. You are my employee. I don't have to ask you anything."

Amazing! Her father's voice coming out of her mouth! She could hardly believe it. But it felt good...incredibly good. She was giddy with it.

Tucker Gates, on the other hand, did not look too happy; the grooves at either side of his mouth lengthened and the tuck between his eyebrows dug deeper. But he kept on as if she—or her father—hadn't spoken.

"If you'd called and asked me about coming out here," he repeated, "I would have told you it wasn't a good idea. This is a real busy time, with calving season and all. There's nobody with the time to show you and your kids around the ranch."

"So?"

"So we can't be entertaining no women and kids," grumbled Deaver. "We got work to do."

"I would hope so," she replied calmly. "I want my employees to work. Mr. Gates—" she turned to him "—if I'd wanted Walt Disney World, I would have taken my children to Florida."

"No fear of having Florida weather here, Mrs. Peters. The weather's unpredictable this time of year. Could be we'd have a blizzard yet. Or mean cold for weeks on end. This isn't the time to see the ranch. You go on back to Chicago tomorrow and come summer, say July maybe August, you bring your kids back here for a week or two—"

"Two?" yelped Deaver.

"—And I'll make sure they get to ride a little, see some of the ranch, things like that. They'll enjoy the visit then."

"Visit?" She mimicked the tone her father had used the one time that new wine captain at Danelo's had offered him an inferior vintage. "I'm afraid you've misunderstood. My children and I aren't here for a visit. We've come to the Double Bar X to live. We're here to stay."

Chapter Two

For such a small thing, this Guinevere Peters packed a hell of a one-two punch. He'd barely absorbed the blow of this wispy woman with the soft eyes and the perfect manicure being the Double Bar X's owner, and she announced that she and her two kids were staying. *Staying,* for God's sake.

That pronouncement even managed to leave Deaver wordless, though not quiet. He bolted out of his chair and stood there spluttering until Tucker thought the older man might explode from the half-swallowed words. Instead, Deaver finally flapped his arms at Tucker in a gesture half of supplication and half of blame, hooked his thumbs in his worn belt and stomped out of the room.

Tucker's eyes met hers, and the humor deep in the soft gray caught him off guard. He felt his mouth ease into a grin and watched her lips curve up. Her eyes seemed to pick up more color, chips of green shining against the softness. The expression eased that impression she gave of carrying worry around with her, like a low-grade infection of some sort. He liked it.

Liked it? What was he doing sitting here grinning at her for? A pain-in-the-neck owner, who'd come to *stay,* for God's sake.

"Mrs. Peters—"

Her smile fled like a startled deer. "You know," she interrupted, standing with a jerk, "I am tired, after all. I'm going to get some sleep, and we'll discuss the details of our moving in in the morning."

Like hell we will. But he said nothing aloud; that would only make this one dig her heels in.

"By the way—" she turned from the door "—it's Ms. Peters, not Mrs. Although it does seem silly to be so formal under the circumstances. I'm going to call you Tucker," she informed him in a voice that reminded him of young Staci Coleman playing Queen Victoria in the high-school play last fall. "And you may call me Jenny."

She closed the door behind her, and he fought another grin. Definitely Queen Victoria bestowing a favor upon her subject.

The grin faded. An owner on the spot was bad enough, but an owner patterning herself after royalty—even play-acting—was more headache than someone who'd done his level best to stay out of the path of trouble for the past decade deserved.

His mood was grim as he headed out to join Deaver checking over the heifers.

"So what are you going to do, Tucker?" Deaver demanded.

He could quit.

She wanted to stay? He could put in his resignation, and let Ms. Guinevere Peters see how she really liked ranching.

Let her worry about finishing the calving, and getting the horses shod for spring work, and feeding the cows if that forecaster was right about the cold front heading this way, and putting that new field in grain and getting the equipment needed for seeding ready. And that was this week.

But why the hell should he quit?

He'd tended this ranch, nurtured this land for over a decade. It was more his than hers no matter what some deed said. Why should he be the one to leave?

Couldn't they both stay?

The temptation whispered from the same part of him that had noticed the soft gray-green eyes, the glint of gold and red in light brown hair, the humor in faint lines at the corners of her eyes, the air of weariness held in check by sheer gumption.

No. They couldn't both stay.

He knew the dangers. He'd first felt their impact as a boy, then bore their full force some fifteen years ago. That's what had drawn him to the Double Bar X in the first place. He might not be a Rhodes scholar, but he remembered a lesson once learned.

No, Jenny Peters and her kids couldn't stay.

"We're going to do exactly what I said before, Deave. We're going to encourage these folks to see that where they belong is back in Illinois, far away from a cattle ranch in Wyoming."

Deaver snorted, but his eyes glinted.

"Subtly, Deave. This has got to be subtle, or I have a feeling Ms. Guinevere might be one to dig her heels in. Understand?"

Deaver snorted again. This time Tucker accepted it as an expression of agreement.

The Peters family would leave. They had to. So Tucker Gates could stay.

* * *

Morning sun had a reputation for bringing strength. It brought Jenny second thoughts as numerous as the dust motes floating in the early-rising beams.

How had she gotten herself into this?

Against the air that had gone from chill to cold overnight, she pulled the covers up over her nose and promptly sneezed. Dropping the covers, she rolled to her side to burrow her face in the pillow. A wave of mustiness hit her olfactory senses, tickling unpleasantly. She rolled back and kept the covers at her neck. Better a cold nose than a string of sneezes that would wake Debbie in the next bed.

She remembered how she'd gotten herself into this. It had started that evening with her father and Liz. Liz had suggested her coming to dinner to distract Jenny from her concerns about the children. Charles Ferrington had carried the bulk of the conversation. He'd changed a great deal under Liz's influence the past few years, but a good business problem still got his juices flowing. And the current juggling of Ferrington assets to avoid a competitor buying out one of his companies occupied his mind.

"... so we're selling those three holdings as a unit, then a single ranch we'd thought we might consolidate someday and—"

"A ranch? Where?"

Her father didn't even blink at her interruption, though her mother would have been appalled—even during the final days of her fatal illness, Alexandra Ferrington had drilled into her daughter that well-mannered women did not interrupt. "In Wyoming. Near the Montana border. When we find a buyer, we'll—"

"I'll buy it."

"—use that income to... What?"

"I'll buy it."

"What on earth do you want a ranch for?"

"I've always wanted to live on a ranch, have horses, you know that." She considered her father and how little they had known about each other until the past few years. "Or maybe you don't. But I have. It was my first dream as a kid. And it would be perfect for Debbie and Greg."

Far away from shopping malls and social cliques of kids with too much time, too much money and too little sense. Far away from bad influences.

"But Edward wouldn't—"

"I think," Liz had interrupted gently, "that is a great part of the attraction."

And of course it was. That Jenny's ex-husband wouldn't fit in on a Wyoming ranch, that he wouldn't bother to make the long trip, that he wouldn't have as much influence over the children and, yes, petty though it might be, that he wouldn't like her moving to a ranch.

And of course he hadn't. Less because he truly regretted his children's being so far away than because he couldn't stand the idea that she made decisions on her own. He'd had his attorney make noises about a custody battle, but it didn't carry much weight when she knew the last thing he wanted was responsibility for two children. Still, for the kids' sake, she'd agreed to a liberal visitation schedule.

But when Edward's attorney made a comment about being sure Edward's money hadn't paid for the ranch, she'd let him have it. The child support Edward paid barely covered the tennis lessons he'd insisted they have, much less the price of a ranch. Besides, it was a ridiculous insinuation when the whole North Shore knew very well how much money she'd been left by her mother, plus the trust from Grandfather Barton.

Charles Ferrington had gone ahead with the sale, although he had looked doubtful right through the goodbye

hugs and kisses. But Liz had supported her. Jenny thought
fondly of her father's wife—it was hard to think of someone not even a decade older than herself as a stepmother.
Liz had supported her every step, helping with the practicalities without taking over and, even more important, en-
couraging when Jenny's spirits flagged.

But maybe Liz's faith in her had blinded her to the plan's
shortcomings, to Jenny's shortcomings.

Sure she'd always wanted to spend time on a ranch, but
what did she *know* about ranches? Nothing. Her mother
and Edward had seen to that.

For as long as she could remember, her bookshelf had
been filled with classic tales of horses— *My Friend Flicka,
National Velvet, Misty of Chincoteague, The Black Stal-
lion.* No matter the book's setting, she had transported them
to a mythical Western ranch she'd created in her mind, an
amalgam of every Western movie she'd ever seen.

Certainly her mother couldn't object to a horse, Jenny
had reasoned as a child. It wouldn't bring dirt and germs
into her house as Alexandra always said a dog would.

Her mother didn't object. She also didn't allow Jenny her
dream.

Instead, Alexandra Ferrington enrolled her in the most
prestigious riding academy on the North Shore, outfitted her
in britches and jacket and applauded her in horse shows.
Jenny had liked it, but it wasn't what she'd wanted.

And years later, in that final year of her marriage when
she'd worked so hard to try to recapture her dreams, Jenny
had suggested a vacation on a working ranch, where they
could get away, get to know each other again. Edward had
taken the plans out of her hands and put them into his travel
agent's, and they spent a week at a spa with a bridle path.
But it had a golf course, tennis courts, a Jacuzzi, abundant

telephones, a computer link to market reports and a fax—
everything Edward needed to be happy.

Manipulated, molded, prodded. That's how she'd felt.
Her mother and Edward had each twisted her dream to fit
their own ambitions.

And she'd let them.

Jenny Peters sat up in bed.

She'd let them.

Maybe she couldn't have stood up to her mother as an
eight-year-old, but she could have later. She could have told
her she wanted to ride the range, not circle an arena. And
she certainly could have stood up to Edward, insisted on her
ranch vacation instead of graciously going along with his
changes and smiling—God, smiling!—about it.

So she didn't know anything about ranches. She'd learn.
And this time she wouldn't be bullied out of her dream. Not
even by her own fears. She pushed back the covers and
stepped out of bed, hopping a little at the cold under her
feet, the noise causing a stirring in the next bed.

No, she wouldn't be deterred.

Not even by a cold floor, or a grim-faced manager named
Tucker Gates.

"Tucker says they won't be staying, but *she* says they're
here for good."

Tucker heard Deaver as he walked down the hall toward
the kitchen. The manager's suite and the kitchen formed a
one-story wing across the back of the two-story house built
in the twenties to replace the spread's original log head-
quarters. The wing was newer, built to accommodate a
wheelchair-bound owner. When he'd died, his young widow
had hired Tucker and taken her kids to Dallas. It had been
Tucker's home ever since. In the main house he only bothered with the office. Otherwise, all his needs were met by the

kitchen and his suite—bathroom and a large room divided by bookshelves into bedroom and den.

"What do you think, Deaver?"

That was Manny. He'd been at the Double Bar X almost six years. He did the cooking and shopping, mostly by default—he didn't gripe as much as Deaver and was less likely to cause food poisoning. But he hadn't been hired to cook and shop, and sometimes Tucker resented the time those chores took, because they sure could have used that other pair of hands.

"Hell, I don't know. Tucker said they'd never show up at all, but here they are. Now he says he can get rid of 'em. He's been wrong before."

"Got a lot of faith in me, don't you, Deave?" Tucker asked without rancor as he entered the room.

Deaver, seated at the large, plain, rectangular table long ago worn down to bare wood, simply grunted. Manny didn't turn from where he was putting grease into a large frying pan. The third occupant of the room, young Karl Wethers, didn't look up from buttering a slice of bread.

Even if they'd followed the social convention of exchanging good-mornings, there was no need. They'd already seen each other, out in the calving shed, in the cold, barely lit hour before six a.m., battling a heifer who'd decided she'd just as soon her calf not get born. They'd won.

Not a bad way to start a day, but it meant the half hour or so of sleep the night-watch sometimes got before breakfast disappeared. Tucker had barely had time to shower and change.

"I don't know, maybe it wouldn't be such a bad thing, having a woman around," said Karl.

Karl had arrived a year and a half before. He juggled his work on the ranch with taking courses at Northwest College over at Powell, leaving the young man little free time.

He worked hard and he listened, but Tucker had noticed a growing restlessness in him, and suspected Karl chafed at the lack of female companionship in his life.

At that moment, Karl seemed to sense the three sets of eyes on him, and looked up. He flushed, but didn't back down.

"You know, somebody to cook—no offense, Manny—and maybe fix up the place a little. And it sure would be nice to have somebody else do the laundry."

"You ain't seen this one," muttered Deaver.

"I wouldn't object to handing over the stove duties," Manny ventured.

Time to stop this right now. Tucker scraped back his customary chair at the head of the table and sat. "Fine, we're all agreed, we'd be real happy to have a housekeeper show up on the doorstep. Especially one who didn't want to get paid. But this woman isn't a housekeeper. She's the owner."

He let that ominous pronouncement sink in. But Deaver had his mite to add. "More likely she'll have you polish her shoes than that she'd be washing your dirty socks."

Manny dished up well-fried eggs, plopping plates in front of them and sitting.

"But you think they'll leave, Tucker? Even when she says they're going to stay?"

He nodded. "The kids don't want to stay, that's clear. And I can't see this woman holding out long against her kids. A little subtle encouragement is all it'll take to make her see she's made a mistake coming here."

"What do you want us to do, Tucker?"

"Just go about your work as usual. They'll soon see we don't have time to entertain them, then they'll be gone."

They all heard the footsteps on the wooden staircase. Everybody turned to the door except Tucker.

"Good morning." Jenny Peters sounded nervous, and determinedly breezy.

Deaver mumbled. Manny said good-morning. Karl stared and swallowed.

"Ms. Peters, let me introduce two more of your employees." Still without looking around, Tucker jabbed his fork to direct her attention. "Manny Whitewood and Karl Wethers."

"How do you do? It's a pleasure to meet you both."

She pronounced each word separately instead of running them together like most people. It made the formula words sound different—special.

"Sit down, and I'll get you a plate and some coffee, Ms. Peters," offered Manny.

"Thank you, that would be very nice." She entered Tucker's view and sat two chairs down the left side of the table. She had on jeans and a green sweater that looked as if it would be soft to touch. It had a pattern in a darker green across the front from shoulder to shoulder. Her hair shone like she'd brushed it, but the area under her eyes was darker than the pale skin around it. She hadn't slept well. "But, please, call me Jenny."

"Here's some coffee." Manny placed a mug before her. Tucker noticed Manny didn't call her anything.

She took a sip just as the old coffeemaker started into its series of peculiar clicks and hiccups. She jerked.

"What's that?"

"What? Oh, the coffeemaker. Damned thing makes enough noise to start a stampede."

From her doubtful look at the substance in her cup, Tucker wondered if her question had been about the noise or the toxic brew. He stifled a laugh.

"You want some eggs, uh, Jenny?" Karl handed her the platter as a tide of red rose on his neck.

"Thank you." She smiled at him, then looked at the cooling eggs. She put down the platter. "I'm really not very hungry this morning."

"Can I get you something else for breakfast?" Manny asked.

"Do you have any fresh grapefruit?"

Tucker had to bite back another would-be laugh at Deaver's outraged expression. Manny was more accommodating.

"No, ma'am. I got a can of peaches somewhere, though. Pretty sure I do, anyhow. You want them?"

"Uh, no, thank you. That's very kind of you to offer. I'll just have some toast."

Karl pushed the clutter of jelly jars toward her, dived back for the butter and put that in front of her, too. Jenny Peters smiled at him, sending another surge of color up his neck, but Tucker noticed she didn't use any of the proffered additions.

The light clattering of feet on the staircase announced the girl's arrival.

Debbie—that's how her mother introduced her, Tucker hadn't remembered the name—looked at each of them in turn without a word.

"Would you like breakfast, Debbie?" Jenny Peters's tone was of forced cheerfulness.

"Want some eggs?" Karl asked, again offering the platter.

Debbie didn't even take it. She looked down at the congealed blobs of yellow and white and said, "Yech! Take that away!"

"Deborah!"

"It's disgusting, Mom. Gross. It looks like—"

"Never mind! You apologize to Mr. Whitewood."

"If I have to apologize for saying it's gross, he should apologize for making it gross."

"Deborah—"

"Sorry." Two muttered syllables could carry a load of sullenness.

Manny Whitewood, who invested no ego in his cooking, accepted the small apology with a dignified nod. "Those eggs'll be stone-cold for the boy." Manny shot a glance at Tucker. "Unless you want me to stick around and..."

"Oh, that's not—"

"Need you to check the calves." Tucker spoke over Jenny.

"—necessary." Jenny gave him a sour look as she finished her statement. The smile returned as she addressed Manny. "I'll fix something for him when he gets up. He can be particular."

Spoiled brats, Tucker thought, confirming last night's assessment. Round here, everyone ate at the same time, and they ate what was served. Not something special, not fresh grapefruit and not dry toast.

Jenny seemed to sense the surprise in the looks she received, and faltered slightly. "That is, if you don't mind me in your kitchen, Manny. I won't—" she flashed a look around the cluttered work area "—mess anything up."

"Can't say I'd notice if you did."

Manny's cheerful answer visibly eased her expression.

"Good. Thank you. In the meantime, I thought I'd see about opening up some of these rooms."

She gave Tucker a challenging look, but he only shrugged. He didn't care what she did in the house. It wouldn't take much to put some sheets back over the furniture once they left.

"*You're* going to *clean?*" Debbie's disdainful disbelief drew looks from Manny, Karl and Deaver, but the child didn't seem to notice. Her mother stiffened, but kept smiling.

"Yes. Would you like to help?"

"No way. Where's the TV?"

"In Tu—"

Tucker cut off Karl. "There's no TV in the family quarters." He stood and looked at Deaver. "I'll call in the order for those plow discs, and the other supplies we talked about, then we'll go look at the fence section you wanted to show me."

As he headed to the office, he heard a concert of scraping chair legs as Deaver, Manny and Karl left to continue their workdays. And he heard the high-pitched whine of a preadolescent deprived of television. He'd have to make sure he kept the volume low on his set if he had it on when they were around. He didn't want them robbing him of his privacy.

He shook his head. God, and he'd thought last night that the girl was better than the boy by a long sight. Good thing he'd be out of the house before that piece of work got himself out of bed.

He sat at the desk and pulled his notes toward him. Without thinking, he glanced up at the chair where Jenny Peters had sat the night before, and an image of her face came clear and sharp. Only it wasn't as she'd looked last night, sometimes harried, sometimes sassy. It was the look this morning. The pained, almost haunted look when her daughter had disappointed her.

So the woman had trouble with her kids. No concern of his. Except it meant they were more likely to nag at her to leave.

And it provided one more reason to get them gone from the Double Bar X and his life as soon as possible.

* * *

Jenny stood in the wide archway that separated the parlor from the hallway and wondered where to start.

Weight tried to settle on her shoulders. The weight of not knowing what to do. The weight of Debbie's poor behavior. The weight of doubt.

Maybe she didn't belong here. Maybe she wouldn't know what to do or how to cope . . .

No! She'd decided this morning, she wouldn't let someone else's definitions of her ability stop her from trying what she wanted—what she needed. Because need definitely described her feelings about shaking her children out of this pattern. They needed to be brought up short, to see beyond their own desires. In other words, they *had* to turn out different from their father.

She was going to try. At least try. If she failed . . . Well, she'd face that then.

First she had to face the parlor. She'd never tackled anything like this. She'd dusted and vacuumed, but for the heavy-duty cleaning there'd always been someone else. What to do first?

She sneezed.

An omen. She chuckled, the feeling almost giddy.

First, open a window and try to get rid of some of this dust. The parlor went from the front to the back of the house, with a double-paned window at each end and a bay window at the side. One porch crossed the front of the house. Another covered the rear parlor wall, then turned to follow the wing. She pushed back the front-window curtains. Morning light picked out the movement of dust, like steam coming off a pot. Opening the window eddied the curtains, raising more dust.

Rubbing her itching nose, she repeated the action at the back window.

Might as well get all the dust stirred at once. She started pulling covers off furniture, piling them in one of the few open spots. A couch, two chairs and a love seat were over-stuffed, square-shaped and plain in dull brown. Lifting covers revealed a wooden settee, a rocking chair, a revolving wooden bookcase, three end tables, a game table with four chairs and a smoking table. No wonder the room had looked like a crowded graveyard.

Worn and faded in areas, and certainly no museum piece to start with, the rug was still a pleasant Oriental-style. Busy mentally rearranging the room, eliminating pieces, swinging the rug around so that bare patch would be under the repositioned couch, Jenny barely noticed the whiff of cigarette smoke. But her own shivering demanded her attention.

As long as she'd kept moving she was fine, but standing still she took the full impact of the strong crosscurrent. She rubbed her arms through the sweater and headed to the back window to cut down the wind.

"What's your name again?" It was Debbie's voice.

"Deaver Smith."

"I'm Debbie. Debbie Peters."

Her only answer was a mumble.

"You shouldn't smoke, Deaver."

Jenny reached the window in time to see Deaver, leaning against a porch post, glare down at his tormentor, who stood three feet away.

"You shouldn't smart-mouth your mother."

Jenny stilled, one hand holding the curtain so she could see without being seen. She forgot about closing the window.

Debbie didn't blink, and she didn't deny it. "Smoking's bad for you."

"Where I come from, so's smart-mouthing your mother."

"Smoking makes you *sick*. It makes your lungs all clogged up with this disgusting stuff and then you can't breathe and you *die*."

"And smart-mouthing your mother makes you a brat, and pretty soon nobody wants to be around you and you're all alone." Deaver's voice, rumbling on the low notes, didn't soften the words any, but there was no meanness in his tone.

Debbie looked at him a long, solemn moment, weighing his words. "That's not the way it is where I come from."

"Well, you're not where you came from anymore, are you?"

Debbie's eyes widened in acknowledgment of that irrefutable logic. She considered the man before her.

"My grandfather's tall, and he plays tennis and wears suits because he's a very important man. He's on TV sometimes, shaking hands with people. Important people. I call his new wife Aunt Liz, and they're going to have a new baby." That drew no response, so she made her comparison more direct. "You're not like my grandfather at all."

At the note of disdainful accusation in her daughter's voice, Jenny tightened her hand on the curtain. Maybe she should go out there. Debbie was about a sentence and half from spelling out for Deaver Smith exactly where in her estimation he fell short of her grandfather.

But she saw that Deaver Smith could take care of himself.

"Stands to reason."

"Why?"

"Because I'm not your grandfather."

"Oh." Debbie considered that. She moved a step toward the man who still smoked steadily. "My grandmother died. I was a baby, and Greg wasn't even born yet. They had a funeral for her, but they wouldn't let me go. I guess I would have been too young to remember it anyhow. My grandfather said she died from cigarettes. She got real sick, and then she died. And they had a funeral.''

Deaver Smith's hand stopped on the way to putting his cigarette back between his lips. He turned his head and looked at Debbie.

"I've never been to a funeral," she added. Her steady regard indicated she saw him as a candidate for her first.

With a jerk, he dropped the cigarette on the porch and ground it out with the heel of his boot.

"I can't waste any more time waiting for Tucker to decide he's ready to get a move on. I got work to do."

Without looking at Debbie, he stepped off the porch and headed toward the barn.

She hesitated a moment, then headed after him, catching up within a few yards. Deaver didn't look around, and as far as Jenny could tell, neither said anything, but at least the old man didn't order Debbie away.

Jenny watched them disappear into the barn, side by side. Releasing the curtain, she turned and gasped.

"Eavesdropping?" Tucker Gates stood just inside the archway. He looked as if he'd been standing there awhile. "It's not real polite, but you can learn mighty useful information, listening to other folks' conversations."

"I don't know what you mean." Listening to Debbie did not constitute eavesdropping. That was her daughter, after all.

His gaze shifted to the window, then back to her face. "You can learn things like what I told you before—that this isn't the place for you and your kids."

She raised her eyebrows with what she hoped would look like hauteur. "Your leap defies logic."

"I always heard mothers got real concerned about the company their kids keep."

Concerned enough to move halfway across the continent. "Say what you have to say, Mr. Gates."

His raised eyebrows acknowledged her return to formality.

"You haven't landed in a monastery here, Ms. Peters." The look he gave her brought to mind myriad sins he might indulge in. But he didn't mention the ones that unfortunately came to her mind first. "We smoke and we swear and we drink. Karl's not around much and I can't speak for Manny, but I can tell you right now I curse when I'm mad, and sometimes when I'm not, and I'm not about to change my ways for a couple of kids and a woman. And I sound like a preacher compared to Deaver. Deaver's got more rough edges than a rusted rowel."

Tucker wished she looked more impressed by that little speech than she did. For as big a fool as it made him feel, it ought to send her screaming from the room. Especially considering who she was.

He'd finally dug out the Ferrington envelopes and read the past month's correspondence. The one that really caught his eye was the formal notice with her full name—Guinevere Barton Ferrington Peters. That explained a lot. He'd heard Ferrington had a daughter.

So that partially answered one of his questions. Like, what kind of woman bought a ranch, sight unseen? Although it left unanswered why she would want a ranch in the first place. But who knew what kind of whim moved a woman whose father would hand over a ranch as a plaything. He figured a little exposure to the unvarnished truth of this situation should send her on her way—and out of his.

But she stood her ground.

Her eyes flicked, as if she was about to look back toward the window where she'd watched her daughter walk off with

Deaver. But just for an instant, then her gaze returned to him.

"There are other kinds of obscenities," she said.

She started out, not breaking stride to add as she passed him, "We're staying."

Now what the hell did she mean by other kinds of obscenities? Obscure words spoken in a raw voice. And why did he want to smooth her hair and try to take the hurt out of her eyes? He let loose one of the curses he'd just owned up to, but only in his mind.

Jenny hoped her voice was steadier than her nerves when she asked Tucker to remain a moment after the rest of the men had cleared out after lunch the second day.

He didn't take off the hat he'd just put on, and his tone qualified as barely civil. "What do you want?"

"I want," she answered rather testily, "you or one of the others to bring in the rest of our luggage." She'd given thought to trying to bring it in herself, but knowing she would get no help from Greg or Debbie, remembering the strain the taxi driver and skycaps had experienced, and considering the wallow of mud behind the rental car's trunk, she'd decided against it. "We are all tired of living out of our overnight bags."

She wished that was the only cause for her children's behavior. Actually, after that first morning, Debbie had been pretty good, complaining about the lack of television only two or three times last night, and not at all yesterday afternoon or this morning, when she had again disappeared in the wake of Deaver Smith. Greg had not been so restrained.

"No time."

She was getting tired of these short answers from Tucker Gates. In fact, she was tired, period. Physically from the toll of heavy cleaning. Emotionally from the sullen silences Greg alternated with periods of complaining.

"You can't spare half an hour?"

"I can't spare half a minute. We got more work to do here than we got time. No way can we get everything done that needs to be done around the place, much less what we'd like to do."

Much less what he didn't want to do, like bring in her luggage. He didn't need to say that, she saw it in his face.

"Why don't you hire more people to help, then?"

"Because owners like their profits."

She opened her mouth to say she wouldn't mind a cut in profits, then closed it. She didn't know what the profit was, so how could she say she wouldn't mind a cut? And how could she tell this man she'd bought a business without knowing what the profit was?

"I'll make you a deal, then, Tucker." And they both knew the return to first names constituted an olive branch. "I will cook dinner, and Manny can use the time he would have spent cooking to bring in the luggage."

The tuck returned between his brows, and she read it easily. He didn't want to accept any further entrenchment, but he couldn't see a way out of it without outright rudeness to his employer. She had him! Jenny fought a triumphant smile. He had tried to maneuver her out of getting their belongings in the house, and she'd flanked him.

"Okay."

He turned to go after that mumbled acknowledgment.

"One more thing, Tucker." He didn't look eager to hear it, but at least he didn't ignore her. "I saw in a description of the house that there's a master bedroom suite." She'd studied the description of the ranch's "improvements"—matching "bunkhouse," "garage," "main barn" and "barn annex" with the buildings she saw from the window of the bedroom she'd taken as her own, though she'd gotten a little lost in the list of miscellaneous sheds. "I'm presuming it's beyond that door in the hallway. Will you unlock it for me, please?"

Some of the other rooms in the house had been locked—closets, storage areas in the basement, too. She'd had to ask him to open each.

"It's open."

She didn't like the glint in his eyes. Somehow the advantage had shifted, and she didn't know how or why. But it wouldn't do to show her uneasiness.

"Good." She smiled brightly. "Because I want to tackle that next. There are plenty of rooms upstairs, but it would be nice to have some privacy from the kids, to have my own area—"

"It's mine."

"What?"

"It's my suite. That's where the manager lives."

"In the *house?*"

His dark brows slammed down. "Yeah, in the *house.* What did you think? I slept in the barn?"

"No. I didn't...I mean, I, uh, I guess I thought you lived in the bunkhouse with the others."

He'd gone stone-stiff.

"You want me to move my things out?"

No—and yes. She didn't want him living in the house with her...with her and her kids. But to kick him out...

"No, of course not. If that's your home... I'm sorry, I didn't know. The information just said a master bedroom suite. It didn't say anything about the manager's quarters...."

"That's the way it's been for more than ten years." She saw something come into his eyes and knew she didn't like it but didn't have time to guess at its identity before he went on. "That's also the way it's been the past two nights, and I've managed to keep from ravishing you in your sleep. I think you can feel pretty secure that won't change. Just not my style to ravish a woman with her kids in the house."

He gave her an insolent smile, turned on a boot heel and was gone.

Chapter Three

Jenny steeled her nerve to face Tucker at dinner. Then she didn't need any nerve because he didn't show up.

Deaver muttered something about Tucker's having gone into town, but nothing else.

She supposed she should have been flattered that Deaver devoted all his attention to her dinner. She'd kept it simple. Baked chicken—without the wine sauce because she couldn't find any wine. Green beans from the freezer—topped with toasted walnuts, an improvisation because there'd been no almonds. Crudités—carrots were the only fresh vegetable she found, with two kinds of olives and pickles from jars. Mashed potatoes—mesh bags of potatoes she'd found in abundance, so she'd closed her mind to warnings about fat and cholesterol and was generous with the butter and milk.

Manny was appreciative, Karl was lavish with praise. Her children didn't praise, but they didn't complain. Debbie even gave her a rather speculative look.

Karl volunteered to do the dishes, which allowed her to deal with the numerous bags he and Manny had wrestled upstairs before dinner.

They'd also helped her redistribute some of the parlor furniture, bringing the rocker up to her room, the rotating bookcase to Greg's, a small chest to Debbie's, and taking the card table with four chairs to the bunkhouse. When Manny teased Karl about leaving a small corner of it free from his papers and books so the rest of them could use it, she'd insisted they also take a small bookcase so Karl had somewhere to store his schoolwork.

So she had plenty to do upstairs. Which freed her from the risk of running into Tucker when he returned.

The trip into Cody provided Tucker with only temporary diversion.

He picked up the supplies he'd ordered the day before. Then, reluctant to return to the Double Bar X right away, he'd found Rebecca Coleman closing up the insurance office where she worked, and asked her out for supper.

That might have been a mistake.

He'd gone to some pains to cool that relationship when he'd realized last fall that people were watching them with expectations of an announcement—an announcement he had no intention of making. Rebecca Coleman wanted a husband and a family. He wasn't cut out for the latter, so he wouldn't saddle her with the former.

So, after watching her younger sister Staci play Queen Victoria in that high-school play, he'd taken Rebecca for a drink, and said he thought they should go their separate ways and wish each other well. She'd cried a little and called him a couple times after, but he'd stuck to it. He'd even felt a little noble—he was doing the right thing, being fair to her, even though it deprived him of the company of an attractive woman—and a damn good dancer.

Tonight had changed that, he thought sourly, as he drove through the star-brightened darkness. The clouds had scurried away in fear of the cold front coming in, and the stars sparkled like ice in the huge blackness above.

Maybe he should have still felt noble, since Rebecca seemed very happy about the new guy she was seeing. A guy who sounded as if he'd give her just what she wanted. Tucker had made that all possible by stepping out of the picture. He should feel good about that. And God knows, he wasn't jealous.

What he was was bored.

Hard to feel noble about giving up a woman so she could find her happiness when you were busy wondering how you'd forgotten how dull she was. Pleasant, attractive, a great dancer...and she stared at him with her eyes wide, her lips slightly parted and not the slightest hint that she comprehended what he was saying.

No, the trip to town hadn't provided much diversion on the plus side. And on the minus side, it had foreclosed on his comfortable delusion that he'd acted with no self-interest in letting Rebecca go last fall.

One more proof Tucker Gates was no boon to mankind. Or womankind.

What the hell, might as well go for a clean sweep and include kids, too, he thought sourly as he opened the door of his room and found Greg Peters stretched out on his couch, feet on his coffee table, heels wrinkling his unread *Beef Magazine* and watching his TV.

"Hey, Tucker, how're you doing?" Greg's bonhomie would have been ludicrous in his childish alto if it hadn't been so obnoxious. "You get pretty good reception for being out in the middle of nowhere like this. I guess that's the cable, huh? But you really gotta get HBO and Cinemax."

Tucker supposed that, despite the words, Greg's obvious discomfort indicated the kid knew he was doing wrong, and that meant he wasn't too far gone. The kid could be saved. But that wasn't Tucker Gates's concern. Kids needed saving, they'd have to go somewhere else. They sure as hell would be better off with anybody other than him.

"Get out."

Greg tried to placate him. "Hey, what's the big deal?"

"This is my room. You were not invited. Get out."

The boy shifted from placate to bluster. "Hey, this whole place is ours. My mom bought it from my grandfather, so I can be anywhere I want."

Tucker took a step forward, and Greg hastily stood up, the magazine cover sticking to his heel an instant, making him look foolish. But this kid was not so easily defeated. He shifted to a hands-back, chest-out, chin-up stance of arrogance. Tucker was torn between annoyance and giving the kid his due for guts.

Annoyance won.

"This is my room," he repeated, low and quiet. "You were not invited." He made sure to meet the boy's eyes. "Get out."

Tucker stepped back and Greg moved from the couch.

"Geez, if I'd known you were such a—"

He broke off as he met Tucker's eyes. He and Tucker were less than three feet apart. Tucker saw a flash of real unhappiness in the boy's eyes before Greg looked away and continued toward the door Tucker had left open. But he didn't go quietly.

"Big man, aren't you? You've got the TV and nobody else can watch it. You think you're so great—well, you're not!" Greg punctuated that by slamming the door behind him hard enough that it popped back open a fraction.

Tucker remained motionless a moment, trying to pinpoint what made him think young Greg Peters had been imitating somebody. Some smart-alecky kid he'd seen on a TV sitcom, maybe? Tucker's mouth twisted as he walked over to the remote left on the coffee table to turn off the TV.

"What was that sound? Did something fall?" Through the barely open door, he heard Jenny's voice as she came down the stairs. "Greg?"

"What?" Greg hadn't moved any farther than the end of the hall.

"Was that you? Were you talking to someone? I thought I heard voices." By the sound, Tucker could tell Jenny had joined her son.

"It was that Gates guy."

"Tucker? What were you talking to him about?" The wariness in her voice held two-way concern—he could almost hear her worrying what her son might have said to him, and what he might have said to her son.

"He's got a television in there, and the selfish jerk won't let anybody else watch it."

"A television? Where?"

"In there. You'd think he was the boss, instead of him working for us. You should fire him."

"In his room? You went in Tucker's room and watched his television? Without his permission?"

"So what? The whole place is ours, so why should I ask him?"

"Go upstairs, Greg."

"You should fire that jerk. Dad would. Dad would—"

"Go upstairs, Greg, before I tell you exactly how disappointed I am in you."

"I didn't do anything wrong." The defensive belligerence wore thin. The voice sounded younger.

"I am ashamed of you, Gregory Barton Peters. Now go upstairs."

"I—"

"Now."

Tucker heard slamming, petulant footsteps mount the stairs, then a quiet out in the hall, like someone gathering herself. Gathering her pride, gathering her resolve.

He missed her footsteps approaching, but heard the quiet knock, soft enough not to disturb the door even though it was ajar.

Damn, he didn't want to do this. Not now. Not tonight. Maybe never. If he ignored the knock, maybe she'd go away. Maybe she and her kids would pack up and be gone in the morning, and he could get back to his normal life.

He opened the door.

She looked composed. Only the brighter color in her cheeks gave evidence of any inner turmoil. It made her look young. So did her hair pulled into a ponytail and the Chicago Cubs sweatshirt liberally marked with dust.

"I came to apologize for Greg's behavior, Tucker."

He looked at her a full thirty seconds. "Want to come in?"

Her eyes darted from him to the room she could surely see beyond his shoulder—included the corner of the bed visible over to the far side, beyond the bookcases.

"Uh, no, thank you." She sounded less certain than a sentence before. As if she had suddenly considered the possibility that he would pounce on her, here and now, with her kids in the same house.

That irked him.

It irked him even more that he'd planted the seed himself. Why had he made that crack about ravishing her in her sleep? He'd been kicking himself about that all afternoon and all evening.

To make her uncomfortable, of course. Uncomfortable enough to get the hell out of here.

But he didn't want to scare her. No woman should feel that way, and the fact that he'd done it to her, even for an instant, made his stomach grip hard.

He shifted. Besides, it was stupid. Sure he didn't want her to stick around, but he also didn't want her to fire him. And she'd be smart to do just that if she really thought he'd harm her.

"You should do something about that kid," he said through gritted teeth.

"Wh-What?"

"You're not doing him any favors letting him think he rules the roost. Make the kid toe the line and see—"

Her first shock solidified to stiffness. "My son is my concern, not yours, Mr. Gates."

"It becomes my concern damn fast when he makes himself at home in my room, with my TV, lady. You got to make those kids of yours stop—"

"I did not come here to be told . . ." She bit it off, but he saw the rest of it in her eyes. She hadn't come to be told how to deal with her children.

Especially not by him, he mentally added. He couldn't agree more, so what the hell was he doing?

He saw her gather in her momentarily scattered poise and wished he could do the same. God, he was tired. He hadn't gotten much sleep. He never did during calving season, but this year, with these three showing up . . .

"I came," Jenny Peters resumed, "to say I'm sorry for the intrusion on your privacy."

"You've said it."

"Yes, I have. Good night."

It was not a good night, or a restful one, for Tucker Gates.

Jenny had driven into Powell that morning—for cleaning supplies, she'd said. What did she think they'd been using to clean? Fairy dust?

Tucker repeated the mental grumble several times during the day. She'd taken her kids with her, so lunch seemed particularly quiet, especially since Karl spent the time staring absentmindedly at the wall and Deaver didn't come in until the rest of them were leaving.

Tucker and Deaver were conferring about a tree stump in the field they planned to plant in grain when they spotted the rental car cautiously approaching on the driveway. A fancy sedan on that surface was like Guinevere Peters at the Double Bar X—neither fit. When was she going to realize that?

The car stopped, the back doors popped open and the kids piled out with several bags each and headed to the house, Debbie pausing to wave to Deaver and get a nod. Tucker was surprised to see them helping their mother tote her cleaning supplies so readily, then he realized they were toting their own purchases. Jenny went around to the trunk and took out two bags, leaving it open—she must plan on cleaning the whole state—while she went into the house.

On her return trip, she detoured to where he and Deaver stood. He'd help her carry in the bags if she asked, but he'd been hired to manage the ranch, not cater to the rich owner, and the sooner she learned that the better.

"We drove into Powell," she said.

That was no news, so Tucker said nothing, but Deaver grumbled, "Did you leave any of it behind?"

"A few sticks and stones," she answered dryly. Apparently Deaver didn't fool her any more than he did Debbie. "I gave the kids some money and set them loose on Bent

Street while I picked up the things I needed. But it was on the way back . . .''

In the afternoon light. Tucker could see flecks of green in her eyes. The brightness took over the gray, sparkling and glowing.

"What was on the way back?" demanded Deaver.

"I took a different road coming back, and we were driving along, with the green fields and neat houses on either side. Then the road took a sudden curve to the right and dipped at the same time, and it was as if we drove into the Twilight Zone. It was a moonscape—hills of bleached white rock and odd-colored pools bubbling ominously and—" she shook her head "—I don't know how to describe it."

Tucker thought she'd done just fine. Her shoulders shifted in a remembered shiver at the eerie grandeur. Her eyes glowed with awe. Her hand swept a line in time to illustrate the impact of the abrupt change in topography.

"I just had to stop the car and look at it. I even turned around and drove back to make sure I hadn't imagined the green behind us, then followed that curve again—and there it was. Amazing."

She looked from one to the other of them, searching for a sign they understood her excitement. Tucker understood; that's why he ducked her look. He didn't want to understand her excitement, to share it, to like the way it looked on her.

But she took no notice. Her attention had been snagged by Deaver's slow nod.

"Yeah, they do a lot of irrigating over that way, 'round Powell. Greens up real nice." With that pronouncement he went over to his pickup and drove away to check another distant fence section.

Tucker knew exactly when Jenny turned from following the truck's progress to him, and he couldn't stop himself from looking back. He'd expected the stunned expression of someone who'd just announced they'd discovered a diamond mine and been complimented on the nice glass. But beneath it, where he thought he might spot outrage or disdain, he saw, instead, humor.

His mouth twitched. Hers lifted into a grin. Then the laughter hit them both.

"Greens up real nice," she said with a gasp, folding one arm across her middle.

"All that irrigating," he told her as solemnly as he could.

Then she put her hand out to grasp his forearm. A simple gesture. Maybe she needed it to steady herself. Maybe she meant it to be friendly. But he knew the danger the instant he saw the motion start. Understanding her reaction, enjoying her excitement, sharing her amusement—that was one thing. He couldn't risk a touch being something else.

He pivoted away before she reached him, laughter echoing toward silence.

"Better get back to work," he announced.

"Yes. Me, too."

He thought she sounded puzzled, but he didn't look back to check.

"Tucker, could I talk to you a moment?"

He nodded to the other three men who hesitated at the door, and they headed out. She was tired of snaring him after meals—this time breakfast—but it seemed the only time he allowed himself to be snared. She certainly couldn't accuse her ranch manager of wasting his time hanging around the house. She had only occasional proofs of his presence, including a book on Wyoming geology appearing on the hall table, marked at the section about the Big Horn Basin.

Jenny knew Manny had had watch duty for cows about to calve last night. But Tucker didn't look as if he'd gotten much sleep, either.

He hadn't said a word through the breakfast Manny had cooked, and the glances she'd cast his way over her toast and coffee hadn't shown a very happy face. It didn't look any happier now that he came back and sat at a right angle to her spot at the table.

"What do you want?"

"I want you to stop shutting me out of the operation of the Double Bar X."

"Don't know how I could shut you out when you own the place."

"You're trying your damnedest." She gestured as if to wipe away her own anger and tried again. "Tucker, this is ridiculous. There's no reason for us to be enemies. True, I don't know much about ranches. But if you told me more about the operation, I'm sure I could help. I could—"

"You want to help Manny and Karl give feed to the cows? That's what they're doing this morning. Because with the cold, cows eat about one and a half times as much feed to keep their body temperatures up. Did you know that? No, I didn't think so. You want to ride with Deaver and me, bring in the new calves closer, so if this cold sticks we can get 'em into sheds quick so we don't lose any of the ones we've been fighting like hell the past weeks to get born? You want to check out the equipment we're going to need for irrigation next month? Make sure it's all ready to go? You want to fix fence out in the Dry Creek section? Because those are the things we would have been doing today if we hadn't had this cold spell making us do other things. Is that what you want to do?"

For someone as mild as she appeared, Jenny Peters had a temper. And Tucker Gates seemed to have a knack at stirring it. Could be because he tried.

"What I want to do is see the books."

"You think I'm skimming the profits? I'd do better robbing the poor box at church. If you're suspecting me of something, you might as well suspect that."

"I don't suspect you of anything. I don't think you're skimming profits. If anything, I think you might be overzealous in not spending the ranch's money. I used that so-called washer and dryer you keep in that closet—" she gestured to an odd section tucked off the hallway between the addition and the main house "—and I wouldn't be surprised to find out they came with the original deed. I can't believe the Double Bar X can't afford to replace them. I have a right to see this ranch's books. And I want to see them."

"You want me to get the books ready for your inspection or you want me to tend the cows so they don't go from the alive side to the dead side on those ledgers?"

She fought for control. If he wanted to make her lose her temper, it was because he thought it gave him an advantage. She'd be damned if she'd hand it over easily.

"I want you to tend the cattle. First. Then, at the earliest opportunity, I want you to prepare the books for me to look at. Is that understood?"

His gaze didn't flicker. "Understood."

They might have gone on glaring at each other, but noise interrupted them.

They heard the clattering of shoes on the stairs. Accompanied by halfhearted sibling bickering, it announced the morning arrival of Debbie and Greg. Still caught up in her confrontation with Tucker, Jenny didn't listen to the text of their squabbling as it flowed past her on their way to the refrigerator. She wondered if even they listened. Sometimes she thought they argued out of pure habit.

"Mom, I'm bored. There is *nothing* to do in this place."

Without taking her eyes off Tucker, she answered Greg's complaint automatically—she'd had practice. "There are books in the case in the living room you might—"

"Books!" Greg slammed down the plate she'd put out for the omelet she'd waited to make until he arrived. "I want to go into town. Karl said there are movies there, maybe video games. And if we're real lucky, they might have heard of indoor tennis, though there's probably nobody to challenge me around here."

It was a self-centered forty-year-old's words in a spoiled nine-year-old's voice.

Tucker's eyes, dark and unreadable, went to Greg. Jenny knew what he must think. It's what she thought, too. That's why they were here. But it still wasn't comfortable to have her son expose his unattractive side.

"No, Greg."

"But I want—"

The crash of a door caught by a gust of wind drowned out the rest of the sentence and gave Jenny an excuse to ignore Greg. And Tucker.

A curse and slam announced Deaver had triumphed over the outer door. He came in from the back hall, muttering.

"Brrr-rrr!" He shook himself, and they could almost feel the waves of chill coming off his shearling coat.

"Cold out there, Deave?"

Tucker sounded perfectly at ease, totally unaffected by his and Jenny's confrontation. Damn him. Well, she could at least fake nonchalance. She picked up her coffee mug.

The older man slapped his hat against his leg and pushed down the scarf he'd wrapped high enough around his neck to protect his ears.

"Cold? It's colder than a—"

In her haste to interrupt Deaver, Jenny swallowed her coffee wrong and the hot, strong liquid added injury to insult by scalding as it went down the wrong way.

She made a strangled, coughing sound that succeeded in stopping Deaver's simile. He glared at her.

"You all right?" It sounded more a demand for an explanation of her behavior in not being all right than solicitude for her condition.

"Fine," she gasped, setting off another flurry of coughs.

Deaver's glare deepened. "Don't just sit there, Tucker, give her a whup on the back."

"No—" she began to say.

Too late. She saw Tucker Gates's long arm stretch her way and felt his broad, warm palm connect against her back before she could repeat the syllable. He didn't hit hard, and he let his hand linger before he lifted it for a second thump to her back, this time lingering longer. Strange that the warmth of that palm against her back could counteract the heat stinging in her throat, but it did seem to help.

"Get your mother a glass of water, Greg." A third pat from his hand. It remained there.

"But—"

"Now."

Greg obeyed, though liquid sloshed over the rim when he clunked it on the table. She sipped gratefully.

Turning to thank Tucker, she met his stare. He looked at her as if she were something foreign—and not something he was at all sure he'd want to import. At the same moment, he drew his hand away from her back, draping his arm over the back of his own chair with studied casualness as he turned to Deaver. It irritated her that his move left a chill the size and shape of his palm on her flesh.

"What's that you were saying, Deave, before Ms. Peters here interrupted you? It's cold this morning? Colder than a what?"

Jenny's glare bounced off Tucker's impervious profile. His voice might have held a glint of amusement, but she was also certain he meant to drive home his point about this not being the best atmosphere for her children. She prepared to stage a belated coughing attack when her daughter joined in.

"Yeah, Deaver, colder than a what?" Debbie asked.

The old man's mouth, opened to answer, closed as he shifted his gaze to Debbie, opened again and closed. Then he clamped his hat on his head.

"Are we gonna get out of here sometime, Tucker, or are we going to spend all day sipping tea in the kitchen?"

"Coffee," Tucker amended mildly as he stood and reached for his coat on the peg.

"But, Deaver—you didn't answer!"

At the doorway, the older man hesitated for a second, before curtly instructing Debbie, "Ask your mother."

The cold broke—everywhere except between Tucker and Jenny Peters. No, better make that between him and the whole Peters family.

From behind the disc plow, raised on blocks in the open area in front of the garage to make an easier job of disassembling it and putting on the replacement discs he'd picked up in town, Tucker watched Greg Peters wander across the yard in the direction of the barn.

The smell of spring in the air had even gotten to him. Or else the boredom had finally worn down his resolve to show no interest in the place.

This was the first time Tucker had seen the boy come out of the house since they'd arrived five days ago. Mostly he saw Greg at meals, but he wouldn't be surprised to learn

Greg hadn't seem him. The boy generally kept his sullen stare on his plate, leaving without a word—also without clearing his place or otherwise lifting a finger to help.

So what was Greg doing heading to the barn? Maybe the boredom that kid complained about unendingly had finally gotten him off his butt.

Well, Deaver was in there, and he'd see to it that the boy didn't get into anything.

He'd certainly been doing that with little Debbie.

Tucker grinned despite himself. Who would have expected that pairing? Not a whole lot of conversation between them, but they seemed to understand each other fine. Deaver had even eased up the smoking Tucker had been after him to quit.

When he'd teased Deaver this morning about not doing his part to encourage the Peters family to leave, the old man had grumbled, "Least she doesn't chatter away to drive a man wild like you used to when I first run up against you. Questions, questions, questions, that's all I got from you from the time I signed up under your pa at the Bristhurst place. Least Debbie keeps most of 'em to herself. Mostly she just watches. Man can't complain about that, can he?"

Maybe not, Tucker thought now. But would Greg Peters be that easy to entertain?

The back screen door creaked open and Jenny came out, carrying an armload of rugs.

She'd gotten Manny and Karl to help her tote out that big rug from the living room earlier in the day and spread it across a section of corral fence. She hadn't needed to do more than crook her finger to get Karl to do her bidding, and not much more than that for Manny since she'd taken to cooking all the lunches and most dinners.

A good part of the morning she'd spent beating on that big living room rug between spells of going back and forth to the old washer and dryer. Since she was now hanging damp rugs on a line, she'd apparently decided nature worked faster than that dryer. He could have told her that.

He could also have told her how the house had a different smell since she'd come—crisp, fresh, a smell that made him breathe deep in satisfaction each time he came in. And he could tell her he noticed the way the kitchen floor didn't make that sticking sound when you walked that he'd always known meant it needed to be washed more. He could also tell her he saw at dinner last night that her manicure was shot to hell and he'd spotted her nodding off over her plate despite the high-octane coffee she had in her mug.

But he didn't tell her any of that. He did his damnedest to pretend the owner of the Double Bar X was still in Chicago, where she belonged.

She looked up, and he dropped his head for a closer look at where he'd fastened a new disc to the plow.

"Hi, Tucker. It's a beautiful day, isn't it?"

He'd ignored her coming around the end of the twelve-foot-wide plow, but he couldn't ignore her greeting. She sounded like someone bound and determined to have a truce.

"Won't last." She shot him a look, clearly amused. She wasn't buying the curmudgeon role today. "It'll get cold again," he insisted, but in a lighter tone. "Wouldn't bet against it snowing."

She shrugged. "But today is beautiful. I'll take that. It *smells* like spring. It must have gotten to you, too. Why else would you bring your work outside?"

"More space."

"But if it were thirty degrees colder, you would have found space in the garage to work on that—what is that?"

"Disc plow. The circles go around, chop up the dirt."

"I know what a plow does," she said with more amused patience. "I am from Illinois, you know. All those cornfields have to get planted somehow."

"Didn't think they had cornfields in Chicago."

"Every other street corner," she said solemnly, her eyes glinting. "Alternating with the lampposts."

He found himself looking into her eyes and smiling. When the smile picked up warmth, he went for caution and shifted the focus to the plow.

Holding a disc in place, he looked for the wrench he'd put down earlier—just out of reach.

"Can I get something for you?" She'd seen his predicament.

"Yeah, if you don't mind. That wrench."

She brought it to him, then took a step back. But not the three or four to return her to where she'd been. Close enough that he couldn't be sure he smelled her scent or remembered it from the instant she'd stood next to him.

He turned his back to her and used the wrench with more force than necessary.

But Jenny, obviously determined to match her mood to the day, didn't leave. "I called the school district. The one for Greg and Debbie. I thought they'd go into Cody, but it's Powell."

The silence hung as if she'd asked a question. What did she expect him to say? He glanced over his shoulder and saw what she expected—she expected him to jump on her. Slightly tense, she awaited an attack on her brains for not knowing the right district, on her kids on general principle or on the ludicrous idea they'd stay here long enough to bother with such formalities as enrolling in school.

God, that's what she expected of him? He wasn't that big a jerk, to make her defend every word she said. He might think she wouldn't stick around, he might not *want* her to stick around, but that didn't mean he couldn't be civil. Did it?

"Can you hand me that hammer?" Her stiffness disappeared; she almost smiled. "The bigger one. Yeah, that one."

She put it in his hand and took the wrench, a simple transaction devoid of contact, but it seemed to ease her.

"The woman at the school district helped a lot. She told me everything I need to get their records squared away and everything. But the spring breaks didn't coincide, so these schools are just going into vacation. It'll be another week before the kids can start school here."

Her silence could have covered contemplation of what to do with her kids, especially Greg, for another week, or another wary pause waiting for him to make a crack. He didn't look around to find out which, but bridged the silence with the method that had worked before.

"Hand me the wrench again, will you?"

He put out his hand. It remained empty.

"Jenny, the wrench?"

When that drew no reaction, he dropped back on his heels and turned to get a look at her. She hadn't heard him either time, too absorbed in staring beyond his right shoulder. He twisted around to see what she stared at.

His mountains.

From the lower hills, covered in tough native grasses softened by distance to resemble velvet, rumpled and folded without pattern yet innately graceful. Up to the rising timbered slopes, their darker, lusher vegetation slashed by outcroppings of the range's skeleton. And finally to the knuckles of raw rock that seemed to shake a fist at the sky in defiance.

"It's beautiful."

He wasn't even sure she knew she was talking, or who she was talking to. Her eyes had turned all green now, the gray chased away by excitement and pleasure. The sun brought out the glints of red and gold in her hair. All the colors that came together in her seemed intensified and polished by her simple enjoyment of the day and the scene.

"And it changes," she went on. "I've seen it. Every day, every hour. The light pinpoints the harshness or washes over it so it almost looks soft—until you remember the spine of rock underneath. Monet could have spent his whole career painting the changes from hour to hour. I can't wait to see the differences the seasons make and . . ."

She swallowed the next word with a nearly soundless gasp and slanted a look at him.

There, now she knew who she spoke to. And regretted having spoken. He saw her worrying how he'd react.

"It's something to see," he agreed.

Neutral all the way—not saying she wouldn't be here to see the changes, not saying she would. But it seemed to ease her concern.

"Do you get used to it? Take it for granted?"

"Two different things. You do get used to it. You have to or you wouldn't get much done for staring off at the views all day. But you don't take it for granted. It won't let you. I think sometimes it loses patience with humans hurrying through their lives, so it reaches down and grabs you at odd times, makes you take a long look and give your homage. Then it's satisfied."

She turned slowly from the mountains to look into his face, her eyes searching.

She was near enough for him to wrap his hand around hers and pull her down, across his knees because he wouldn't want her chilled by the ground. And it would be nice to hold her. He wanted to know what it would feel like to have her arms go around his neck, to test the softness of her hair, to discover if the scent of her skin changed when it made contact with his.

He'd once been on a bucking horse, competing in a high-school rodeo, and he'd had this clear, blinding impulse to find out what would happen if he just let go. It would be disaster, but it enticed him. He could almost feel himself being thrown from the horse, flying through the air, crashing into the uneven dirt. It would mean pain, disqualification. But the urge pulled at him.

Thinking about it after, he figured the instinct for self-preservation overrode that impulse to reach into the fire. Self-preservation worked again now.

He looked away.

What was he doing telling her things like that, anyhow? Hell, she probably looked so impressed because she hadn't thought he knew words like *homage*.

"I'd like to ride up there," she said. "Take the time to see it up close. See it slow."

He could show her places that would make her eyes go grass-green with excitement and sparkle like... What the hell was he doing? He didn't want her to see those places, didn't want her to draw more ties with the Double Bar X or the mountains or Wyoming. He wanted her and her kids gone.

He shouldn't tell her things, he shouldn't show her things, he shouldn't wonder things. She was the owner. She and her kids were separate from him and the others. He'd learned that lesson long ago. He didn't need any more instructions on that one.

"Too dangerous. There are wild animals—bear, coyote. The trails are rough. This time of year, you've got tree-falls, muddy ground that can slide away to nothing, flash floods from melt-off. It's nowhere for a novice. It's nowhere for you."

The softness of a minute ago hadn't entirely left her eyes, but now they held more of the snap he'd come to expect.

"I am not a novice. I can—"

"Mom!" The shout came from the barn.

Tucker straightened, muscles bunching to react. There were dangers . . . He'd known how to face the dangers as a kid. But some kids didn't. Some never learned. Some never had the chance to learn.

A light touch on his arm stopped him—body and mind.

"It's all right, Tucker." She smiled. All he could take in was the light prickle of sensation under her fingers. "That was a two-syllable Mom-call—*Mo-om*. That's the my-brother/sister-is-being-mean-to-me, life-is-unfair, I-want-to-play-the-video-game-now call. Not the call-the-ambulance call."

She took her hand away, gave him a final smile and headed to the barn. Obviously she was feeling a little superior.

No need, Jenny. I forfeit. No contest when you're going against somebody who doesn't know anything about kids, doesn't know anything about families. And won't ever learn.

No contest against somebody like me.

Chapter Four

She had been on the Double Bar X a full week and she hadn't ridden a horse.

She'd aired, dusted, vacuumed, swept, polished, and washed. She'd peeled, sliced, baked, fried and roasted. But she hadn't ridden a horse.

This afternoon would remedy that situation. She could just take one of the horses, she supposed. But she didn't know which belonged to the Double Bar X and which belonged to the individual employees; Tucker, Deaver and Manny each had a horse. And Tucker might have plans to use one or another for something special. Besides, she didn't want it to look as if she'd gone behind his back—worse, to look as if she didn't want to face him.

She crossed the yard, skirting the long narrow building she now knew was the calving shed, where Tucker and the others spent so many late-night hours. But he'd said something at lunch about checking a horse's shoes, so she headed to the lean-to off the barn, graced on official papers by the name of barn annex.

Jenny shaded her eyes with her hand to see into the shadowy dimness beyond the open double doors. She made out Tucker Gates bent over, examining a horse's foot.

"Tucker, I want to ride."

He didn't look at her but released the horse's leg, slowly straightened and began putting away his equipment.

"It's ridiculous not to—" she began.

"I watched Tucker shoe the horse, Mom." Debbie's voice from the darkened corner deflected Jenny from her purpose. Squinting, she made out Debbie, with Greg next to her, seated on crates.

"You shod him?" she asked Tucker.

"Yup." He laid the saddle blanket on the horse's back and turned for the saddle that rested atop the divider wall that closed off the tack room.

"Do you always do your own shoeing?"

"Mostly."

"Why?"

He continued saddling the horse without pause. "Gets expensive having somebody come out here, and there's times you don't want to wait. Don't worry. I know what I'm doing. I'm not endangering your property. I took courses at Montana State. Can show you my grades if you want."

"I wasn't objecting to your doing it. But with everything else you have to do, the expense isn't—"

"He cut off part of the horse's *foot*," Greg announced over his mother's words.

Maybe Alexandra Ferrington's strictures on well-mannered women not interrupting had merit, especially if they could be applied to males.

"It wasn't his foot, stupid. It was his hoof." Debbie spoke from the superior position of having spent five more days hanging around the barn than her brother. "I told you, Deaver says it's just like your fingernails. They've got to get trimmed sometimes. If you never trimmed your toenails, your feet would hurt, too."

"I don't care, it was gross and . . ."

Without a word, Tucker led the saddled horse out of the shed, into the open area, and away from her children.

Jenny trailed after. "Tucker, I understand how busy you are, but it's ridiculous that you won't—"

"Get on." He'd circled the horse around so the stirrup was right in front of her.

"What?"

"You want to ride? Get on the horse."

"Now?"

"Right now."

"But I'm not dressed." Her wave took in her jeans and tennis shoes. "I don't have boots—"

"Look dressed to me." His voice cut sharper. "'Round here, we don't need fancy clothes or polished boots, we just get up on the horse."

His swipe at fancy clothes hit home.

She glared at him and stepped up to the horse. She put her left foot in the stirrup, then hesitated. She'd ridden so seldom since her marriage. Edward hadn't encouraged it and she'd wanted to show she could share his interests, so she'd spent her time developing her tennis game and going to parties. Then when the kids were born . . .

"Get up."

Tucker's command jolted her into action. She swung her right leg off the ground.

Tucker's palm against her fanny jolted her in other ways. She wasn't sure if he legitimately meant to propel her into the saddle—help she didn't need—or if the touch was meant to be derisive. Either way it unbalanced her, making her fumble a little in finding her seat. But that was the physical reaction. Another reaction bothered her more—emotional, chemical, hormonal? Who knew, but its precise nature seemed immaterial compared to the way it fizzed through her blood.

She turned to relieve her feelings by snapping at Tucker, but he'd stepped back, and something in his stance made her pause.

From the direction of the open shed door, she heard a snicker. Greg and Debbie. Great, just great. At least they weren't privy to what went on inside her, so they laughed only at her clumsiness.

The saddle felt odd. Cumbersome, a barrier between her and the horse.

"You gonna sit or you gonna ride?" Tucker's bland inquiry drew another titter from the doorway.

Automatically, she took up the reins and instructed the horse to turn to the left.

Nothing.

Cutting a look at Tucker, she caught him pressing his lips tight, fighting a smile.

She squeezed more firmly with her knees and gently pulled back on the left rein.

Nothing.

And the sounds behind her became outright laughter.

Leaving subtlety behind, she made her movements stronger. The horse shifted under her. Took one step forward, and stopped.

The laughter swelled.

"Might help if you didn't saw at his mouth that way," Tucker said. "And give him a poke with your heels instead of being so worried about hanging on. Boomerang's not going to run away with you."

Run away? She'd be lucky if she could get the slug to walk.

"I am not worried about . . ."

When she turned in the saddle to glare at Tucker, she caught a better look at his face and realized the horse's sluglike nature was exactly why her ranch manager had put her on him. Tucker's expression shifted as he looked over at her children, first thoughtful, then frowning. Then the door of the calving shed came open, followed by a bellow from Deaver.

"Tucker! Get on over here. We got one coming backwards."

Before the words drifted away on the breeze, Tucker started toward the calving shed at a lope. He didn't look back before disappearing inside.

But in his absence, his words echoed. Words about sawing at the horse's mouth and using her heels.

Jenny looked down at the reins in her hands. One in each hand—English-style—instead of held together in one hand in the Western style.

Rushed by Tucker, she'd automatically adopted the riding style she knew best, a style developed for lightweight English saddles and used for horse shows and jumping. No wonder the horse hadn't responded. Her knee commands had been useless against the bulk of the Western saddle, and she'd given him instructions in a language he didn't understand.

She shifted the reins to her left hand, laying the right one against the horse's neck, as she loosened her knees and clicked her heels against the horse's side.

Boomerang stepped forward. Reluctantly, true, but a full step, followed by a second, and a third.

A stronger urging and she got him into a trot, slow and bumpy, but a definite trot. She let him slow to a walk and looked around with a triumphant smile.

The yard was empty.

Tucker knew somebody was at the stall door from Sayers's reaction, but he didn't turn. Whoever was there would speak up when they wanted to be heard bad enough. In the meantime, Tucker continued combing the chestnut mane, picking out burrs and untangling knots.

Soothing work after a long, tiring day. They'd saved the calf and the mother—a day's worth of stress packed into too few minutes. Then he'd taken Sayers to ride the herd, checking new calves for signs of sickness. He'd spotted one showing early signs of the scours. Once he secured the calf, he got the medication down him fine with the pill gun. Not strenuous but no picnic, either.

Now it was near dinnertime, and he wasn't really postponing going in and facing Jenny Peters, but these moments alone in the barn tending to Sayers were going by too fast.

"Tucker?"

Going, gone. That voice, edging between politeness and resentment, belonged to Greg Peters. Tucker turned his head altering the rhythm of his movements.

"Yeah?"

"I want to talk to you." There, he sounded like some big businessman trying to cut a deal. Didn't the kid ever sound like a kid?

"Then talk."

"I, uh, Sayers is your horse, isn't he? I mean not part of the ranch."

"Uh-huh." Somehow Tucker didn't think Greg had come out here to talk about Sayers's ownership.

"Sayers—that's an odd name." Tucker volunteered nothing, so Greg asked, "Where's it come from?"

"Football player. Great runner, just like this guy."

"Gale Sayers? He was a Bear—a Chicago Bear."

"Uh-huh." Tucker didn't like the way the kid made it sound like that gave them a connection. Admiration for two great runners had prompted the name, that's all. It didn't build any bridges between him and a strange kid. "What did you want to talk to me about, Greg?"

"Oh." He shuffled his feet in the straw. "I, uh, I want to learn to ride." He'd almost made it with that, then he ruined it. "I might as well, since there's no way I can keep up tennis. I would have gone to regionals next year in my age group if I'd kept—"

Tucker interrupted ruthlessly. "Why not ask one of the others to teach you to ride?"

"They all said I had to ask you."

So he'd checked out every other possibility before coming to Tucker. The boy wasn't stupid.

Under Tucker's scrutiny, Greg straightened, raising his chin. Though the boy's mouth stayed rather sulky, Tucker could, for the first time, see something of Jenny in Greg Peters. Something about that air of facing a firing squad—in the person of Tucker Gates—with chin-up back-straight pride.

He'd done Jenny a disservice today by setting her up like that on Boomerang in front of her kids. Maybe he owed her.

"I'll teach you to ride in exchange for chores around the place."

"Chores!" Greg sounded more astonished than Tucker would have at winning a lottery, and considerably less pleased. "We own this place. Why should I do chores?"

Tucker shrugged. "Up to you."

"But I want to ride—"

Tucker turned back to him, slow, but with enough authority to stop the flow of complaint. "What you want isn't going to decide this. Chores for learning to ride—that's the deal. Think it over."

Then he walked away, hoping luck was looking out for him, and the kid would decide the price was too high.

Tucker lingered at the table after the rest had gone their ways, all except Jenny, who was cleaning up.

Manny had gone to his sister's up in Red Lodge for a couple days to celebrate her birthday, Karl was in the bunkhouse studying, and when Debbie had asked Deaver to show her the calf delivered this afternoon, Greg had gone along.

Tucker wouldn't put it past Deaver to tell those kids some of the details of how they'd hooked the cow up with a chain and OB straps, then levered out the calf with a calf-puller. With a calf coming feet first like that, you didn't want to let it take too long or you'd lose it, sometimes the mother, too. Afterward, they'd hung up the calf by its back feet, head down, to help drain excess fluid from its lungs. If Deaver told the Technicolor version, the two kids could come flying through that door any second now.

But for the time being, that left only Jenny and him.

Vaguely he was aware of the kitchen being a lot cleaner than it used to be. Less vaguely he was aware of a soft, clean scent that came with her when, without a word, she periodically came over and filled his coffee cup.

He hoped Jenny Peters didn't do anything foolish like think he'd stuck around for the company. Or worse, think he'd stuck around to apologize for the episode with Boomerang. He was too beat to move, that's all. He needed to sit here awhile, his only motion bringing his cup to his lips for a steady infusion of caffeine into his system, to get him through his turn of night-watch.

She wiped a towel along the counter and put it down. Without looking, he sensed her hesitation. She went to where the temperamental coffeemaker clicked away, and brought over the pot.

"This is the last of it. You want me to make more?"

"Yeah." She didn't deserve rudeness, so he added, "That would be nice. Thanks."

With her back to him, she set about making the coffee. "How can you sleep after drinking all this coffee?"

"Not sleeping's the whole idea. It's my turn to watch the heifers."

"Heifers are the young cows, right?"

The caffeine had done its job—he had enough energy to nod. "Right. Two-year-olds, having their first calves."

"And they need help?"

"A lot of them. Even the ones that don't, we like to handle some, so they're used to it. That eases things if they have a rough calving down the line and need doctoring."

"So what do you do when you watch the heifers? I mean, is there anything technical you have to do?"

"No. You just look them over, see if any of them look as if they're getting ready to calve—"

"How can you tell?"

"They're not exactly stoic about it. They let you know. They bawl a good bit." She turned to face him, leaning her hips against the counter, the coffeemaker making its strange sounds behind her. He looked at the liquid half filling his cup. "So you check around to see if any of them are ready. If none of them are, you go try to catch a little sleep in the shed so you can get up in a while and check again. Until one of them's ready. And it always seems as if it's never just one. It's two or three at the same time. And then you're so busy, you can hardly remember the last time you breathed."

"I could watch tonight, so you could rest."

He shouldn't have touched her this afternoon. Ever since, at the damnedest moments, his palm had itched and his mind had fevered with the urge to know what it would have felt like to be pulling her toward him instead of boosting her into a saddle.

The *thoughts* would be bad enough in the long hours of the sleepless night ahead of him. He sure as hell didn't need the real thing around to torment him.

"Yeah? You learn to pull a calf while I wasn't looking?"

"I said watch, didn't I? Or weren't you listening?" She jerked away from the counter and strode to the table. The coffeemaker hissing behind her seemed to match her mood. "Watch, I said. I could watch. And if something started happening, I could come and get you. Or Deaver. Or Karl. That's all. That's what I was saying. Thinking maybe I could help so you could get a little more sleep. It couldn't hurt your disposition any."

"I don't—"

"Look, Gates, I may hold a horse's reins in two hands instead of one, but I am not a novice. And I am not stupid."

His crack about her pulling a calf might not have been fair, but it didn't seem the kindling for all this heat, either. Heat that crackled in her eyes and glowed against the creaminess of her skin. Heat that was fast transferring itself to his body. Damn.

"I've never said you were stu—"

"And another thing—I may lack all the skills you've been so busy pointing out, but I can learn. I'm through apologizing for what I don't know. I'm learning, and until I'm done learning, you just have to live with it." She turned away from the table, then spun back so fast, he didn't have time to blink. "And I'd like to see you try the same thing, Tucker Gates. I'd like to see you trying to adjust to the city."

She leaned forward, palms on the table. Her breasts pressed against the fabric of her blouse. He could see the outline of their curve, the slight demarcation of her bra, the point of her nipple. When she pulled in a deep breath to start off again, he felt the physical impact on his own body.

"I'd like to see you do the things I've done. I'd like to see you have a sit-down dinner for twenty-four in your dining room, when the woman you've hired to help comes down with the measles the day before, and the afternoon of the dinner you realize you don't want to be married to your husband. But you have all these people coming, and they're not going to be happy with peanut butter and jelly sandwiches. And when you think you *might* survive this night, the chairman of the board of your husband's firm gets looped and tries to corner you in the powder room—"

He could imagine holding her in the corner with his body, pressing against her softness, so he could understand the chairman of the board. And he'd beat the tar out of him if he ever met the bastard.

"—But you *do* survive. And you do it so well, your husband doesn't have the least idea anything's wrong and everyone has a wonderful time. Except you. I'd like to see you do that! And until you can, I don't think you have any right to say anything about my not knowing how to get along in your world."

She straightened, turned away. Again, she spun back, adding punctuation by banging her fist on the table. His cup jumped. He couldn't take his eyes off her.

"And another thing—I will not be laughed at."

This time when she turned away, she kept going, leaving him no opportunity to point out he hadn't laughed this afternoon. And he certainly had no inclination to laugh now.

"What're you doing?"

Jenny ignored Tucker's question as she tightened the

saddle's girth strap around Flash—it figured she'd pick Flash. Not a mean-spirited horse, but young, and he could get squirrelly. This was worse than he'd expected when Jenny hadn't shown at breakfast, worse than the suspicion that bloomed when Debbie mentioned her mother had gone to the barn. He'd remembered a need to go there himself, first thing.

"What does it look like I'm doing?"

He ran an eye over the rig, looking for loose straps, undone buckles, but between the barn's dimness and her movements, he only caught glimpses.

"You could take Boomerang—"

"Forget it. I heard why he's called Boomerang—he returns to a dead stop as soon as you release him. No thanks. I'll take Flash. We'll get along just fine."

"Hey, look, I don't think—"

"That's quite all right, Tucker. You're not paid to think."

She put her left foot in the stirrup. He started forward, but she'd easily swung her right leg up and over before he could reach her. She tapped her heels into the horse's sides and moved through the opening he'd left.

"Jenny—"

"See you later, Tucker."

Later was an eternity.

He stopped counting how many times he looked in the direction she'd gone only to realize what had caught his eye was a tree teased by the wind. She'd missed lunch, which caused a lot of griping by her kids. Not from worry, but because Manny wasn't due until tonight and that left Tucker to fix lunch. They'd groaned about the peanut butter and jelly sandwiches he fixed. He told them to take it or leave it. It sure wouldn't hurt his feelings if they went hungry.

But it made him think of Jenny's tirade the night before about dinner guests who wouldn't have been satisfied with peanut butter and jelly. And about a husband—ex-husband—who'd clearly given her a rough time.

She'd been upset. Probably not paying much attention to the trail or her riding. Debbie had said something about thinking her mother used to ride as a kid, but the girl was short on details. Jenny had said she wasn't a novice, but she hadn't looked too comfortable on Boomerang, and Flash was a lot more horse to handle.

"...So whaddya wanna do about it, Tucker? Tucker?"

"What?"

Deaver slapped a hand against his own hip in disgust. "You weren't listening to a word. Not a blamed word. You've been worthless all day, Tucker. Hell, you'd have to work dawn to dusk just to get *up* to worthless."

"She's been gone four and a half hours."

Deaver looked at him more closely, then eased next to where Tucker sat on the top rail of the fence, and spoke evenly. "There's a lot to see out there."

"There's a lot that can happen out there, too."

Deaver didn't try to deny it. He simply sat there looking at him until Tucker couldn't stand it anymore. He dropped down from the fence.

"I'm going after her."

Tucker was far enough away that he could pretend he didn't hear Deaver's parting grumble, "That's what I'm afraid of."

Jenny rode off her anger, but it took nearly two hours.

The old Jenny never used to get angry.

But the old Jenny had been created by years of her mother telling her what girls like her *don't* do and her husband telling her what women like her *can't* do.

The new Jenny seemed to ricochet from uncertainty to the giddy belief that she *could* do things. And the new Jenny got livid when other people expressed her own doubts.

Tucker's face when she'd pounded the table popped into her memory. He must have thought she'd gone crazy.

But it was worth it. Shouting the words had made her see the truth, to believe it—even the old Jenny had been capable. Tremendously capable, no matter how those capabilities had been devalued. Even by her. She wouldn't do that anymore. It felt good to think of what she'd accomplished already, without really being aware of it.

It felt very good.

So did the horse under her, the sun above her and the space around her.

After she got the feel of the horse, she'd stayed in open areas, letting Flash canter and gallop out his pent-up energy and her anger. Now they'd both cooled off, and she pointed him to the tree-covered rise that formed the first notes of the mountain crescendo she'd admired from the house.

The slow-going path allowed plenty of opportunities to look back at the territory she'd covered. When she climbed higher, she might be able to see the house and other buildings around that fold, but for now the panorama held no sign of humanity other than widespread fences and fading jet trails. Scattered cattle grazing as they wended their way toward another patch provided the only movement in the vast landscape of Double Bar X land.

Her land.

She took in the air, sharper than yesterday's but still springlike, and the words. *Her land.*

This was the fabric of her childhood fantasy... except all her fantasies included at least a snippet of dust and tumbleweed hurried along by a dry wind. That, she suspected, would come after summer dried out land now fresh and green. She'd never looked forward to dust before.

How would Debbie and Greg take to dust?

She thought they were starting to come around to living in Wyoming. Well, they were at least *starting* to start to come around. Debbie showed more interest in ranch life. She'd really waxed enthusiastic about the calf born yesterday. Even Greg had talked some. Not a huge breakthrough, but a step forward.

A welcome change from all the steps backward she seemed to take with Tucker Gates.

What did she expect? He was another domineering, sure-he's-always-right male, just like Edward—

She slowed Flash to a walk, winding along a rising path near a stream rushing downhill.

Better also slow your accusations, Jenny Peters.

Tucker Gates was not like Edward.

Edward had always manipulated her, trying to get her to do things without asking for them. She suspected he'd thought he'd *handled* her.

Tucker made no bones about his opinions—that she had no business being on a ranch, that she should do something about Greg. And he said straight out what he wanted. To be left alone. For her to go far away and take her kids with her. No ambiguity there.

But there was a question. *Why* did he want that?

Tucker had figured she'd take the main trail up the mountainside. The way she looked at the peaks every time she came out of the house, it was the closest thing to a sure bet you could get with a woman. With little stock out this way yet and the ground soft enough to hold Flash's hoofprint, it didn't take long to know he was right.

Coming around a curve in the trail, he caught sight of Flash placidly cropping grass—with his saddle empty.

Worry hadn't even solidified before Tucker caught sight of Jenny sitting on her jacket beside the stream, tucking a wrapper into the pack from her saddle.

Relief ebbed fast. What was he doing chasing around after city-bred owners out for an afternoon picnic? He drew a breath to order her back on the horse, then she turned and smiled at him. It stopped the words. He dismounted before he considered the wisdom of walking over to her side.

"Hi, Tucker."

"You should be more careful," he said grimly. "I could have been anybody coming up on you like that. Or an animal. Grizzly's not unknown around here."

She shook her head. "Flash didn't spook, so I knew it wasn't an animal. He nickered a little and Sayers answered, so it seemed likely it was somebody from the Double Bar X. Besides, this is all Double Bar land, right? What would someone else be doing here? You want an apple?"

He waved away the offer but dropped next to her on the ground.

"That's just the point. This is Double Bar land, and if it hadn't been one of our guys, it could mean trouble. I'm not saying it's the Wild West and it's probably a damn sight safer than any city, but..."

She wasn't listening.

But she did seem aware of the silence, because she filled it.

"God, it's beautiful." She sighed and shifted, the movement bringing that particular scent of hers to him. What had he been thinking sitting so close? She faced him just then.

"Tucker, I'm glad you came up here. It gives us a chance to talk. Really, it gives me a chance to apologize. About last night, I'm sorry—"

"You don't—"

She didn't seem to hear, so intent on what she had to say. "I know I said I was through apologizing. But I really am sorry for spouting off that way to you last night. I'm afraid you got caught in a delayed wave of anger at my ex-husband. That wasn't fair."

"Doesn't matter."

"Yes, it does. I shouldn't have—"

"Let it lie, Jenny."

She met his eyes, and for an instant, he drowned in hers. He looked away to find a blade of prime spring grass to stick between his teeth, and to let them both pretend that look hadn't existed.

Tucker stood. "We ought to get back."

He extended his hand—a gesture of peace, and friendly assistance. She looked at him a moment before accepting it.

She rose with a slight groan and a wry grin.

"Sore?"

"A little. I haven't ridden this much in years."

He exerted the exact amount of pull to get her to her feet. It wasn't as though he'd tugged too hard and she took an extra step that brought them together. So he didn't even have that excuse when he took her in his arms.

It was the moment in the yard, it was the instant on the rodeo bronc. Only this time, self-preservation lost out. He didn't let go, he held on.

"Tucker." Her voice held uncertainty, caution.

He couldn't hear it. Not now.

He stilled doubts—hers and his own—with his mouth. Her lips were soft, slightly sticky from the apple. He licked at the sweetness. His hands sought another kind of sweetness, feeling the small points of her shoulder blades under his palms, roaming up to tangle with her hair and cup the back of her head as her lips parted for his tongue.

He needed her closer.

The sensation seemed to drive all the air from his lungs. He had to release her mouth, just long enough to regain oxygen. Then he would taste her mouth again, feel the smooth ridge of her teeth, slide his tongue along hers—

Her gasp brought him back to reality.

Only sternly disciplined muscles kept him from jumping away from her as if he'd been scalded. He eased back carefully, staring at the stream, urgent with the spring melt but rushing no faster than his blood.

"That shouldn't have happened. It won't happen again."

The words sounded stilted; it was the best he could do. He wanted to tell her he knew his place, knew the line between employer and employee was not meant to be crossed. That he truly understood that, and had lived by it for more than a decade. But he'd just have to demonstrate those words by keeping his hands the hell off her. Keeping his mind off her . . . well, his mind would have to fend for itself.

"Tucker, I think we should talk a—"

"No."

"—bout this."

"No." He didn't want to talk about it. And he didn't want to stay here another minute, alone with her and the urgings of spring. "It shouldn't have happened. It won't happen again. If you want to fire me, that's your right."

"Fire you? I just want to talk abo—"

"And I don't." He watched gray swallow the green in her eyes and stood rock-still. The words came out despite him. "Why the hell did you come here?"

"I just wanted some time alone up here. I didn't—"

"I don't mean . . ." He clamped down every emotion and said his piece. "Look, I've got better ways to spend my time than chasing up here after you. I spent most of the night tending a pair of heifers not at all sure they're ready for motherhood, and now I've got a ranch to run. Your ranch. That's the way it is. So let's forget this happened, get on our horses and I'll get back to my work.''

She examined his face another thirty seconds, long enough for him to feel sweat filming his forehead. Wordlessly, she picked up her jacket and pack, then walked past him. Not looking at him, but close enough that he held his breath against the temptation of catching her scent.

She'd mounted before he jerked himself out of immobility. He followed her down the path, trying not to watch her straight back that had felt so pliable under his hands, trying not to see the sunlight weaving with her hair that had felt so soft threaded through his fingers.

Maybe this would scare her off. Get her and her kids off this ranch. Out of his life.

First thing the next morning, Jenny Peters drove into Cody and turned in the rental car.

Then she bought a four-wheel drive vehicle.

Let Tucker Gates stew over that one for a while.

Fire him. As if he thought she'd be too afraid of what he might do if he stayed around . . . or too afraid of what *she* might do? Either way, it wasn't flattering of Tucker Gates to think she had so little backbone in one case or so little self-control in the other.

She'd wanted to lay their cards on the table. She would have pointed out they were both reasonable, mature adults. She didn't want to get involved with anyone. Her independence was too new, too fresh. Her children needed her attention. Just as clearly, he did not want to get involved— at least with her. He might be mad for some local woman. Her, he wanted living under a new zip code.

Those were the important facts, she would have told him. But Tucker Gates wouldn't hear of it.

Because he'd kissed her to scare her off?

She didn't like the idea. What did it say about her if he'd meant to scare her off and her reaction was that she wanted more, *more?* But she considered it. And she began to see its benefits.

It was certainly less volatile than chemistry and it explained his reaction. Her reaction? Well, she hadn't had much experience with men, with a grand total of two dates since the divorce, and Tucker was attractive—and annoying. Not the type to override her determination not to get involved.

One more thing—if he'd kissed her in his campaign to scare her off, it explained why he didn't want to talk.

Extending her shopping in Cody, Jenny bought a microwave, a coffeemaker with a timer—and no strange noises—and sheets. Then she made an appliance store salesman's month by arranging delivery and installation of a dishwasher, washer, dryer and hot water heater. She considered a TV, then decided against it.

At a printing shop, she found a fax machine and requested the records transfer for enrolling Greg and Debbie in school. She also stopped at the county courthouse for detailed topographical maps of the area, and in the process happened upon some very interesting information she would take up with Mr. Gates in the near future. No, on second thought, she'd get the process started now, since he didn't care to talk.

Then came a no-holds-barred trip to the grocery store and a gift shop for dishes, table mats, a shower curtain, candles, several scatter rugs and bubble bath.

"I couldn't resist," she told Liz on the telephone.

Calling Liz was something else she couldn't resist.

During the day's spree in Cody and Powell, she'd felt powerful and energized, but driving up to the house, which looked rather dingy and deserted in the late-afternoon sun, she'd felt her assurance bleeding away.

Maybe she was flirting with danger here. Maybe Tucker Gates hadn't kissed her just to scare her off. Maybe she didn't want that to be his reason. Maybe she shouldn't have gotten mule-headed about this. Maybe she and the kids should catch the next flight back to Chicago.

"Good for you." Liz's staunch approval braked her plummeting mood. "There's no reason you should suffer without those things. And there's no reason to wait for someone else to provide them when you can yourself."

"I'm not sure how Tucker's going to take it." That escaped before she would check the words.

"Tucker?"

"Tucker Gates. He's manager of the Double Bar X."

"The manager. So he's your employee, right?"

How could she explain to Liz? "Right."

"How old is Tucker Gates?"

"I don't know. Mid-thirties, maybe."

"Single?"

"Yes."

"Ever married?"

"I don't know. I didn't interview him, you know. I came here, and he was already in charge." Very much in charge. "It's not like I hired him."

"Anything else? Say, like whether this—"

"I don't know what—"

"—Tucker is good-looking? Or if he's giving you a hard time?"

"He doesn't want me and the kids here. He's run the Double Bar for years, and it's like he thinks we're intruders. As if we had no right to be here. He's always pointing out I don't know anything about ranching. But he's not giving me a chance. I want to know about the Double Bar, and I *am* learning."

"Maybe he's scared of what will happen if you learn too much."

"You mean he thinks I'd kick him out?"

"That's one possibility. You're also a very attractive woman, who's—"

"Liz, that's not—"

"We're not going to start that again. I have to get going. For now, listen and you can argue on the next call. You're a very attractive woman. You're also his employer, have money and come from a world he probably thinks is very different from his. That could scare almost any man."

"I really don't think Tucker is—"

"One more thing, Jen."

She gave up trying to change Liz's mind. Liz would have to meet Tucker Gates to know how ludicrous the idea of his being afraid of her was. "What?"

"You *are* learning. You most definitely are learning."

Chapter Five

Tucker ignored the appearance of the new four-wheel drive—quite a feat since the topic dominated dinner that night. Karl and Manny discussed her choice in detail, with a few asides by Deaver, while Greg and Debbie focused on her treachery in going into town without them.

Tucker remained silent, but not, Jenny thought when she noticed the tuck back between his eyebrows, oblivious.

The tuck deepened over the new coffeemaker and microwave.

By the next day, with the arrival of the washer, dryer and dishwasher, she thought the furrow might have taken up permanent residence. But he didn't say a word, not even when she casually let it drop that the hot water heater would be another week because it was on back order. Not even when the plumbing work required for the dishwasher meant lunch and dinner menus of microwaved frozen dinners.

A telephone call came as the men arrived for dinner, looking less than thrilled about the fare. Tucker answered, then held it out to her.

"Jenny? Are you there? Are you all right?"

"Dad! I'm fine. Why would you—"

"Liz told me about this manager you've got there." *Liz, you traitor.* "She said he's giving you a hard time. Is he?"

"Yes and no."

"She said he has you doing manual labor."

"*He* doesn't *have* me doing anything. I've chosen to..." The strained quality of the silence behind her reminded Jenny of her audience. "It's nothing I can't handle, Dad."

"I had my people check this Tucker Gates today—"

"Dad!"

Outrage didn't deflect Charles Ferrington from his purpose. "—that's why I didn't call until now. He comes back clean. I'm not surprised. If he hadn't, we wouldn't have kept him on after we bought that place. It also looks like he's done a good job with the ranch. But if he's causing you trouble..."

This was the one drawback of Liz's influence—sometimes Charles Ferrington, in regret for missing being a real father to her years ago, tried to recapture those days by treating her as if she were still under voting age.

"It's all right, Dad. I'll take care of it."

"I know Liz says I should have faith in you—"

"You should."

"I do, Jenny, I do. But you know, if you need help..."

"I know, Dad. Thank you. And if I do need—" with a glance at the back of Tucker's head, she changed her word choice "—anything, I'll call. Now how are the parents-to-be?"

From there, the conversation became strictly family, with Charles exchanging hellos with his grandchildren before hanging up.

The dinners had to be reheated, which did nothing to improve their taste, nor Tucker's grim mood.

At least the coffee was good. Maybe that would offset how he'd surely feel about her taking any steps that affected the Double Bar X.

That happy thought died the next afternoon when she returned from riding. Tucker came out of the garage as soon as she rode into the yard, as if he'd been watching for her.

"I want to talk to you." From his tone, it wasn't to ask if she'd had a nice ride.

Jenny stayed mounted. Why give up the advantage?

"After dinner," she said.

"Now."

"If we talk now, Tucker, dinner will be late. It will have to wait until after dinner."

He glared, but stepped back. "After dinner. In my office."

As he walked away, she smiled slightly—she'd stood her ground, without even having to think much about it. That felt good, even with that last phrase reminding her Tucker Gates knew a thing or two about holding ground, too.

Maybe that was why she insisted on cleaning up the kitchen first. You own the Double Bar X, she reminded herself, wiping the counter. You're an intelligent, capable woman. You can have an intelligent, reasonable discussion with this man.

He's not Edward. He won't put you down. You don't have to defend yourself.

Still, as she gave the refrigerator handle a swipe, then headed to the office, her muscles tightened.

* * *

"You wanted to talk with me?"

How could the woman standing in front of his desk possibly have two children? She looked more as if she were a child herself, a child sent to the principal's office for the first time. He'd purposely sat behind the desk, but now his gesture smacked of pettiness. She looked so...

No, it didn't matter how she looked. She was the owner. She was butting in. And she was clearly not about to butt out—he'd caught her subtle shift from his saying he wanted to talk *to* her, to her saying talk *with* her.

"What's this?"

He slapped the forms he'd received in the mail today on the desk in front of her, then tried to stifle guilt when she flinched slightly.

But her hands remained steady and her face calm as she picked up the papers and took them over to the wing chair she'd used the first night, bypassing the seat by his desk. It put a good part of the room between them, and the chair back obstructed his view of her face, even when she looked up from the papers and spoke.

"They appear to be applications for grazing leases for government property."

"I know what they are. What I—"

"Then why did you ask?"

He ignored her question. "What I want to know," he resumed, rising and going to the front of the desk to prop his backside against it, so he could see her face, "is why they were sent to me."

"I asked them to be sent to the Double Bar X."

Another of her fine distinctions—for all practical purposes, he and the Double Bar were one and the same.

"Why?"

"I had an interesting discussion with a gentleman at the county courthouse, then I checked with the forest service and found out more about leasing government land for summer grazing. All the leases are pretty well set, but once in a while they open up. And getting the application in now couldn't hurt for next season. Some leases are right up the mountain from Double Bar land, so it seemed—"

"You didn't think that might have occurred to me in more than ten years of running this place?"

She nodded. "Yes, I did. But I checked and there are no leases held by the Double Bar."

Leaning forward, he rested his hands on his thighs. "That's because I worked long and hard to wean the Double Bar from government leases my first eight years here."

"Why? The land's right here and everybody says the grazing should be real good this year. A lot of the ranches use the government leases, so why—"

"And a lot of ranches get into financial trouble. Or didn't *everybody* tell you that? You know how narrow the margin is between making it and going broke out here?"

"I would if you'd let me look at the books." A hit, a definite hit, he'd give her that. "But that seems all the more reason to use the government leases, especially if the fee's reasonable and the grazing's good."

"And what if next year the fee goes up again, like it has before, and the grazing's not so good?"

"Go somewhere else."

"You and every other rancher in the region. All trying to go somewhere else, scrambling for those few 'somewhere elses,' driving up the price of those 'somewhere elses,' taking whatever you can get no matter how far you have to spread your operation because you've got to feed the stock you've built up thinking you'll have the government land to lease. And that's only looking at what happens with a bad season. How about it they cut off leases completely? You know, there are organizations fighting to get all cattle off government land permanently?''

That surprised her into an interruption. ''Why?''

''Because they've taken a few worst-case scenarios of overgrazing and turned it into the rule, not knowing or not caring to listen that undergrazing can be as bad in its way for land as overgrazing. But facts don't always matter. They've got their agenda and they've got the power to put on pressure. So, say they get the leases outlawed. Then what happens to all the ranchers who've relied on that grazing? Maybe that won't happen, but I'm not gambling the Double Bar's future on it. So, from the time I came here, I started replacing the grazing acreage they'd been getting from government leases. Buying some, otherwise leasing from individuals. Two years ago, I finally got independent of all the government leases.''

He nodded to the papers Jenny held. ''Then those showed up.''

''I'm sorry.'' She put the papers down carefully on top of the same papers she'd moved off the chair that first night, still in the spot where she'd placed them. ''I wanted to help. I didn't know—''

''I know you didn't know.'' And he'd be damned if he'd feel guilty for letting her know. He straightened and crossed his arms across his chest. ''In the future, check with me before you go wasting your time and mine on some idea you've hatched about ranching.''

She stood, drawing up to her full height, reminding him again of the queen with a ramrod back.

''Other than this edifying little conversation, I don't see that you've wasted any more time than opening an envelope.'' Her cold dignity melted fast under the heat of temper. ''And in the future, don't you make the mistake of thinking that because I don't know all the fine points of this world—"

Getting tied up with government leases didn't qualify as a fine point in his book since it could have a lot to do with whether the Double Bar X would survive without the safety net of being part of a corporation, but with her under this head of steam, he had no chance to bring that up. Besides, he wanted the right time to broach that topic.

"—that that means I don't know anything, that I'm incompetent."

"I didn't—"

Her disbelieving glare shut his mouth more effectively than the twinge that said he might have conveyed that feeling because he wanted—needed—to believe it.

But she clearly had no interest in any inner battles he might be waging.

"I will have you know, Tucker, that I know how to do a lot of things that you would probably fall flat on your face trying. I know how to hail a cab—"

"You've told me..." But she wasn't listening, and he suspected she needed to say this, even if it was exactly what she'd said before. Sometimes one cleansing didn't get out all the pain. That ex-husband must really be a piece of work.

"—on Michigan Avenue. I know how to organize a charity bazaar to make the most money and feed the most egos. I know how many layers to wear for a November football game at Soldier Field and I know how much skin to show at Orchestra Hall. I know the perfect blend of deference and friendliness when talking to the chairman of the board and his wife, and for every level on the corporate ladder down to the night janitor. And I know how to cross four lanes of traffic when you forget to tell me this is the exit until nearly too late because you're so busy talking about yourself and your precious career—again—even though it's

Debbie's birthday and you left this morning without even mentioning it and I had to dry her tears and convince her that her father hadn't really forgotten and you had, you bastard, you had. And I know how to—''

"Jenny..." He stood and reached for her shoulders, any amusement he'd felt at her tirade evaporating as the anguish poured out. And he didn't like it a bit that somehow he'd become a stand-in for her ex-husband.

But his placating tone and steadying hands had the opposite effect from what he'd intended.

Starting to slump, she immediately stiffened, knocking away his arms with an abrupt move. "Don't you condescend to me, Tucker." At least she knew who he was. "Don't you dare, you...you—''

Before his mind comprehended what she intended, his gut absorbed the blow.

Good God, the woman had punched him!

Punched him hard enough to gust the air out of his lungs and to trigger the instinct to double up to protect his middle—and below.

"That's something you didn't mention you knew," he managed to say.

He could swear she'd left the imprint of her knuckles on his gut, but mostly he felt torn between amusement and a reluctant admiration. When he straightened, he saw her expression was also divided—although her mix held horror and self-satisfaction.

She didn't seem prepared to say anything, so he added, "That was a hell of a roundhouse right."

Her expression changed in an instant, the self-satisfaction inexplicably crumbling. "A roundhouse?"

"Yeah," he confirmed cautiously, not sure of this new mood of hers but keeping an eye on her fist.

"Oh, God, I couldn't even do that right..."

The words trailed off and he desperately wanted to wrap her in his arms. He settled for a brushing touch to her shoulder.

"What do you mean, honey?"

"I didn't even punch you right!"

Emboldened by her failure to bristle at either the touch or the slip-of-the-tongue endearment, he returned his hands to her shoulder, rubbing in gentle, soothing circles.

"Sure you did. You hit me just fine."

"No, I didn't." Her head fell forward, muffling her voice some, but the words and tone were stubborn. She showed a tendency to let her forehead rest against his chin, which he encouraged with a firm palm curved around the back of her head. "My self-defense teacher said never telegraph your punch. She said women do that all the time—they wind up and by the time they're ready to swing, the other person can see the punch coming and can stop it easily. And that's what a roundhouse is—a big windup. I know that much."

The last was said with a rasp, as if he were the one saying her punch hadn't been up to stuff.

"Believe me, Jenny, I didn't see it coming." None of it. Not her humor. Not her backbone. Not her determination. Not the way she'd tasted by the stream. Not the way he reacted to her now.

Her only response was a sound of disbelief.

"You don't think if I'd had the chance, I would have stopped that punch? That came too damn close to leaving me singing soprano for a while."

She stirred and he felt her breath, warm, soft and slightly moist, against his neck. He gritted his teeth. She wasn't the only one stirring.

"What do you mean?"

"Jenny, if I hadn't ducked right at the end or if you had been a couple inches shorter, that would have been one hell of a damaging punch. Your aim might not be the best, but roundhouse or not, you pack a hell of a wallop."

Without lifting her head completely, she slanted a look at him. "I know."

His turn to ask, "What do you mean?"

"I meant to hit you right where I did. I didn't want to really hurt you, but you deserved to *worry*."

It was too much. In a few short minutes he'd seen her wary, he'd seen her angry, he'd seen her discouraged. Now he saw her teasing. How could he stem his emotions when hers spilled over, tugging him first one way, then another?

He took her face between his palms. "Jenny," he said, as if she were the one about to make the mistake instead of him. He covered her mouth before she could respond.

"Jenny."

She heard him say her name a second time—for real or only in her head? His lips were occupied with pressing against hers, sliding along hers, traveling to her cheek or chin, then returning, so how could he have spoken? But her name had sounded different, soft and a little surprised.

Maybe the surprise was hers. Surprise that he was kissing her, that he was allowing to happen what he'd said could not happen again. Surprise that she had wanted so badly for it to happen. Surprise that it felt as good as she remembered.

There was less strangeness in this kiss, more certainty. Tucker Gates was a man who knew what he wanted, and what his lips wanted right now was to please and to be pleased. She kissed him back, not forgetting her irritation with him or any of the other emotions of the past few minutes, but putting them second.

She parted her lips, and he made a deep kind of growl in his throat. It didn't slow him from taking advantage, sliding his tongue into her mouth with a slow pervasiveness that sent shimmers of reaction through her. Oh, yes, he knew what he wanted.

When he leaned against the desk again, his arms stayed tight around her and she stepped in closer between his spread thighs. The adjustment in their heights allowed her to put her arms farther around his neck, so she could slip one hand into his hair and the other along his upper back.

He responded by dropping one hand to her fanny, pulling her flush against him, so her breasts pressed into his chest and she could feel the growing ridge of his jeans against her abdomen. His tongue set up a rhythm—new, yet familiar, and so tantalizing. A rhythm she answered without even knowing she knew it.

The phone rang.

Like a dreamer tuning out an alarm clock, she didn't recognize the sound until he broke away from her and swore, the curse all the more heartfelt for being under his breath.

His hands at her hips set her far enough away from him that he could twist around and pick up the receiver.

"Double Bar X." He sounded gravelly, though even someone who knew him wouldn't think anything was wrong. But when he flashed a look at her, she knew *he* thought there was something major wrong—them.

She was backing away when he added into the receiver, "Just a minute," then held it out to her. "It's for you."

She took it without looking at him.

"Hello?"

"Jenny, what the hell is going on out there?"

"Oh. Edward."

She felt an insane urge to tell her ex-husband that what was going on was she was necking with the ranch manager and if he hadn't called, she probably would have been on the floor making love with him. Or maybe on the desk.

The urge died when she heard Tucker moving away.

"What are you talking about, Edward?"

"I am talking," he started to say in the portentous tones he used when he didn't think she'd given sufficient weight to his pronouncements, "about your son."

That got her attention. "Greg? What about Greg?"

"If you kept better control over your children, you'd know. But ever since you ran off to Wyoming like some irresponsible—"

"What about Greg, Edward?"

"He called me this afternoon." She mentally echoed Tucker's curse word of a moment before. "At work."

Ah, Greg's real sin. And the reason for this call.

"What did he call you about, Edward?"

"It wasn't very clear." In other words, he hadn't listened to his son—Greg was rarely oblique about expressing himself. "But what is crystal clear is that you are not maintaining good discipline over those children. Why you had to go out—"

"I will talk to Greg about calling you at work, but I will also remind you that they got your answering machine when they called Saturday morning at the agreed-on time—the time you set up. They were very disappointed."

"Something came up. I had to change my tennis game time and didn't have a chance to let the children know."

"Tennis, Edward?"

He had the conscience at least to sound defensive. "The international vice president asked me to be his doubles partner. I couldn't say no. This is a very important time in my career. It is not the time for Greg to be calling me at the office."

"I'll talk to him."

"Good." There was a pause, like a car shifting gears, or Edward Peters shifting from peeved to patronizing. "So how are you, Jenny? Are you and the children enjoying your little adventure in the Wild West?''

"We're fine. The children can tell you all about it this Saturday. Good night, Edward."

"I was just trying to be—"

And succeeding. "Good night, Edward."

She hung up softly.

It took a couple deep breaths before she could turn around. But Tucker had gone.

She should have guessed. If he hadn't wanted to talk about that kiss by the stream, he sure wouldn't want to talk about this. Locking it away and never opening that door again seemed more Tucker Gates's style with things that made him uncomfortable. Like her.

If this had been a ploy to scare her off, her reaction must have frightened him to death, she thought with a grim smile. And his own reaction. That hadn't been acting.

When she climbed the stairs, she knew the night was not over yet for her.

A bar of light showed along the edge of Greg's door.

She pushed it slowly open. He had a book propped against his bent knees, the pillow behind his back. She used to sit like that as a girl, reading in bed, finding her fantasies. A glimpse showed her Greg was reading a cartoon book. Definitely different fantasies, yet the dreaming remained.

Her son. A swell of love rose in her. He looked so sweet sitting there. Fresh-scrubbed from a shower and younger-looking in the plain T-shirt he wore with pajama bottoms as a concession to Wyoming's still-chilly nights. No sign of sulkiness or a sneer on his face.

The shifting light from the opening door brought his head up, and he frowned.

Stifling a sigh, she went into the room and sat on the edge of the bed. "Greg, we have to talk. That was your father on the phone."

"Is he coming to get us like I asked?"

Double-edged pain slammed into her heart—once because he wanted to leave, the second time because he would always be disappointed by his father.

"You know that wasn't the agreement. You and Debbie are to live with me. You'll visit your father this summer."

"Then what did he call for?"

Greg sounded almost exactly like Edward in that moment. She took an extra breath, for patience.

"He called because another part of the agreement is that you and Debbie won't call him at the office."

"I didn't agree. He just made it a rule. And I think it stinks."

Her role had always been to calm, to mediate, to buffer her children from their father's selfishness. She didn't know she was going to bend that role until the words were out. "Frankly, I think it stinks, too."

Greg gawked at her. He looked so astonished, she couldn't help but grin. He grinned back, just for a moment.

"But," she went on when his mouth's curve slipped downward. "Whether it stinks or not, that's the way your father wants it. So no more calling him at the office. I checked and you and Debbie can call Saturday and everything should be fine this week."

"But he still won't come and get us?"

"No, he won't come and get you. We're staying here, Greg," she added firmly. "I hope you'll like it after a while. You'll start school in a few days and then you'll make friends and that will help a lot. Plus, as you get to know how things work around the ranch, I really believe you'll like living here more."

He said nothing for a moment. At least he didn't repudiate any chance Wyoming might rise in his estimation or he might ever like the ranch—a real step forward.

"That Tucker Gates thinks he knows everything."

The shift in subject caught her, both unprepared and on a vulnerable spot. She stepped carefully.

"He certainly knows a lot more about ranching than you or I do," she answered wryly.

Greg didn't say anything, and she could tell by his expression his thoughts again were following their own path.

"I want to learn how to ride, Mom. Horses," he added as if she might not figure that out on her own. Jenny held her breath, waiting for her son to ask her to teach him to ride. "But Tucker says I have to do chores before he'll teach me. Can he do that?"

She swallowed her disappointment. "I suppose he can. It's his skill and his time, so he has the right to decide what price to put on them."

"Geez!" Greg turned and punched his pillow to a better shape, then slid deeper under the covers. "Chores!"

"It's your decision, Greg."

"That's what *he* said. Chores . . ."

Jenny wouldn't be surprised if he grumbled the word in his sleep all night. She would have other matters disturbing her dreams.

Tucker watched Jenny's shadow cross in front of the window in Greg's room. The light went out, and in another minute the light in Jenny's room came on.

He sure as hell wasn't going to stand here in the spring-night chill and watch those shadows.

He turned and headed for the calving shed. He wouldn't get much sleep, anyway—might as well give Karl a break tonight. Maybe the cold air would work like a cold shower and get his mind and body off those moments in the office with Jenny.

He'd already cursed himself for being every kind of fool in the world. After he'd sworn some more at Edward Peters's timing, he'd grudgingly accepted that he should really thank the bastard. Another couple minutes and there wouldn't have been any stopping. His gut clutched at that thought, as his mind tried to bury it, fast.

But they had stopped. For good. And now the thing to do was forget all about it. And pretend it never happened. Starting right here, right now.

"Hey, Karl. Why don't you go get some sleep? I'll take the watch."

Tucker didn't find it surprising that he had plenty of work to keep him out of Jenny's path. He'd spent a couple days getting two irrigation canals ready, clearing brush, removing the winter's accumulation of debris.

"Giving that top priority, are you?" Deaver asked.

"Needs to be done."

"Just surprised you're doing it right now."

Tucker hadn't answered. Working on the irrigation canals seemed the safest plan. Because what did surprise him was how many times he had to turn aside the impulse to go into the house for something even though he knew he'd run into her there. And how often he found himself watching for her when she went out on Flash most afternoons.

For the first time, he thought he understood how his father might have felt all those years ago, something he'd always dismissed as a basic weakness of his father.

But he'd be damned if he'd repeat his father's mistakes. He was stronger than that, and smarter. Fifteen years ago he'd missed the similarities between his father's history and the situation he got himself into until it was too late. But he'd learned from that, had seen the line between employer and employee was not for crossing under any circumstances. Most especially not the circumstance that had him wondering about what might happen if he went after Jenny, and came upon her alone beside a stream once more.

Her outings got later when Greg and Debbie started school, because Jenny drove all the way in to pick them up every afternoon just as she took them in every morning, instead of letting them take the bus like other kids.

This afternoon, when she got back, she took Flash and headed out. He wondered, but he didn't follow.

Tucker was near the open tack-room door when he heard Debbie's voice. He hadn't seen much of her lately. He slowed unconsciously.

". . . and I think math's dumb."

"Gotta know math," returned Deaver's grumble.

"Why?"

"What if you're a vet like you were talking about. How could you figure how much medicine goes to a horse that weighs half as much as another horse?"

"Maybe I won't be a vet, then," she said defiantly. "I could run the ranch instead."

"Still gotta know math. Figuring how much seed you need for how many acres. Ordering feed for stock. And keeping track of your money."

Tucker grinned. He'd received a similar lecture from Deaver, although he'd been a good deal older than Debbie, and Deave's goal had been to get him to take college courses instead of keeping an open mind to grade-school arithmetic. He wouldn't bet against Deaver's getting his way again. Deave was even wily enough to know when to stop arguing—at least with Debbie.

"What else you doing in school? You making friends?" After a pause Deaver added, "Why not?"

"They treat me like I'm from another planet."

"You are."

"Deaver!" The unhappiness of the previous sentence was lost in a giggling protest.

"You sure look like it to me sometimes when I see those clothes you wear to school." Having dropped that seed, he moved on. "Isn't there anybody you talk to?"

"Michelle Downs talks to me some. She's nice, and she's in my class. Her grandparents have a ranch near here."

"Sure, I know the Downses, nice spread."

"Michelle said their calves were all born weeks ago. They're all done, and we're not. How come?"

"That's how they planned it. It's not a race, you know, it's just how you want to run your operation."

Another pause, and Tucker could visualize Debbie's serious eyes as she distilled that information. "How do you make the cows have the calves when you plan it?"

Now the pause came as Deaver sputtered in search of an answer. Tucker grinned—served the old coot right.

But Deaver recovered.

"Ask your mother. Now, are you going to help me put this wound dressing on Boomerang like I promised Tucker or you going to jabber all day?"

Come to think of it, "ask your mother" wasn't a bad answer. Tucker had some questions he'd like to ask Debbie's mother himself. Like when she was going to get out of his life and leave him in peace.

Jenny intended to ask Tucker straight out.

She wouldn't make the mistake she had about the leases

on government land. She would ask him directly about some of the impressions she'd picked up in town. Nothing overt at first, just a feeling, a few raised eyebrows and hesitations when she mentioned the Double Bar X's orders in passing.

She hadn't wanted to ask these new acquaintances. Partly because she felt a little silly—the owner not knowing her ranch's operation. But also she intended to face Tucker with this, and bring it out in the open.

As she pulled into the driveway and the kids scrambled out to check the doings in the barn—always their first stop—she vowed that for once Tucker Gates was going to talk to her about the Double Bar X.

"Why don't you buy things in Cody? Or Powell?"

He looked up in surprise from where he sat on the edge of the desk chair, leaning over some papers. He had on a light jacket, liberally streaked with dirt.

Almost immediately, surprise gave way to another reaction in his eyes. She thought it was irritation that his effort—up to this point successful—to avoid her had failed. But before she could be certain, he looked down at the invoices laid out on the desk, picking up one.

"Where do you think I do my shopping? Beverly Hills?"

She shook her head impatiently. "For the Double Bar X. You aren't buying supplies for the ranch from the people around here."

"No, I'm not. Not some things."

"Why not?"

He put down the invoice. "Because one advantage of being in a group is it's more cost-effective to buy in bulk."

She just looked at him, waiting for more. She knew this tactic of expectant silence worked on Greg and Debbie—

Tucker shifted in his chair—and it was going to work on Tucker Gates.

"I first managed the Double Bar X for a woman whose husband had died, the guy they built the wing for when he was in a wheelchair. She remarried and moved away. The ranch barely got by, but she didn't care because she didn't need the money. That's why she was willing to take a gamble on a kid like me, too. As long as it didn't cost much, she kept the ranch in case her kids wanted it. When they got old enough and didn't want anything to do with ranching, she sold to Etienne de Salare. You heard of him?"

"The French clothes designer?"

"Yeah." He said it with such disdain she wondered what he'd think if he knew of her Etienne gowns in storage back in Illinois.

"Yes, I've heard of him."

"He must have found a lot of women willing to spend a fortune on their clothes because he has a wad of money."

"Not just clothes. Perfume, handbags, shoes—"

"—and eventually ranches. The Double Bar X was his fifth in the U.S. Some adviser told him it was a good investment or tax break or something, so he started buying up spreads like I'd buy a belt."

She heard bitterness deep in his voice.

"Anyway, old Etienne didn't mess with us any. But one of his financial consultants did point out that if all us ranch managers got together, we could get a better deal on some orders. He was right. And the Double Bar benefited. So when we got sold to the Ferrington Corporation, we did the same thing with the ranches they own."

He'd stopped, like that ended the story.

"But Ferrington doesn't own the Double Bar X anymore."

He shrugged. "Near enough."

"What does that mean?"

"Charles Ferrington's your father, right? I figure there won't be any problem ordering through them."

"No."

He looked across the desk at her. "No what?"

"No, it's not near enough, and no, we won't buy through Ferrington Corporation."

He looked annoyed. "This is a painless way to cut expenses without hurting the ranch."

Dimly she recognized that the slamming of the kitchen door probably meant one of her children had come in, but her attention remained on the issue—and the man—before her.

"At the expense of a lot of long-term goodwill."

"Most owners prefer short-term profits to long-term goodwill."

I'm not most owners. How can you lump me with the rest of those absentee owners you kept at such a distance?

But she didn't say the words, because that was exactly where he wanted her, too—at a distance. Instead, she leveled a look at him. "I thought we settled that when you explained about not using government land. I agreed with that decision because I *am* in this for the long term."

"Mom!" Greg's call held no urgency. She ignored it, waiting for Tucker to dispute her or to acknowledge what they both knew—that they were talking about more than the ranch's profits. He said nothing. So she spelled it out.

"We are going to do business with the people around here. Bargain for the best deal you can get, but do it with the people around here. Our neighbors."

How could they continue to prosper if the county around them didn't? This wasn't a business you could pick up and move. The welfare of the Double Bar X was as interlocked with the welfare of the area as it was with the weather and the earth and the seasons.

He said nothing for a long moment. The creases deepened around his mouth in what might have been meant as a smile, but didn't much resemble one. He slowly settled his hat low on his forehead, shading his eyes. He stood and went around the desk to the door behind her. His voice came back, even and cool.

"That's damn fine and noble of you, Guinevere Peters. And what happens when your neighborly instincts run the Double Bar X's profit margin down to zero and your daddy takes back the little toy you've ruined? What happens then? I'll tell you one of the things that happens—one Tucker Gates is out of a job because he let a profitable ranch turn unprofitable."

She turned around, only then realizing that Greg had come down the hallway and was openly listening. But for the moment, her attention focused on Tucker, looking him over coolly. The jerk, the unmitigated jerk, to think she'd lay blame on him, to think she'd let her father bail her out, to think she was so muddleheaded and naive.

"All the more reason to cultivate good relationships with the people around here. Since you'd be asking them for a job."

But he got the last, insolent word in before striding away. "You're the boss."

She wanted to sink into a chair and release her frustration in tears. But Greg still stood in the hallway. She straightened her shoulders and started past him.

"Are you firing Tucker?" Greg's interest smacked of ghoulish as he followed her toward the kitchen.

"Greg, this was a business discussion between Tucker and me. It's not your concern, and you shouldn't have been listening."

112 NOT A FAMILY MAN

"Oh, yeah, like you know about business. You don't even work."

The kitchen screen door slapped closed and she saw Tucker's back as he crossed the porch. He would have had to have worked real hard to miss Greg's words.

Suddenly, it was more than she could take.

"Go to your room, Greg."

"What?"

"You heard me. Your room. Right now."

"Why?"

"Because I've had enough of your disrespect, your outright rudeness. Now get up there."

If he defied her, could she physically haul him up those stairs?

She was spared finding out. He stomped down the hall and up the stairs, the noise not quite masking the mutters.

With slightly shaking legs, she sank into a chair and dropped her head into her hands.

Tucker had just finished getting off the worst of the mud accumulated on his work gloves from rolling the heavy propane bottle from the corral corner, where it had spent the winter, to near the back of the pickup. He would get Karl to help him load it up later, then get it filled in preparation for branding. He'd been checking his memory against last year's invoice when he'd been interrupted earlier.

Jenny's voice came from behind him.

"Where's Flash?"

He turned around slowly, not hurrying to answer. "Karl's out on him, checking the calves."

"You said he was too young to do that."

He rubbed his gloves against each other, crumbling off dried mud. "Needs seasoning. That's what he's getting."

"And it just so happens he's getting that seasoning at the time I usually ride? I don't think so, Gates. I want Flash available in the afternoon for me."

Tucker peeled off one still-encrusted glove. "This is a working ranch. And to keep it working, I need—"

"Flash is to be left available in the afternoons. As you so kindly pointed out a little while ago, I am the boss. I will take the responsibility if that bankrupts the Double Bar X. As I will take responsibility for maintaining good relations with our neighbors if you don't feel that is within the range of your abilities."

With that she turned on a heel and marched out.

"What was that about?" Deaver demanded, coming out of the storage room where he'd been stowing away the jar of horse-wound dressing Jenny had picked up in town.

"Miss High-and-Mighty finally showing her true colors, that's what it was about." Tucker slapped the gloves against the door frame, spattering dirt. Deaver watched him without a word. "As if I don't have a good relationship with people round here...."

Another slap and another spew of grit.

Deaver leaned against the wall out of range.

"She said that even after you told her about teaching that free course in horse-shoeing? Or those two seminars you got brought out this way? And about getting that account for all the Ferrington business in with Joe Purdy?"

Tucker whapped the gloves again. "Didn't tell her."

"Why not?"

"I'm not going to go trying to impress the boss."

"Nobody could accuse you of that."

Tucker turned, the extreme dryness in Deaver's voice serving to lower his temper.

"Seems like you've done about the opposite," Deaver added.

Tucker tried to dismiss the whole issue with a shrug. "She wouldn't have heard me, anyhow. She was still stewing over Greg mouthing off to her. That boy treats her like an addle-brained servant."

"Who you think taught him that?"

"His father." That was a no-brainer. "This Edward Peters must be a real piece of work."

"Don't doubt that for a minute." Deaver went past him, but turned around for a final observation. "But seems to me, the boy's been better since he came. Might even have broke that habit total if he didn't have fresh prints to follow."

Tucker followed Deaver's logic too damn fast for comfort, and guilt followed right behind. Even taken aback by Deaver's implicit criticism, he remembered the incident in the yard with Boomerang and Greg's expression a little while ago as he'd absorbed Tucker's stinging words to Jenny in the office.

And Jenny's expression.

Yes, he wanted them to leave, but he never wanted to see that hurt in Jenny's eyes. And he never meant to cause it.

He couldn't wipe it away, but he wished he could make it up to her.

Chapter Six

"All right, Tucker. I want to learn how to ride."

Greg's words had a peculiar effect on Tucker. Dread, that came first. Then a sort of fatalistic acceptance that this was his opportunity to make up to Jenny any disservice he might have done in her relationship with her son. Finally, a reminder to himself to be careful of what he wished for in the future, because sometimes he got it.

"Chores first."

"Geez, don't you trust me?"

"Let's say you don't have a line of credit here."

"What does that mean?" the boy demanded.

"It means chores first."

He set Greg to feeding the two ailing cows he had in the corral in order to keep an eye on them. When Greg returned, Debbie trailed behind.

"I want to learn how to ride, too, Tucker," she announced.

What the hell, two couldn't be much worse than one.

"All right. Feeding's got to be done twice a day, so one of you takes mornings and the other afternoons."

"*Every* day?" Greg demanded. "We have to feed them *every day?*"

"You like to eat every day, don't you? What makes you think a cow doesn't?"

Debbie cut to practicalities. "You take afternoons, Greg. You always oversleep. I'll do mornings." She turned to Tucker. "When's our first lesson?"

"Now."

"Good." Greg started toward the barn.

"Where you going?"

"To where you keep the saddles and stuff."

"That's called the tack room. But we don't need it for this lesson." He headed for the pasture. Debbie came right behind him, Greg followed more slowly. At the fence, Debbie started climbing up. When she put out her hand, silently asking for his to steady her, he hesitated an instant before accepting her small, warm palm on his. She matter-of-factly found a seat on the top rail, and released his hand. No big deal, Tucker reminded himself.

"We aren't going to get on one?" Greg asked. He climbed to the top of the fence, too—with less aplomb than his sister, and also without asking for or receiving any assistance.

"First you have to know what you're getting on."

"But all the kids at school can ride and I want—"

"You're not going to keep up with the kids at school, not for a long time," Tucker said flatly. "The ones on ranches have been around horses as long as they've been alive. Most of the ones from town aren't much behind. You've got some making up to do, Greg. There's no way to skip that."

"But—"

Tucker went on as if there'd been no protest. "First thing is to remember a horse doesn't think the way you do, but that doesn't mean you should underestimate him. That can get you in a lot of trouble faster than you can get yourself out. So let's start with the head . . ."

Greg subsided, but Tucker couldn't tell how much he took in about terminology for parts of the horse.

When he declared the first lesson over and Debbie and Greg headed toward the house, Tucker wondered how they would react when they found out they wouldn't get on a horse for several more lessons; first they'd have to deal with such unthrilling issues as safety and catching your horse. Tucker gave a sigh. What had he gotten himself into?

Jenny leaned against the fence, watching her children on horseback.

They'd been there before—some of the resorts Edward had favored for their rare vacations had nose-to-tail trail rides. But this was different. Although Debbie and Greg rode only inside a ring and under Tucker's supervision, it was the first time he'd had them actually riding.

A graduation of sorts.

He couldn't take time every day for lessons, and when he did, he took his time emphasizing safety, caring for the horses, equipment, the proper way to saddle and unsaddle, then one whole session working on mounting and dismounting.

Jenny thought he was being unnecessarily methodical. She'd picked up a lot of that long after she'd been riding. And from what she could gather, many kids around here were in the saddle practically before they could walk, much less worry about proper stirrup adjustments.

But from what her children relayed and what she'd overheard, Jenny knew Tucker's comments touched on areas well beyond basic horsemanship—riding in snow, dealing with wildlife, safety in the mountains, telling directions from local landmarks, warnings about snakes. It made sense, on the ranch these rules were about as basic as the warnings she'd given her kids when they were little—to look both ways before crossing the street and not to wander away in a store. But it felt odd for anyone else to instruct her children.

She shook her head at herself. What mattered was the kids advancing. Debbie listened intently to Tucker's advice about handling the reins, frowning in concentration as she laid the right rein across the neck of Deaver's old roan, Tally, and added pressure from her right leg.

Greg was borderline.

"Stupid horse..." Jenny caught that phrase when his mutterings of frustration over the motionless Boomerang gained volume.

Two strides took Tucker to the horse's head. He took hold of the rein.

"How you figure that, Greg?"

"Figure what?"

"That the horse is stupid."

Greg looked first surprised by the question, then a little flustered and finally defensive.

"Because I gave him an order, like you said, but he didn't do it."

Tucker tipped his hat back, gaining a clear view of Greg.

"You're the one learning, not Boomerang. He knows what he's doing. He's the veteran. It's more likely you're making mistakes than he is. So before you go blaming him again, you better be sure you're not at fault. Otherwise, the lesson ends right then and there. Understood?"

Greg looked sulky, but his tone wasn't too bad when he mumbled yes. Tucker resumed, and by the time they ended, no sign of Greg's sullenness remained.

Tucker did have a knack with Greg, Jenny acknowledged, ignoring a twinge at the thought. But she decided she wouldn't watch any more lessons. Greg and Debbie didn't need their mother hanging around.

Jenny returned from her ride, cooled down Flash and brushed him, then headed toward the storage shed. Karl had said he thought he'd seen a couple old currycombs there. She found the one in the tack room awkward. It fit fine into a hand the size of Tucker's, but not hers.

Twenty minutes later, she came out with no currycomb, but willing to acknowledge that the back porch no longer qualified as the biggest accumulation of junk she'd ever seen. At the sound of Tucker's and Greg's voices she slowed, closing the shed door quietly without thinking about why.

"...You don't like any of them. Not a single one?" Tucker asked with no sympathy in his voice. She spotted them by the garage. The big overhead doors were closed, but the side door was open and Tucker stood before it, as if he and Greg had been about to part ways.

"No."

"Why not?" Count on Tucker to be direct.

Greg would clam up now, defensively draw in and—

"They're dweebs."

"Every one?"

"They don't know anything. They're so stupid. It's like they've never done *anything*."

Tucker contemplated Greg in silence while the boy shifted his feet and looked off down the driveway in assumed unconcern before darting a look at the man beside him.

"You know when white folks first came out here—"

"Is this a history lesson or something?" Greg interrupted with an attitude Jenny recognized as Edward's.

"Yes."

Greg subsided under the effect of Tucker's quiet tone, backed by his direct look. The boy didn't look happy, but he made no more cracks and he leaned back against the garage's wall.

"When white folks first came out here," Tucker repeated, "they passed right through. On their way to California or Oregon. Or later, looking for gold up in Montana. They looked at this land and saw no lumber like the redwoods on the coast, no gold like in Alder Gulch. Not even corn and wheat like the good farmland they'd left back East. They looked at this land and said it was worthless. But the Indians didn't say that. They'd been living on this land a long time, and they saw how it provided for them. They looked for what it gave them—the buffalo—and they made the most of it."

"What does this have to do with those dweebs at school?" Sullen, but at least Greg was talking, asking.

"You see dweebs. What I'm telling you is what you see depends on how you look."

"You mean it's my fault they don't know anything?"

"It's your fault if you don't stop and see what they *do* know."

"Sure—it's always my fault. The horse knows more than I do, the kids at school do. I'm the only stupid one."

Greg stomped away a few yards, then darted a look back, as if expecting to be stopped. When Tucker said nothing, he dropped his head and kept going.

Tucker's eyes followed Greg's foot-scuffing departure for a moment. Then he took off his hat, dropped his head forward and finger-combed his hair. He stayed that way an extra beat, as Jenny wondered what was going through his mind.

When he straightened, he shook his head, jammed the hat on and strode into the garage without another look at Greg.

So he missed what Jenny saw—Greg pausing by the fence near the barn and staring out across the pasture beyond it to the rising mountains, solid and dark against the fading light of the western sky. Greg stared with the same intensity he would have applied if that particular view were a new video game.

Then he disappeared into the barn, and Jenny leaned back against the shed wall.

Tucker had told Greg exactly what she'd been trying to convey for the past week. Greg hadn't shown any blinding transformation, but he had seemed to listen. Maybe.

She hoped he had. She really did.

Jenny paused with her finger on the light switch.

The kitchen was clean and neat. The rest of the interior was clean and neat, with each of them settled into a comfortable bedroom and the parlor rearranged to her satisfaction. She'd even made inroads on the porch's debris, with help from Karl—and hindrance from Deaver, who kept finding reasons to keep items she saw no earthly use for. The exterior needed painting, but with no experience and two stories, she thought even the new Jenny might need assistance there. And the patch of earth encircled by the driveway would have to wait for warmer weather.

Her riding had rounded into shape, along with several muscle groups that did a little less complaining each day. And she was coming to know this land—*her land,* she always thought with a clutch of some deep, unspecified emotion.

She had to find something to do or she'd go nuts.

Unless—or until—Tucker Gates loosened up and let her contribute to the running of the ranch, she had only one room left to tackle.

Without allowing time for second thoughts, she flipped off the kitchen light and went to the office.

The door was open, light on and desk chair occupied.

From the doorway, she considered Tucker Gates, as she had that first night. He didn't look quite as tired as he had then—calving season was letting up. But the grooves beside his mouth were deeper, and his mouth, if anything, was grimmer. Then, she'd thought he wasn't an easy man. Now, she knew he wasn't.

The tuck appeared between his brows; sure sign he'd sensed her presence, she thought with a mental grimace. But she waited until he looked up to speak.

"I was thinking . . . I know how busy you've been lately and haven't had time to keep up with, uh, keeping the office in order." She glanced around the cluttered, dusty room. "So I thought maybe tomorrow I'd do some spring-cleaning." He said nothing. "If you don't mind."

"It's your house."

"In other words, you'd rather I didn't, but you won't say it. Why don't you just say it?"

"It's your house," he repeated grimly.

"It's your office."

"It's the Double Bar X office, and you own the Double Bar X, as you've reminded me several times."

"It's the Double Bar X office, and you're the manager, so it's your office."

He nodded slowly. Even that level of acceptance represented progress. "In that case, I'd rather you left it alone."

"Okay."

He broke the look first, dropping his eyes to the papers spread on the desk and drifting into a pile. But Jenny sensed his attention remained on her. He sure didn't make any progress in reading the sheet in front of him as she went over to the bookshelf by the fireplace. Stacks of magazines, and several years of old phone books, anchored the bottom shelves. But she spotted some book titles that looked as if they might be regional history.

"Mind if I borrow some?"

"Help yourself," he said. He hadn't looked up yet still seemed to know what she referred to:

"I'm enjoying the one on the area geology, though I have to take it slow and reread sections because it's not something I'm familiar with."

He didn't acknowledge he'd left the book out for her. But neither did he deny it by asking what she meant. In its way, this silence, too, was progress.

She took three books. On the way back to the door, she paused by the wing chair where she'd sat the first night. The papers she'd moved still topped the stack next to the chair. She picked them up absently, an idea forming.

"You know, I was thinking..."

"No."

Only someone poised to pounce could have gotten it out so fast.

She glared at him. "How can you say no? You haven't heard what I was going to say."

"I don't have to." Finally, he looked up, his dark eyes cool. "You're the one who wanted me to say things right out."

"Yes, but I'd like you to *listen* first."

"I told you, I don't have to. You're thinking about a computer."

He was not only not an easy man, but a downright irritating one at times—especially when he was right.

"A computer would help a lot around here, with the record-keeping, finances and taxes, and especially that special breeding you were talking about with Deaver the other night. If you weren't so set against modernization—"

"Who's against modernization? Where modern works best, that's what I use. When the old ways work best, that's what I use. It has nothing to do with being against modernization."

"Well, if you're concerned about using a computer, I could take care of that and..."

Her words trailed off as he shook his head. No, of course he wouldn't like the idea of her contributing.

"Winter before last I took a course. Computer doesn't bother me."

"Then I could buy one and—"

"That—" he slapped his hands on the desk, stirring the papers "—is what bothers me."

She jumped at the sound but didn't back down. "That makes no sense. You don't mind a computer, but you do mind my buying one? Explain that."

"You're infatuated with the ranch right now and you want to come in here and buy all sorts of toys. Maybe I should let you, take advantage of your open checkbook before you go back and leave us to creep along on our own means like Etienne de Salare and Ferrington did. But that doesn't seem real honest. And that's where I draw the line. I've always been honest with the people I work for."

She wasn't sure what made her angrier. The accusation of buying toys, the presumption that she would leave, the association with impersonal corporations or that word *infatuated.* It all added up to his dismissing her, and her feelings for him.

She stood up.

Feelings for him? She didn't have feelings for Tucker Gates, except extreme irritation. He was so pigheaded.

"Draw the line? You're always drawing lines. But it has nothing to do with honesty. You slap down all those lines to keep space between you and the rest of humanity."

"Not drawing them. Recognizing them. And being smart enough to know that people who try to ignore them get hurt."

"How? How do they get hurt?"

"They get hurt by thinking they're just like anybody else, that they can fall for a woman or be a friend to a kid and it doesn't matter. That the differences between them don't matter because they're all just people. But they're not. They're not individuals. They're labels, labels that decide where you fit. And trying to break out of them messes up everybody concerned. Foreman or hired hand or—"

She watched him pull in his emotions, watched him force his words through the narrow channel of deliberation.

"Or," he went on coolly, "manager or ranch owner . . ."

For an instant, when he'd mentioned falling for a woman and being a friend to a kid, she'd felt a mix of panic and hope. But those final words told her clearly: the rare show of emotion was reserved for events in his past. For her, he had only the dispassionate description of their business relationship.

"Those are the lines that can't be crossed."

He met her eyes, and if she thought she caught a shadow of regret in the blackness of his, she had to accept that it was her imagination.

"You know, Mom. You must be pretty smart."

She stared at her daughter. "I guess I do all right," she said cautiously. "But I'd be interested to know what makes you say that now."

"Well, the teacher told us today that when you want to know something, you go to the library to ask the books, because books have all sorts of knowledge in them."

"Yes." Although she hadn't gotten the connection to mothers yet, Jenny followed the logic so far.

"Well, I figure Deaver's smarter than any book. I mean, books can't tell a calf's sick just by looking at it. And almost any question I have, Deaver can answer, but—"

Oh, Lord, what had her ten-year-old daughter been asking that good-hearted but most decidedly earthy man?

"—a couple times when I've asked him a question, he's said to ask you. So he must think you're pretty smart. And he said Tucker's being a danged fool. But when I ask him what about, he wouldn't say."

Debbie looked at her, not expecting an answer, since she was obviously satisfied with her own deduction, but her expression conveying that she had a new slant on her mother.

"See you, Mom."

"Bye."

The back door closed, and Jenny let loose her laughter. Tucker would get a kick out of this....

The laughter trailed off. What had made her think of sharing that moment with Tucker?

"What's so funny?"

She spun around at the voice, staring as if her thoughts had called up a vision, instead of the living, breathing man standing behind her, leaning his ranging frame against the doorjamb.

"What are you doing here?"

"Didn't know I wasn't allowed in the house."

An image would certainly be less prickly. "I thought I was alone in the house. You startled me."

"Sorry. I'll fix that right now."

"Tucker, I didn't..." But he'd gone. What had possessed her to think she could share anything with him?

"There's something out there."

Nearly finished with replacing a belt on the tractor, Tucker didn't lift his head at Jenny's voice, though he'd been aware of her riding in on Flash. He'd already lost too much time explaining the basics of what made a tractor run to Greg. God, the kid could ask questions. "Out where?"

"By the stream, on the far side of the canyon, among those pines."

"What is it?"

"I don't know. But Flash was really worked up. Dancing and shying. I could hardly keep him from bolting. He just wanted to get out of there."

"He's young, probably just had excess energy."

"No, it wasn't like that. He kept looking back like he expected to find something chasing him."

"Aw, c'mon, Mom." Greg gave Tucker a knowing, man-to-man look and grinned. "Are you saying the bogeyman was out there? Or the Abominable Snowman?"

Jenny said nothing, but Tucker saw her mouth go tight and her eyes reflect pain. He closed the tractor's side panel, put on his hat and started for the barn.

"Where are you going?" demanded Greg, who had run after him. Jenny followed more slowly, leading Flash.

"To see what's out there." Greg gawked at him, but Tucker pretended not to notice. "Want to come with?"

Tucker also pretended he didn't see Jenny's frown as she unsaddled Flash, rubbed him down and turned him out to the pasture. As she watched them finish saddling up, she answered his questions about where exactly she'd been and how Flash had acted, but she didn't look happy.

So he pretended that didn't bother him, as he and Greg headed out. What did she want from him? She came and told him there was something out there and he was going to look.

Tucker reined in Sayers and shifted in the saddle for a better look across the canyon, to be sure what he'd seen hadn't been from his own movement or the shifting shadows.

"I thought Mom said she was over by the stream when she started hearing things."

"She did."

There. He had it. And it wasn't shifting shadows or from his own movement.

"So why're we stopping here? Why don't we go over there?"

Tucker pulled out the field glasses from his pack and handed them to Greg.

"See the bent pine on that outcropping? Okay, follow it straight down to just above the stream. See anything?"

"There's a sort of brownish patch. Like a bush, maybe? It's fuzzy."

Tucker leaned over and twisted the focus ring. Greg's hand came up and took over. "I see the stream and a tree and—"

"To the right a little."

"—a brown sort of—it's a bear!"

"A grizzly."

"A bear!"

"Her cub's there, too. Behind her and to the right."

"Oh, my gosh. Oh, my gosh." Greg lowered the glasses and turned wide eyes to Tucker. "What are we going to do?"

"Nothing. Except keep our eyes open over there the next few days.

"Aren't you going to shoot him?"

"Why shoot her?"

"He—*she* might eat the cows."

"Nah. Unless the cows bother the bears, the bears won't bother them, and cows will work away from a bear. Best plan is if you see bear, you go your way and they'll go their way. You just don't want to surprise them, or back one into a corner, or come between a mother and her cub."

He was thinking about those words in another context as they rode into the yard. Greg had been very quiet all the way back.

"It looks like Mom knew what she was talking about, doesn't it, Tucker?" The boy sounded thoughtful.

"Yeah, it looks like she does," he said, deliberately broadening the tense to cover more than this incident.

Greg glanced his way, but Tucker didn't turn, and in a moment the boy busied himself with caring for Boomerang as he'd been taught.

Tucker had some thinking of his own to do.

If finding the bear provided a lesson for Greg, it introduced another one for Tucker. Because he *wasn't* surprised. She'd said there was something out there. He might have believed it wasn't anything much to worry about, but he hadn't doubted for a second that she was right.

So when had he started respecting Jenny Peters's judgment?

They'd decided to curtail rides up to that area for a few days to give mother and cub a chance to move on, so Jenny had planned a shorter ride. Then a fast-moving storm washed that out, too. She was dashing back from the barn when Tucker's pickup came into the driveway. He honked as she reached the porch.

Surprised, she waited there, wrapping her damp sweater around her in the abruptly chilly air.

He held the truck door open with one booted foot while he grappled with something beside him on the seat. When he came up the porch steps, she saw he held something tucked inside his slicker, against his chest. She opened the door for him, then wished she could have let it slam in his face, as the first words out of his mouth were criticism.

"You're all wet. You should have worn a slicker. Didn't you see the storm coming up?"

"Gee, I guess I'd turned off my radar."

This man could draw more smart-aleck answers from her than she'd ever known she possessed. Then she saw the quirk of humor at the corners of his mouth.

"Just don't want you to get the puppy all wet."

"What pu—"

Then it was there, in her hands—she didn't even remember putting them out, but now they held a ball of cinnamon fluff the size of a cantaloupe, but considerably more active.

"A puppy..." she said, guessing she wore a stupid grin to match the stupid tone of her voice.

"That's what I said."

"But where did it come from?"

He shook his head. "If you don't know where puppies come from, we could have a problem, since Deave told Debbie to ask you about how we arrange when calves will get born."

"I don't mean..." She started a gesture, leaving her bundle restrained by only one hand. The puppy took immediate advantage by nearly squirming himself into a nose-dive to the floor.

Tucker stepped in close, his chest blocking one avenue of escape and his big hands reinforcing her hold. The puppy settled, but Jenny's heart didn't, especially when Tucker didn't move.

"I meant..." she said, some automatic part of her bringing out the words when the rest of her was conscious only of the smell of rain on him, the warmth of his body against the back of her hands, the prick on her neck of a drop released from the brim of his hat. "I meant, where did you get the puppy?"

"At the Emmitts, the folks who want us to do some planting for them this spring, for a percentage of the grain come fall." She nodded, remembering that dinner topic. "They had these puppies. Australian sheepdog. Molly Emmitt says they're real good-natured, good to have around."

She lifted her eyes to his face. For too brief a moment to measure, they looked at each other, standing close enough to feel what happened when they crossed his line.

Tucker backed away, breaking the look.

"Tucker."

Before she could say more, Debbie, with the instinct for cute, cuddly baby animals that operates strongly in those who never yield mop or vacuum cleaner, appeared at the kitchen door behind her.

"What's that, Mom? What have you got? A puppy! You've got a puppy!"

"Tucker brought it," Jenny said. She was pretty sure he hadn't gotten it for himself, but he'd have to say it.

"It's yours?" Debbie demanded.

He took another step back, as if to prevent Jenny from thrusting the puppy at him.

"No. He's for your... for here, for everybody."

Jenny almost smiled at hearing Tucker Gates brought to stumbling for words by the combination of a ten-year-old girl and a handful of puppy.

"Molly Emmitt says they come in real handy. They're good to have around the place." Tucker had regained his balance, she could hear it in his tone—and in his putting the good of the Double Bar X first. "Molly says just the scent of a dog around keeps the rabbits and such from overrunning her flowers and vegetable garden."

"I suppose so." A vegetable garden. There'd been gardeners and landscaped yards, but her last vegetable garden was a tomato plant in a homemade greenhouse for a grade-school science project. The idea tempted her now.

Jenny held the warm little body up to get a better look at the melting brown eyes, fuzzy pointed ears, black-button nose and tiny pink tongue intent on making contact with her face. "So Tucker plans to make you work for your keep, you hear that, puppy? You're going to be a ranch dog, what do you think of that, puppy?"

"Can I hold him, Mom? Can I?"

"I'm not planning anything," Tucker objected as Jenny handed the puppy over to Debbie and turned to face him. "It's up to you what to do with him. In fact, it'd probably be easier to keep him as a house dog."

"Easier?"

"For when you leave."

A punch wouldn't relieve her emotions this time.

Even when he came the closest to crossing those lines of his, Tucker pushed her away, reminding her he expected—wanted—them to leave the Double Bar X. To leave him.

Walking to the side and half a step behind Greg, Tucker kept a hand on the boy's shoulder. Not enough to insult him but enough to have a grip if he started to go down again. The half a step back was so Greg wouldn't see if Tucker lost this battle he waged with a grin.

Inside the back screen door, he let his hand drop so they could both toe off their boots. He half expected the boy to bolt for the solitude of his room. Instead, he gave a smothered sort of groan and came to a halt.

Jenny stood in the narrow passageway between the corner of the counter and the long table, a plain white apron wrapped around her waist, an empty measuring cup in one hand, in the other a spatula lumpy with a dollup of something that promised to shape up into cookie dough and a smear of flour across her bared forearm.

"Well, I wondered where you all got off to. I haven't seen a hint of you or Debbie since we came back from church. And now you come wandering in looking as if you've been playing in a trough. How'd you get all wet?"

When no response came to her teasing, her smile faded and she flicked a look at Tucker but immediately looked back to her son.

He had meant the puppy as a peace offering, but clearly she wasn't putting all her trust in it yet. He couldn't blame her—he didn't know what had possessed him to say sure when Molly Emmitt asked if he wanted one of the puppies for the new folks she'd heard were living at the Double Bar X.

What he should have said was they were just here temporarily, just visiting, moving on any time now.

"Where've you been?"

"In the calving shed."

This time she met Tucker's look for more than a blink, and apparently whatever she read in his expression reassured some motherly-worry. Her shoulders eased, and she moved to the counter to put down the cup and spatula. With her closer, he smelled the flour, the butter, the sugar she was mixing, and under it a sweeter scent he told himself was vanilla or some such flavoring, because the alternative was too potent.

"Why were you in the calving shed?" she asked. "And how'd you get wet?"

Tucker shifted away from the counter so the back of a kitchen chair propped up his backside. He could leave, now the boy was in safe hands. On the other hand, what could it hurt if he stayed? Only as a spectator. Or maybe he could cut Jenny off before she made the kid expose himself. Give the kid some support. Strictly moral, of course.

"What were you doing in the calving shed?" she asked more insistently. "Is that where Debbie has been?"

"Yeah. We were just watching."

From his new vantage point, Tucker could see Greg had his eyes fixed on Jenny's hands. Hands that she was wiping dry on the white apron across her flat abdomen.

"What were you watching?"

The boy was paling fast. Tucker could almost follow Greg's thought process as he put together what he'd been watching with his sister's comments about babies and now the presence of his mother in front of him.

Greg mumbled something and bolted past Jenny.

"Greg . . . ?" She started after him.

"Let him go." Rather to Tucker's surprise, she stopped, turning to him.

"What on earth's gotten into him? What's going on out there?"

"Well, if I hazarded a guess, I'd say what got into him was a whole lot of respect for what his mother went through in bearing him." Her eyebrows shot up and her eyes rounded, but she said nothing, so he went on. "And as for what's going on out there, Greg just witnessed his first calving. In fact, he assisted a bit."

Jenny went almost as pale as Greg. He wondered for a second if he'd have to catch her.

"Oh, my God," she muttered, and started again in the direction Greg had gone.

Tucker shot his left arm out in front of her, securing her with a hold on her opposite forearm. Under his palm her skin felt soft and warm. The silkiness of the pale hair on her arms ticked his flesh. He could feel the hair on his own arm rising as it brushed so slightly against the apron and the loose fold of her blouse just above her waist.

"Let him be a while, Jenny."

The words came out closer to a whisper than he'd meant. She turned her head and her eyes were almost even with his. She was so close he could see those green flecks. All he'd have to do was reach out his right arm, slip it behind her and pull her to him. And in her eyes he saw her recognition of that. Knew that she saw the same possibilities, that she had the same questions. But her doubts... they were very different.

It was his doubts that made him drop his hold on her. And it was her doubts that made her turn away, snatching up the spatula and measuring cup and returning to the mixer.

"Well." She didn't seem to like the way that had come out, so she tried again. "Well, that must have been quite an experience for Greg."

"Guess so." Tucker welcomed back his equilibrium and wished to God he didn't lose it so easily around her.

"When I brought the kids out here, it was with the idea of having them learn life's realities, but I didn't imagine the lessons would get quite so, uh, basic this fast. I didn't consider how they'd handle that."

"He did okay. For a city boy." He saw her spine straighten and felt a little more at ease. "Course, he's not the natural Debbie is."

Jenny shot him a look, partly horrified, over her shoulder.

He shrugged. "She's still out there with Deaver tending the new calf. I think seeing his sister there put Greg on his mettle. As I said, he did pretty well. Even helped pull the calf free when we got into a bit of trouble." Jenny lost some of the color she'd just regained. "He started to breathe a bit fast—Greg, not the calf. And Debbie spoke right up and told him not to be such a sissy, that a woman went through this every day."

Jenny still stared at him, but her mouth twitched a little at that. "Well, not the same woman every day. They usually get at least nine months off in between."

Tucker nodded, fighting his answering grin. "But it had a lot more impact the way Debbie said it, especially when she told him if you'd been as big a sissy as him, he never would have been born. That made him straighten right up."

"I suppose so," she murmured a little weakly.

"In fact, he did fine from then until we started back this way. It was when we stopped at the pump to wash up—I didn't think you'd want us in the house in that state. Anyhow, I suppose he started thinking about what he was washing off and how it came to be on him, and..."

He shrugged again.

Perhaps in gratitude for his tactful omissions, she took up the conversation as she turned back to the mixer.

"Yes, I can see how that would happen with Greg. From the time he was a baby, barely able to crawl, he'd steam right into things before he'd see what he was getting into."

She turned on the mixer, the noise blocking conversation. He should get back ... He stayed put, watching Jenny's movements with a strange sort of satisfaction.

"It's odd what distinct personalities they have from the moment they're born," Jenny said when quiet returned, still working with her back to him.

"Like Rambo," he offered, prepared for her to object to her children being compared to a puppy.

Instead, she nodded. "Exactly like that. The kids said the name was short for rambunctious, but I think they saw his personality right away, too—lots of action and no subtlety. And that's the way it is with babies. They're individuals right away. At least mine were. Debbie was a very quiet baby, but she watched the world around her with great curiosity. And she's stayed that way. She's my observer. She doesn't say as much, but she sees what's going on."

Something made him turn his head, and he met the wide, serious eyes of Debbie, who'd slipped silently into the kitchen. He hadn't been around her as much as Greg, not with her latching on to Deaver from the start. And he wondered now what the girl was like.

Debbie looked at him, and for a reason he couldn't explain, he winked at her as he spoke to her mother.

"Oh, yeah? She sees things? Like what?"

"Lots of things. Like the animals and the sky and the flowers and ..."

As her mother wound down, Debbie looked straight at Tucker and added, "Like the way you watch my mom when she walks past and you don't think anybody's watching you."

He heard the clatter of the spoon falling out of Jenny's hand as she spun around, and he felt her look go from her daughter to him and back. But he didn't take his eyes from that serious little face staring at him, telling him without words but in no uncertain terms that she wouldn't fall for a wink. Or anything less than the truth.

"I suppose I do, Debbie." He hated like hell admitting it—to himself or to Jenny—but Debbie gave him no choice. "Your mother's a very attractive woman. I wouldn't be human if I didn't notice that—or at least I wouldn't be a man."

Debbie stared at him, unblinking, a moment longer, then gave a nod that made him want to sigh with relief. "I've seen Karl do it, too. He turns red."

"Well, there you have it." He wasn't going to argue, though Debbie's lumping of Karl's crush on Jenny with his reactions was ridiculous. His feelings for Jenny were . . . He gripped the back of the chair hard, braking the thoughts.

"All right, that's enough nonsense," announced Jenny, wiping her hands again. "You are a mess, Deborah Barton Peters. You get upstairs and get cleaned up." She shepherded her daughter toward the stairs without looking at him. "We'll get you in the shower and then you can help finish these cookies."

"Why doesn't Greg help? Just because I'm a girl—"

"No, just because they're for your class tomorrow. He'll help when the cookies are for his class."

The voices faded and Tucker, alone in the kitchen, slowly ungripped the back of the chair.

Chapter Seven

Jenny hadn't followed a lot of things Tucker Gates had done in the four weeks she'd been at the Double Bar X, but taking her into his office that night immediately after dinner, seating her in one of the wing chairs amid a partially cleared room before a small fire and handing her a stack of manila folders topped all the other mysteries.

"What's this?"

"You wanted to see the books? This is the best I can do. We don't keep a book. These are financial statements from tax returns the past few years. Inventories of cattle, inventories of equipment. Everything I've sent to Etienne de Salare and Ferrington. That what you wanted to see?"

"Yes, I did—I do. Thank you." She sank into the chair with the thick folders in her lap. "Uh, thank you."

"You're welcome."

For a few minutes after he left, she listened to the distant sounds of the kitchen cleanup crew. She caught Tucker's low notes and heard Manny and Karl. But could that be Debbie and Greg? Cleaning? Yes, if Tucker had asked them to help.

The thought brought a twinge of something too close to resentment for comfort.

Contemplating his influence over her children would have to wait its turn. Right now she had to grapple with this sudden capitulation over her reviewing the Double Bar X finances.

It would be so nice if it meant he'd accepted her presence, no longer waited day to day, hour to hour for her to pack up and leave. Nice but not believable. Not from Tucker Gates.

So why had he given her the financial statements? Was he trying to maneuver her into something?

A sigh dropped her shoulders. She suspected he wouldn't reveal his reasons until he was good and ready. But in the meantime, she might as well take advantage of the information he'd finally provided her.

She tuned out the sounds beyond the office, slipped off her shoes and tucked her feet up beside her as she opened the top folder...

The welcome aroma of fresh coffee roused her as she compared a figure in the final folder to one in the first.

"Thought you'd be ready for a break."

She looked from the mug under her nose to Tucker's face. How long had she been studying these figures? The house was quiet, and the stiffness in her back and legs said at least a couple hours.

"Thanks. Smells great." She put the mug he handed her on a table unearthed from a drift of paper. First things first. She untucked her feet, raised her arms over her head and stretched out the kinks of concentration.

Tucker turned away abruptly, taking the other wing chair and dividing his interest between his mug and the fire.

Feeling better, she took a sip, then a second. "You've done a fine job here."

"Always nice to hear praise from your employer."

She didn't react to the pointed remark. "I see it here—" she tapped the folders "—and I've seen it day after day— you work the Double Bar X as if it were your own place."

He met her eyes. "It will be someday. I've always had in mind to buy it. I've been saving. It's sooner than I figured, but Deave and I have talked... I want to buy the Double Bar X from you, Jenny."

Her first reaction was shock at his straight-out statement of what he wanted. Her second was how hard it must have been for him to watch the place he tended and loved get passed from hand to hand. The burst of empathy left her a little flustered.

"If I'd known that, Tucker, I wouldn't have bought it. Because you can't help but feel... But, really, it wouldn't have made a difference. It was going to be sold, anyway. Ferrington Corporation had made that decision before I ever came into it, and if another firm had taken it, they probably would have consolidated and then you never... But that doesn't matter now. I did buy it and—"

"I'll give you a fair price. You'll get a small profit. Not bad for owning such a short time."

He might as well not have spoken; Tucker knew that before the words had even finished forming. She sure wasn't tuned in to concepts like fair price and profit. He could see her steady herself, grab her resolve and hold on to it.

"I did buy it, and we're here now, and we're staying. I'm sorry, Tucker, I really am. I know you care about this place. But the Double Bar X isn't for sale."

He knew this afternoon that he had to make a move to get her away from here. When a ten-year-old saw things he didn't want to admit to himself, drastic measures were needed. To get Jenny to sell, he had to show her the finances, that was only fair.

"I won't lie to you, Jenny, I—"

"I know you won't."

The words were soft, the look so brief it almost didn't exist. He wasn't sure of the import but he felt the impact all the way to his bones. And as quickly locked it away. That wasn't for him.

"I won't lie to you," he repeated, almost coldly. "I don't think you're going to last here. I want to buy when you go."

She shook her head. "You're wrong. If you weren't, yes, I'd sell to you. But you *are* wrong, Tucker. I'm here to stay."

"Why?"

"I need it."

He sat back, more sure than he'd been a moment before.

She didn't need the Double Bar X. Not the way he did. Not the forever way he did. She'd sought it out as a temporary refuge and eventually she'd recognize that, and see that she and her kids belonged somewhere else. They'd move on and he'd remain, with exactly what he wanted. If he could just be patient. And careful. So that when they moved on, they didn't take too much with them.

What he had to do was help her see the truth. This was a good time to start.

"Why did you come here, Jenny?"

"I don't know what you—"

"There's a charge for seeing the books, Jenny—that's it. I want the truth. I want to know why you came here."

Thoughts slid past her eyes, he watched them. Watched her reluctance, then her decision that telling would help persuade him to her way of thinking. Fine, let her think that. Because he was certain in the end, telling her story could only help her see the truth of what he knew: the Double Bar X was a temporary stop for her.

"I came here—we came here—because I wanted to get my kids away from my ex-husband."

With no time to put up a guard, something powerful gripped him. "He hurt them?"

"No, no—not the way you're thinking."

She reached across the gap between their chairs to put her hand on his arm, and he consciously eased muscles he hadn't been aware of tightening. It wasn't enough. He stood, went to the fireplace to give the embers a few useless pokes while Jenny continued.

"Physical abuse isn't Edward's style. He's more subtle than that." Her mouth twisted. "More like Chinese water torture—the drip, drip, drip that erodes self-confidence. I couldn't let that happen to Greg and Debbie."

"You married him, had two kids with him. You must have loved him." His words came out harsh, but she didn't flinch. It was almost as if she'd expected the harshness. "All of a sudden that love turned off? You suddenly saw—"

Almost as if she'd expected the harshness.

His own thought echoed, rankled. Expected it from her ex-husband or from him? Either way, he didn't like it.

"Suddenly saw that I didn't love him anymore?" she took up his words. "No it wasn't like that. I don't know when I realized I'd stopped loving him. But I know when my marriage ended."

He returned to the chair, perching on the arm, one elbow hooked over the wing and his legs stretched out. He could see her face, but could move away if he needed to.

"It was at the tennis club," Jenny said. "The third one Edward had joined. I liked the second one, made friends and really enjoyed it. But Edward wanted to 'move up.' So we moved on to this club..." Her eyes lost focus, along with their usual softness. "Greg had a match. I'd finished earlier, and watched the end. The other boy wasn't as strong as

Greg, and Greg knew it. He expected to win. But the other boy was patient. He waited for Greg to show his weaknesses, and then he took advantage. So Greg lost.

"When Greg came off the court, all he talked about was how he needed a new racket. His shoes didn't fit right. And the lights were bad in this club, why couldn't we join a better one? He knew a place where the people were much better. Better... He didn't mean their tennis ability. Eight years old...

"I sat there looking at my son and realizing I loved him to the core of my being, but I didn't like him very much, and I wouldn't like him at all if he kept becoming more and more like his father. That was the moment my marriage ended, no matter what the legal documents say."

"Why had you married this guy?" *None of your business, Gates.* He waited for her to say the words, to put him in his place.

"That's not a very flattering story."

He said nothing, knowing he shouldn't ask, letting his silence tell her he'd listen if she wanted to talk.

"What it really comes down to is my mother liked him."

Tucker considered that. "How about your father?"

"My father didn't approve or disapprove. To tell you the truth, I don't think Dad considered what Edward was like until I told him about the divorce."

This didn't match the man she had long conversations with on the phone. She must have sensed Tucker's doubt.

"My father's changed a lot in the past few years under Liz's influence—that's his wife now. I've changed a lot, too, under her influence. She's helped me see things, why things happened, that I never saw at the time."

"Like you and—like getting married?"

"Like getting married. My father wasn't around much then. All his energy went into business. So Mother was the one I went to for approval. Mother had very strong ideas about how women of our class should behave—that's how she talked—so I had very specific expectations to meet to get her approval. Edward met those expectations.

"He came from the right kind of family, had the right kind of bank account, the right kind of job and the right kind of ideas. In other words, he and Mother saw eye to eye. Most especially on me.

"We married when I was twenty. He was thirty-two. I wanted to wait a year, until I'd finished college, had my diploma. He and Mother said there was no reason for me to delay the wedding to get something I would never put to use. It wasn't as if I'd ever go out and work."

She sank back in her seat, lost in the past.

"I think they were a little annoyed when I took extra courses and managed to graduate before the wedding. But of course, they were right, I never did go out and work. I played tennis, volunteered for charities where I would meet women who were good connections for Edward's business and got pregnant almost immediately.

"For a very brief time, I felt as if I were really doing everything right, and I had my mother's total approval. Then she got sick."

A vague memory of a woman, soft and warm, pushed at the edge of Tucker's mind. He'd been young when his mother died, but Jenny had known her mother and relied on her. "That must have been tough on you."

Jenny met his look, and he saw that doing it taxed her courage.

"It was tough, but not the way you mean. I don't deserve sympathy, Tucker. I was angry, so angry at her for getting sick. It was as if she'd broken the bargain. I had done everything she wanted—everything—and now she was deserting me. Looking back, I think I even got pregnant with Greg before I really wanted a second child because I imagined the pregnancy as some sort of bargaining chip to make my mother stay around longer."

She spread her fingers across the cover of the folder, then drew her fingers in to a protective ball.

"She died five weeks before Greg was born. And I was lost."

Tucker had steeled himself against touching her in desire, but this... He went totally still, afraid any movement would end with his taking her in his arms and rocking away the pain.

He could see that she wanted to stop, to pretend she'd never made any of these revelations, to hide them away, to smooth it over and keep up good appearances, to do all the things she was undoubtedly raised to do.

She kept going.

"By that time, I knew I didn't love Edward, not the way I wanted to, not the way I needed to keep doing things I didn't care about just to win his approval. His approval didn't mean as much as my mother's."

She didn't spare herself, telling him of the deterioration of her marriage as the old Jenny slowly sank under the weight of all those old expectations.

Edward had excused her for a year, discounting her behavior as depression over her mother's death. Then he'd lost patience. Feeling cheated of the docile woman he'd married, he'd started cutting her with slighting remarks, dismissing her efforts and abilities. And she'd believed him. For a long time, she'd stopped trying.

The first step out started with running into an acquaintance from those early volunteer days, who had turned a stint at the Art Institute into a career at a gallery. Her enthusiasm was contagious. Jenny had signed up at the Art Institute without consulting Edward and over the next three years had ignored his belittling, winking comments about her "dabbling in the art world."

Dabbling or not, she'd learned, and she'd loved it. And she had thrived in an atmosphere where she was simply Jenny Peters. Not Alexandra's daughter or Edward's wife or even Greg and Debbie's mother.

The second step had really been her father's. Charles Ferrington had a business lunch with Liz Sharon to discuss her employee relations workshops and fell in love. Liz was a whirlwind in their lives. A beneficial tornado, that picked up the far-flung pieces of their father-daughter relationship and brought them together.

For the first time, Charles Ferrington put something— and someone—ahead of his work. And for the first time, Guinevere Barton Ferrington Peters had someone who asked what she wanted to do, what she liked instead of telling her what she should do, what she should like.

Jenny didn't tell Tucker all this, but he heard it. In the tone of her voice, in the softening in her eyes, in remembered fragments of conversation he'd heard over the past weeks.

Jenny also didn't tell him the other conclusion he drew from her story. This woman had guts. The guts to change herself and change her life.

"God, it's nearly one. I didn't mean to talk your ear off." Jenny stood and took two steps toward the door, which brought her near enough for him to see the sheen in her eyes. She stopped by his right knee. "Thanks for listening, Tucker."

"No problem."

He could have left it at that. That would have been safer. But he made himself face temptation by meeting her eyes, looking up slightly from his seat on the chair arm.

Mistake.

She was so close, he could see the gratitude in her eyes, and the indecision. Something else, too, something he was man enough to recognize, but didn't risk examining. Besides, he'd already been caught by the indecision.

He saw what she wanted to do and what she was afraid of doing. *My God, she's been married, had two children—is she really so uncertain about initiating a kiss? Yes.*

He could have stood up, looked down, broken the moment. Instead, he held perfectly still.

She dipped closer, hesitated for an instant that hung like torture over him.

Her lips brushed his, soft and quick, then retreated. She looked at him from too close for comfort and a hell of a lot too close for safety. But he didn't back away. He stayed right there, looking into gray-green eyes gone wide with self-discovery.

She accepted the truth with wonder.

Jenny Peters, drilled in demureness from babyhood, wanted to kiss a man. This man. Wanted to kiss him long and wet. Wanted to explore his mouth with her tongue. Wanted to feel his tongue in her mouth. Wanted to hint at the union and passion the kiss could imitate. Wanted... Jenny Peters wanted.

More amazing yet, she took.

She looked past the wariness in his eyes and kissed him. Not softly this time.

She slid the tip of her tongue against the stern line of his top lip, a caress and a request. He opened his mouth, but that might have been in surprise. He held so still under the grip she'd taken on his shoulders. Then she slipped her tongue along the ridge of his teeth, and deeper, and he jolted.

He made a sound. It vibrated with desire, communicated directly from his mouth to hers. He met her tongue, stroking against it, drawing it deeper. At the same time, he gathered her to him, one hand tunneling under her hair to cup the base of her skull, holding her while their tongues thrust and retreated, thrust and retreated.

A charge sparkled through her. Like heat lightning in a midnight-dark sky, its pattern had a logic of its own, not following the ordinary pattern of nerves or muscles. A prickle as sensuous as the skin of a peach brushed at her breasts, tightened between her legs, but also across the back of her shoulders, along the front of her thighs, inside her ankles.

In the urgency to come together, they had paid no attention to the niceties of position, but now she became aware that she stood almost astraddle Tucker's leg, and the charge deepened.

He lowered one hand to cup her bottom, the pressure rubbing her more firmly against his leg. When he slid forward on the chair arm, his leg slid deeper and higher between hers, and she gasped. Her knees seemed to loosen and she leaned into him.

He muttered something that sounded like instructions, but she could only follow the lead of his body. As he swung his legs around and dropped onto the cushion, she cooperated, ending with a slightly skewed seat in his lap, one arm around his neck, the other grasping the front of his shoulder. When he put his arm around her, she felt his large hand against the bare skin at her waist exposed by her pulled-up sweater. She remembered the sensation of his palm on her back the day she'd choked on Deaver's intended words. It hadn't prepared her for this.

The earlier charge intensified, a zing that pervaded her skin and her bones. She wanted more of that touch.

He provided it.

Her sweater rode higher as he explored the previously innocuous skin of her side, back and midriff. She rubbed against him, loving the feel of his hard legs under hers, his solid chest against hers. And she explored as well.

His textures fascinated her. The sturdy softness of the hair that curled at the nape of his neck, the vulnerable smoothness of the skin there, protected by hair and collar, and such a contrast to the tough, whiskered jaw and chin he presented to the world. The sleek ropes of muscle at shoulder and arm that she felt through his shirt.

But she didn't want his shirt. She wanted to learn his skin, the way he was learning hers. She tucked her hand inside the open V of his shirt collar, experiencing two buttons' worth of his skin, toughened by the elements, warmed from inside, prickled with hair that beckoned her lower.

A third button gave way, but she could swear she hadn't done that—or undone it.

And still they kissed. Long, slow, deep matings that brought his head over hers as she half lay in his hold, stretching and arching to answer a rhythm his touch and his kiss communicated to her body.

The roughened surface of his strong fingers contacted the curve of her breast, and the sigh she gave into his mouth had the tone of "at last." His palm covered her breast, delivering heat and sensation through the silky material of her bra. Then he brought the same to her other breast. She marveled at the intensity of each light touch, the pleasure when his fingers slid under the material to meet her skin, the jolt of desire when he stroked her nipples. She wanted his mouth there, and knew that should shock her, but shock would have to wait.

Her hip brushed the bulge under his jeans, and he went motionless for four heartbeats. It made her want to move all the more.

"Hold still ... Please—"

She didn't bother to answer; she showed him she didn't want to hold still.

His touch strengthened, and it seemed that all her sensation focused on her breast.

She was wrong. She knew that when he dropped his hand lower, first drawing her closer with a firm caress against her hip, then sliding across her abdomen, tracing the path of her jeans zipper. And lower. He made a low sound in his throat that never escaped the union of their mouths as his hand cupped her at the base of the zipper.

This time shock punctured the haze of sensation. Not at his touch, but at her own reaction. What was she doing? What was she *feeling?*

She broke away from his kiss and gasped a word. She could never remember later if it was "Wait" or "No," but he reacted as if it were "Freeze" and backed by a shotgun. He went ice-solid.

Then, before she could assimilate either her desire or her instant of panic, he went into action—removing his hand, smoothing her sweater down, practically pushing her off his lap, standing her on her feet and snatching his hands from her hips as soon as she had some balance.

"You better go." It sound more an order than advice.

"Tucker, I'm sorry. I don't know..." She couldn't begin to list what she didn't know—how she felt, what she wanted, how she wanted him to feel—so she let it hang.

"Don't be." The stiff words matched his body language. "I shouldn't have let it happen."

"You? You didn't. I did. And that's why I think we have to talk about this. To—"

He ignored that. "I promised it wouldn't happen again." He stood, keeping some distance from her, his mouth twisting into a parody of a grin. "I don't know if you'll believe me, not with my record, but I'm saying it again. This time it'll stick. But—"

"Tucker, that isn't nec—"

"—right now you better go."

"—essary. That isn't what—"

"It sure as hell is necessary. We've each got a role here. Nice and clear. You're the employer and I'm the employee, and this—" he left *this* for her to fill in "—is not part of those roles. Not any part of them. So it's stopping. Right now."

"Another line you're drawing between people, Tucker?"

"That's right. A line that can't be crossed. Now, if you're not leaving, I am."

"What are you going to do if you ever do own the Double Bar, Tucker? Then you'll be the boss. Will you suddenly feel different about Deaver? Or Karl or Manny?"

"That's not—"

"How would you keep yourself separate from the people who make you nervous then? If you couldn't draw lines between employers and employees? Why do we make you so uncomfortable, Tucker? What are you so afraid of?"

But he wasn't answering. He was leaving.

"Tucker, don't be a stubborn ass. If we can talk this out—"

But he was gone. Jenny watched him, pieces of her scattered among desire, regret, admiration, frustration, fear.

At least *she* knew what she was afraid of—the way she felt around Tucker Gates.

The temptation to sink back into the passive ways of the old Jenny hummed a Siren's song to her over the next several days. To sit back and let matters develop around her, without facing issues and choices. To drift.

She fought it.

First, she went to the Buffalo Bill Museum in Cody and volunteered as a docent. The impressive collections focused on William F. Cody's times, the Plains Indians, historic firearms and Western art. The Whitney Gallery especially caught her, with the work of artists who had captured the special light, the sense of space and grandeur that never failed to demand her homage, as Tucker had said.

With her experience from the Art Institute, the education director said that, while her formal training would wait until fall, she could do the ten-minute spotlights—researching a special topic to present to visitors. The director and curators approved her first three ideas. That inspired her to dive into the research.

The Buffalo Bill Museum wasn't her only project. She had an informative discussion with an instructor at the college in Powell, taking home a personally tailored reading list on ranch and livestock management.

If the weight of the books equaled knowledge, she would have had both areas licked the first day.

Instead, she plugged away, some days with only the determination not to slip back into her old ways.

Facing the issue of Tucker didn't apply, since she saw mostly his back. Anything that required a trip to town or a far corner of the spread he took on himself. When he was in the house, he stayed behind closed doors. The only times he spent more than passing-through time in the same room with Jenny were dinners—for those he arrived last and left first.

She recognized the symptoms. She'd spent a lot of her life denying emotions; had she been as obvious as Tucker?

As much as that irritated her, and as much as she believed they needed to talk, Jenny couldn't deny feeling some relief—because she had no idea what Tucker was hiding, what he really felt for her.

So, she made no attempt to cut off his retreat. And she tried to ignore that even Flash couldn't gallop off this sense that her emotional barometer was plummeting and a storm rolling in. The old Jenny would have avoided that at all costs.

What would the new Jenny do?

She didn't know. That unsettled her. Yet, in a way, it also exhilarated her.

Coming up the driveway at past midnight on his return from Billings with the tractor part, Tucker frowned at the light showing in the parlor window. Who was up this late? It could be trouble. One of the kids sick. Or Jenny. Or a problem with the ranch he should have been around to handle. Or...

Or Jenny asleep on the sofa.

The light blazed over her head, an open book rested on the cushion by her hip and two more were spread on the floor below for easy reference. But Jenny was curled on her side, her head resting on the arm pillow.

She looked tired. Her skin was pale, the smudges that she'd borne when she'd first arrived were back under her eyes.

Even the little he'd seen her lately, she'd acted tired, too. Less patience, fewer smiles, more thunder.

What was she trying to prove, driving herself this way?

Greg had let something drop about Jenny's volunteering at the museum. From the little he said, it sounded as if she'd jumped into it with both feet. Then Karl mentioned that Jenny had borrowed some of his texts to "read up."

Tucker glanced at the dense, technical pages. There were easier ways to pick this up—if she really wanted to. Maybe he'd say something to her...

No. He wouldn't say anything to her, and he wouldn't let himself worry about her. He'd stick to what he knew was right. And safe. Which was why he resisted the urge to stir her awake so she could go upstairs to a comfortable bed; he was already thinking too much about Jenny in the comfortable bed down the hall in his room, awake.

Tucker considered her a moment longer. He also didn't move the books or turn out the light. But he did pull the quilt she used as a covering for the dull sofa off the back and over her, carefully avoiding touching her.

"Liz had the baby this morning. It's a boy. Everything's fine. The baby's fine—perfect!"

"Oh, Dad, I'm so happy for you and Liz. If you and Liz need me, maybe I could find someone here to look after the kids..." Tucker flashed into her mind, then disappeared. He was more than capable, but she couldn't envision herself asking him, or him saying yes. "... or take them out of school for a few days and help out. Especially when Liz comes home and—"

"No, no. There's no need for that. Liz has it all arranged—you know how she is. Her mother's coming for a few days, then I'll take a couple weeks off and it'll be just the two of us with the baby. After that, the nanny will come in. Besides, you have your hands full out there."

Jenny looked down at the spatula she hadn't put down when she'd picked up the phone. Yeah, she had her hands full—with another batch of cookies. For Greg's class this time. Those kids were going to OD on sugar.

Extending the long cord, she put two prepared cookie sheets into the oven and twisted on the timer.

Her father went on detailing the arrangements he and Liz had made. He was right—Liz didn't need her. Who did?

"So there's no need for you to come." No, no need for her. "You don't need to start playing big sister yet."

"Sister," she repeated in a whisper too soft for the long-distance line and her father's abstraction. Somehow she'd never quite put it into words. It felt odd. Like trying to get her land legs after a lifetime at sea.

"The one thing we haven't decided on is a name for your little brother. I'll let you know when we do. I've got to get back. Give my love to Greg and Debbie."

"Of course. And you give our love to Liz."

"I will."

The line disconnected, the dial tone came, and still she held the receiver.

Rambo hurtled into the room with all the rug-scrambling energy of a four-month-old puppy, and ran straight into the trailing phone cord, jerking the receiver from her hands.

It clattered to the floor, setting up a startled howl from the untouched dog. Rambo's self-defense maneuvers involved spinning around as fast as he could, picking up speed when the cord snagged one of his paws.

Jenny was kneeling, trying to untangle puppy, cord and receiver when Tucker's boots came into her field of vision. She hadn't heard his approach over Rambo's noise.

"You need to keep better control of this beast," Tucker said dryly, holding up a well-chewed Agriculture Department flyer.

Need. That word lit a flare in her. "It was your idea to make him an indoor dog. You're probably already planning to pack him off, too, when you succeed in driving us away. Then you'll have all your ends neatly tied up and be rid of every reminder of the Peterses."

He hooked his thumbs in his front jeans pockets, rocked back slightly on his boot heels and considered her. "I just suggest you keep him out of the office. There're papers in there we don't want to lose."

The "we" did not placate her. She released Rambo's paw from a final coil, stood and slammed the receiver home with unnecessary force.

"Then close the damn door. That's how you keep the Peters family from watching your precious TV, so it ought to work on our dog, too."

The oven buzzed, or she might have said more about Tucker Gates's policy of separation. Instead, she switched off the buzzer, banged open the oven door and retrieved the first of the two sheets of cookies.

"Smells good," Tucker ventured cautiously from behind her. She ignored him. "You make real good cookies, Jenny. If you ever needed a job, you could open—"

She spun on him, spatula held like a lance. "Open a bakery? Hold bake sales? How cute!"

He held up his hands in surrender, which might have ended it, if he hadn't also muttered, "What did I say?"

"I am capable of more than this, you know. No matter what you think, Tucker Gates, I am not an idiot. It's not that I mind baking cookies for Debbie's and Greg's classes, I don't. But I'll be damned if I'm limited to that. I can do more. Why won't—"

But he'd reached the end of his tether, too, and cut in. "Like making it so your kids don't have to lift a finger to help themselves?"

"You don't know what you're talking about. The divorce was difficult for them and—"

"It was harder on you." The flat words sounded angry. "Look, maybe those kids were learning being self-centered at their father's knee and you were right to get them away, but you're not helping the situation any."

"What's that supposed to mean?"

"It means you do all the chores. It means you make meals when they want to eat. It means you take care of Rambo. It means you ferry them back and forth to school at their convenience. My God, they hardly knew the meaning of the word *chore* before they wanted to learn to ride. Your ex-husband might have started this, but you're the one spoiling them now. No wonder they aren't fitting in at school. Driving them instead of making them take the bus isn't doing anybody any favors—not you and not your kids. You're using up your time, you're spoiling them and you're making them different from the other kids. Debbie can probably get past that, but Greg—"

"I don't need you to mediate between me and my son, thank you very much."

"I wasn't—"

She tried to pull in her anger, to be fair. But even knowing he was the source of only some of her emotions couldn't stop her venting them. She was hurt, confused...and scared. He was responsible for that. Because one of the things she feared was that he was right.

"I don't need a daughter who thinks I'm smart only because Deaver Smith tells her to ask me questions and a son who tolerates me only because you kindly indicate I'm not an idiot. I see how he looks up to you, and I know you've been a good influence on him. But I didn't get him away from his father just to have him aping someone he hardly knows. Oh, I'm not saying you're not an improvement when it comes to role models. But that doesn't mean—"

"*Role model?*"

The stark emotion on Tucker's face more than his voice brought her up short.

"Yes, you have to know how Greg looks up to you—"

As an undercurrent to her words, she heard the whine of the screen door opening, but Tucker was too caught up in his thoughts to hear anything.

"I'm no damned role model. Last thing on God's earth I want to be is a role model to your son or any other kid. I'm no charity to help straighten out your kid and I'm no role model, so keep him the hell away from me, and all this will be just fine."

The screen door slammed, punctuating the end of that speech, and both turned in time to see Greg's back as he ran down the steps, away from the house.

Tucker swore, and headed out the door himself, swiping at a chair back in his way and toppling it. Outside, he took the opposite direction from Greg's.

Jenny stared at the blankness beyond the screen door until the combination of Rambo's crying and a pair of odors reached her. Rambo's housebreaking had just suffered a setback. And the second sheet of cookies, left in the oven during her argument with Tucker, had turned the color of his eyes.

Chapter Eight

The curator's telephone call to praise her preliminary research, though welcomed, did not lighten her mood. Because immediately she thought of telling the Double Bar's manager of her small triumph. And the instant after that, the idea of sharing anything with Tucker Gates shook her.

During her late-afternoon ride, her mood ricocheted like a bullet in a canyon.

First— She was crazy to think of sharing anything with Tucker, including the air they breathed and the ground they walked on.

Then— Hell, why not? She'd tell him. There was something between them—*something*. Wasn't there?

Then— No, there was nothing between them. She'd practically thrown herself at the man, and being human, he'd responded, but that didn't count as *something*.

Then— Wait a minute. Even if she discounted every kiss, every touch, there was something. The laughter, the caring she'd seen in small ways and, more important, the dignity he accorded her by his honesty. Even when it hurt.

And finally— What could have hurt Tucker to make him so determined to stay apart from people? Or at least certain types of people—families. She knew even small wounds left untended could fester or could build scar tissue more disabling than the original injury. What had happened to him? Would he ever risk opening up enough to tell her?

By the time she brought Flash in, she had a roaring headache that made her grateful Manny was making dinner tonight. She desperately wished it were as simple as Debbie's interpretation of Deaver's words—Jenny was smart and Tucker was a danged fool. But it wasn't that clear-cut. Tucker's intelligence was undeniable, and she certainly had her share of foolishness. Maybe he was right about this.

No, it wasn't simple at all.

Any thought of trying to talk to Tucker died at dinner.

First, Manny had already heard from his cousin, who worked with the sister of the curator's assistant that the staff thought highly of Jenny and was most impressed by her topics and research, and he announced it at the table.

Karl and Manny congratulated her, with a small addition from Debbie. Even Deaver mumbled something about hoping those museum people would be smart enough to know an experienced hand when they saw one, and Greg gave her a tentative smile.

That smile was particularly precious. She'd tried to talk to Greg about what he might have overheard this morning, but he'd denied hearing anything. Whether Tucker liked it or not, this pretend-nothing's-happened role Greg played was definitely modeled on him.

Tucker didn't look up from his plate and didn't say a word.

He continued eating methodically, as if he weren't wearing noticeably new jeans, a crisp white shirt, a fancy tooled belt and polished boots. A black cowboy hat with a silver band that she hadn't seen before sat on the table by the back door. It all screamed the news that Tucker Gates was going out tonight.

Her headache surged, and she lost the thread of the conversation until she heard Karl telling Debbie and Greg about a dance that night at a regional community center.

"In Cody?"

"No. It's out a ways. There's not much around it at all—except nights like this when there's a dance, then there're vehicles all over the place. Folks come down from Montana, a few even from Idaho and all around Wyoming."

"And none of 'em will dance any better than Double Bar X's manager, eh, Tucker?" Manny's teasing also held a strong note of pride.

"You should see him," Karl interjected, before it became awkwardly apparent Tucker didn't intend to respond. "He really is good. I remember last summer watching Tucker and Rebecca Coleman on the Fourth of July. Lots of folks just stopped dancing so they could watch."

"Watch dancing?" Greg asked, disbelieving.

"You bet. I wish I could go watch," said Manny, who planned another trip to Red Lodge.

"We can go watch," announced Debbie. "You could, too, Manny, if you stayed here instead of going to Red Lodge pretending to see your sister when it's really to see that widow who lives next door to her."

Dull red spread across Manny's cheeks while Karl laughed, Jenny hid a smile and a chuckle could even be heard from the direction of Tucker's downcast face.

"Blabbermouth. Last time I tell you anything," muttered Deaver, but a quirk of his mouth gave him away.

But such levity did not distract Greg.

"Okay, we'll go watch," he announced.

"It's not for kids," Tucker said.

"But—"

"No. This is for adults."

"I'd like to go."

Jenny's announcement drew surprised silence. For a tick of the clock, she was as surprised as anyone else. Then she was a shade irked at the others' surprise. She was outright shocked by Deaver's response.

"I'll look after these two." He nodded to Debbie and Greg.

Tucker cast him a glance Jenny couldn't see. He didn't look at her even when he spoke to her.

"You wouldn't like it."

"How would you know?" Her harsh demand drew looks from around the table, except from Tucker. Automatically, she softened her next sentence. "It sounds like a lot of fun."

"Not your kind of people." A veiled insult even in his telegraphic style. "And women don't go alone."

That drew stares from Manny and Karl that informed her without a word that the second part was untrue, but she figured the first half needed to be addressed first.

"Most of the people I've met here in Wyoming have been very much my kind of people. Of course there are exceptions," she added, with a pointed look in the vicinity of Tucker's shoulder. "But I'm sure I would enjoy it very much. So—"

But before she could do more than turn toward Karl, Tucker cut in.

"You've got watch tonight, Karl."

"But calving's just about done."

"Just about isn't done."

"But, Tucker—"

"You heard me."

Yes, they all heard him, Jenny thought. And they all knew his intention. That did not mean they would listen. At least she didn't intend to.

The man had radar.

Jenny walked in the door of the recreation center with Karl and had the dubious pleasure of meeting Tucker Gates's eyes from the far side of the room. He broke the look first, but only to glare at Karl, who seemed to shrink by her side.

"It's all right, Karl. Remember, I'm responsible. I gave you a direct order."

"Yes, ma'am."

Jenny gave him a particularly warm smile, perhaps not entirely altruistic. "Jenny, remember?" she said with a soft touch to his arm.

"Hey, Karl. How's it going?" That greeting started a stream of exchanges that allowed for no further private conversation.

For the first time in a long time, she benefited from the lessons in sociability her mother and ex-husband had impressed on her, because concentrating on the people she met helped distract her from Tucker's presence.

She received hellos from two people she'd met at the museum, a secretary from the grade school and the college instructor who had helped her. Karl seemed to know everyone, producing a number of introductions that resulted in nearly as many invitations to dance.

"I'm sorry, I don't know how," she answered.

Some gave up easily, some lingered for conversation, some come back to ask again. One, named Bryan Felton, was the most persistent. Karl, who grew more relaxed as Tucker remained across the room, yet never left her side despite her encouragement to go dance, frowned when Bryan Felton headed off with the promise that he would be right back.

"Feltons got a big spread."

"Oh, really?" she answered absently. Tucker had just been joined by an attractive young woman with a stunning fall of glossy brown hair. The young woman's smile said they were not strangers.

"Yeah. Feltons have a lot to do with the museums and hospitals and such." Karl sounded neither impressed nor particularly happy about the Feltons' philanthropies. "Family's pretty big deal 'round here, though maybe not as big as Bryan Felton thinks."

"Mmm-hmm."

"Ma'am—Jenny—are you listening to me?"

"Of course." She turned from the sight of the brunette putting her hand on Tucker's arm in a familiarly coaxing way. "What is it you're trying to say, Karl?"

Before he could answer, Bryan Felton returned and once more asked her to dance.

"I'm sorry, I don't know how."

Bryan smiled as the band started an easy, traditional waltz. "I bet you know how to dance this," he said. "That's why I asked them to play it."

"Thank you, but—"

"Uh, Jenny..." Karl turned his back to Bryan and muttered under his breath. "Tucker doesn't like him."

So, Tucker Gates didn't care for Bryan Felton. What a shame.

"I'd love to dance with you, Bryan."

She felt the looks as they took the dance floor. Most reflected idle curiosity at seeing a newcomer with one of the well-known residents. A few, from the women, were speculative, perhaps a bit jealous. The one from Karl was a gawk. The one from Tucker was a glare.

The dance was pleasant, though this music didn't draw nearly as many dancers as previous songs had. Bryan Felton danced easily. He held her closer than she liked at first but accepted the added distance she created. His conversation reminded her of a laid-back Edward—a Western twang added to the ubiquitous "I-my."

Song over, she thanked Bryan and rejoined Karl, who shuffled his feet and looked even more worried.

"Tucker doesn't get mad often, but when he does . . ."

She agreed with the second, unspoken part, but she disagreed with the first half. As far as she could tell, her ranch manager spent plenty of time being peeved at her.

Karl brightened when the band struck up the next song.

"Wait until you see this," he said.

"See what?"

But he didn't need to answer. The crowd obviously knew what to expect, some easing off the dance floor, others setting up a wide circle, leaving a few couples in an inner circle. Those select couples included Tucker and the dark-haired young woman. The song spoke of *dancin'* and *romancin'* and the couples put the words to motion. Especially the lanky figure in the white shirt and new black hat, partnered by the brunette. They formed a striking couple.

"Good, aren't they?" Karl's question, tinged with reflected pride, required no answer.

Jenny couldn't take her eyes off the dance.

The brunette circled under Tucker's raised arm, trailing her arm around his waist as she slipped behind him, then came out on his far side. With a saucy smile, she snatched his hat off his head and put it on her own before they started off on an intricate passage of side-by-side footwork. Tucker didn't protest.

The dance dipped and swirled, their bodies meeting and retreating in a choreography made possible only by practice. A lot of practice and familiarity.

Jenny couldn't take her eyes off them.

On another pass, with their hands linked over their heads, the hat was transferred from the woman's head back to Tucker's, though Jenny couldn't tell which of the dancers performed the transfer. It didn't much matter, because in another chorus of music, the hat returned to the woman.

It was peculiarly intimate. A sign of things shared, of give-and-take.

The movements ruffled Tucker's hair, leaving it a little wild. The way it would look if a woman had been running her fingers through it. The way it had looked a few nights ago when her fingers had experienced its texture.

Jenny couldn't take her eyes off him.

Even when the music wound down, applause rose around them, and the brunette put her arms around Tucker for a hug that he returned.

Even when he looked over the young woman's shoulder and met Jenny's eyes, with a dark, unfathomable intensity.

Beside her, Karl's nervousness condensed into dread.

Between the interruptions of milling dancers, thirsty party-goers headed to the bar and others crossing the room to greet friends, they saw Tucker say something to his partner, leave her and start toward them.

"He's going to kill me." Karl's resigned statement activated Jenny's protective instincts.

"I'd like a soft drink. Would you get me one, please?"

"Now?"

"Now."

"But—"

"Right now, Karl. A soft drink, please?"

He looked from Tucker's approach, slowed by exchanges with many of the people crowding the room, back to her. "You're sure?"

"Yes."

"Okay." He ducked his head. "Thanks."

He departed quickly. She cut another look toward Tucker. Giving Karl a way out didn't mean she had to wait like a prisoner for the judge's arrival. She pivoted and headed toward the door. Her one glance back told her Tucker had altered his course, and now closed in on Karl. He had a brief exchange with the young hand, which didn't look too intimidating from this distance, then turned toward her.

With no real thought to where she would go, other than *away,* she was out the door.

She had reached the end of the wooden sidewalk that ran along the front of the recreation center when she heard footsteps coming fast behind her. She knew the cadence of the boot heels on the boards as Tucker's. She kept going.

Just as she stepped from the dusty gravel parking area into the sparse, tough grass where the latecomers had parked, he caught her, one hand wrapped around her arm above the elbow, stopping her, then using her own momentum to swing her around to face him. Just the way she'd seen him use his dark-haired partner's motion to guide her into a spin.

He was already drilling questions at her.

"Where do you think you're going, Jenny? What do—"

"None of your damn business."

To keep herself from coming up against him, falling into his arms, she raised her free hand, the heel of it striking him hard in the breastbone. He gave a grunt, but finished his demand.

"—you think you're doing here?"

"And that's none of your damn business, either. But if it were, I'd tell you I was invited, and told by several people how glad they were to see that I'd come. *Some* people don't seem to think I'm a social pariah. *Some* people don't seem to think I should be kept from having any fun. *Some* people *enjoy* my company. But it's *not* any of your business."

Trying to wrench her arm free gained only a pain that promised a future bruise.

"You made it my business when you got one of my hands to disobey my express—"

"One of *whose* hands?"

He went still and dangerous. "That's right. That's right, isn't it? That's what this all comes down—"

He broke off, and his head came up, hearing the sounds before she did. And before she'd fully recognized them as sounds of someone approaching, he took hold of her other arm and wheeled her into the narrow, deeply shadowed canyon between a pickup's cab and a van.

The weight of his body wedged her against the side of the van. On some level she recognized his urge to keep their argument private, even knew that it was as much for her sake as his own—maybe more, since she was the newcomer.

But that was the very small portion of her not ruled by her senses.

The van's surface was cool and smooth against her back, a stark contrast to the heat of Tucker's body against her. The heat built up from the dance's exertion and his anger seemed to roll off him and into her. She could smell the sweat overlaying the scent of soap, and a faint, lingering whiff of leather. Her hands had automatically gripped his arms to maintain balance, and now they absorbed the slight dampness that had soaked into the cotton of his shirt. One of his thighs pressed against hers.

He held utterly still.

Low voices came nearer—a man and a woman, laughing a little. Nearer still. Started to pass. Faded.

She didn't breathe.

She closed her eyes and she could see him dancing again, could see the rhythm of the dance, could feel the rhythm of the dance.

She never knew how, but it changed then. He was no longer pinning her against that van, he was holding her, gathering her in. His thigh was between hers now and she accepted it, welcomed it. His eyes were dark, so dark and intense. And then his lashes started lowering, and she couldn't see the intensity, but she could feel it as he looked at her mouth. He was going to kiss her. Really kiss her. And this time he wouldn't stop with a kiss.

And then he wasn't.

He didn't move, but he squeezed his eyes closed, and he let out a hiss of words too garbled to identify. But they were curses. If he felt half what she felt right now, they had to be curses.

He wrenched himself away from her, and in the near dark, they stared at each other. He glared, and his jaw clamped so tight she could practically hear his teeth grinding. She suspected her expression looked every bit as unfriendly as his.

"C'mon."

His grip on her already-tender upper arm made her wince as he started towing her along.

"Where?" That was all she had breath to get out.

"Away from here. Anywhere."

"But Karl—"

"I told him I'm taking you home," he said grimly.

She gathered more breath. "You're hurting my arm."

He slowed long enough to shift his grip lower.

"We've got to talk about this, Jenny. We've got to get it settled. Now."

As if I've been the one refusing. As if I've been the pig-headed one about this.

But she didn't say that. She didn't say anything as he bundled her into his truck and barreled along in the dark on narrow, unmarked roads. The speed and the blackness that immediately swallowed the narrow swath of the truck's lights, fit her mood exactly.

Damn the man. He was driving her out of her mind, and driving her body into a perpetual state of frustrated frenzy.

Well, no more. This was it. This was the showdown.

The storm the new Jenny had awaited.

He stopped the truck with a jerk, then sat silent, stiff, facing forward.

She had a vague impression they were on Double Bar land, though she hadn't kept track of their route, and they certainly hadn't come down the drive. With the headlights off, it was dark, with no moon, and the stars not fighting their way through a covering of pines.

The man next to her was about as easy to make out as the landscape.

Well, she'd been the one who kept saying they should talk, so she might as well.

"Tucker—" she cleared her constricted throat "—all right, Tucker, here's what I've been wanting to say. I think we should say this out, so it's clear, and then we can go on."

No response to that introduction.

It was up to her. "Okay, I will say it, get this out in the open so we can deal with it—I'm attracted to you. But that doesn't mean anything, not really. I mean, you could be all wrapped up with someone and I wouldn't even know it, because you don't bring anybody back to the Double Bar, but of course you could be doing anything you wanted on your own time away from the ranch, and I would have no way of knowing you'd been seeing somebody a long time, maybe were real serious about them.''

"Rebecca and I broke up more than six months ago."

"Oh." Should she be glad he'd known what to answer without her asking? "You danced very well together."

"Don't go putting something into that that's not there. She's not pining for me, and I'm not pining for her. She's seeing someone, real serious, as you said. We just like to dance together."

"I'm not putting anything into anything. All I'm trying to do is get this clear so we know where we stand instead of trying to guess what the other's thinking. Then we can work together more easily, without this tension." Righteous indignation over his accusation faded. "So I've said it, and that's it. Done. Because nothing would ever really come of it. You've been very clear, and I won't put you in an awkward position. I just wanted you to know that. Because when it comes right down to it, with my being your employer, it would be sexual harassment, wouldn't it?"

"Sexual harassment? What the hell are you talking about? You're a woman."

"It doesn't have to be only a woman, you know. A man could be sexually harassed. That's why I'm telling you that your job as Double Bar X manager would never be in jeopardy because of whatever there is between us personally. I mean if we're angry at each other, or... or not angry, it doesn't change that you're very good at your job."

"You're giving me a freaking job review? Now?"

"No, I'm not giving you a job review. I'm just trying to be open about this, and you're not making it any easier."

She deliberately laced her fingers in her lap to avoid any more revealing gesture—maybe wringing her hands like an old-fashioned melodrama heroine about to be tied to the railroad tracks. Lying in bed nights, she'd imagined this moment, even when she'd tried not to. This wasn't the way she'd envisioned it.

Where had all those graceful phrases and situation-soothing insights she'd addressed to the ceiling gone?

"I've never been very good at this sort of thing and you keep ramming it down my throat that I'm the employer and you're the employee, so I figured with this thing not being mutual, I just wanted to make sure there wasn't any—"

"Are you crazy?"

She frowned at his hoarse interruption, but her pulse picked up speed. "What do you mean?"

He still stared straight ahead as he started with precise, driven words. "I mean—" without moving his head, he cut his eyes to her "—that I want to lie you down on the ground and bury myself deep inside you damn near every time I see you, including when you're carrying an armload of soggy rugs, for God's sake. Is that mutual enough for you?"

"Oh." His words called up her memory of the day and a look in his eyes and allowed no more answer than that for an instant. "But then why—"

Tucker hadn't meant to say anything, at least not anything of what had been said. He'd meant to drive her back to the house, tell her in no uncertain terms that she had her world, and he had his and they just didn't mix, and put an end to this whole crazy desire for her.

Instead, he'd driven her here and told her too much of the truth not to keep going.

"I'll be damned if I'll have people saying I'm sleeping with the boss."

"Oh." This time the syllable carried hurt. "You think people would say things like that?"

"Hell, yes, they would, if they're human. But it's not just for my ego. Nothing good ever comes of that sort of thing. Nothing good," he repeated with bitterness. "I'm looking out for my side, but it can't be all that different from your side. Think about what your family and friends would say about you sleeping with the hired man. Not the sort of thing they do at the tennis club."

That drove her upright and made her grip his arm, apparently trying to jerk him around to face her. She didn't budge him, but he did turn to look at her.

"I am sick and tired of thinking about what the people at the tennis club would say. That was my mother. And Edward. But not me. For the first time, I'm learning to think about what *I* say." She became even more emphatic. "And don't give me that crud about your being the hired hand. You know you're no such thing. That's a dodge, a way to hide. And, besides . . ."

In a blink she seemed to deflate. Her voice dropped, but he heard her determination to finish what she'd started.

"And besides, you're *not* sleeping with me."

He reached toward her, hesitated, said "Ah, Jenny . . ." in a strange, soft tone he hardly recognized as his own. It made her turn to him, and he reached out to her again. He pushed her hair back from her face with a gentle hand.

"I won't have you feeling sorry for me, Tucker. I won't take—"

"That's not what I'm feeling."

He barely had time to wonder if she could sort out the self-directed wryness in his tone from something more fatalistic—he couldn't—before his lips touched hers, and sorting out thoughts gave way to taking in pleasure.

Cupping her face between his palms, he held on to her like an anchor, while she swamped his senses and his sense. Her hands came to his wrists. Something hit him low and hard at the possibility that she meant to pull his hands away. And when, instead, she spread her fingers over his, sealing his touch, he was lost.

He touched his tongue to her lips and she opened to him, greeting his invasion with a soft touch of her own, further loosening the clamp he'd had on his desires. Her shyness faded as the touches became thrusts, slow, deep declarations of intent. She accepted, she answered, she reciprocated.

Tasting the softness beneath her ear, he kissed a path under her chin, then down her throat. He fumbled with the buttons of her blouse, his fingers not nearly fast enough to satisfy the burning in his gut, stoked higher by the light brushes of her fingers as she worked his shirt buttons open.

He didn't bother to finish the job, but spread the sides of her blouse so he could cup her breasts, gently brushing his thumbs across the tightened nipples. She sighed and arched, and he lowered his head to kiss her there, as he'd wanted to for so long.

Her bra, with no lace or bows, was of some plain, silky material that covered her like a second skin. He traced the shape of her nipple with his tongue, and she clutched his shoulders. He took it into his mouth, and she rocked in the rhythm of his touch. He tended her other breast until he thought he might explode. Rising, he felt the points of her nipples, the material over them damp and heated, rake twin paths along his chest.

Angled across the seat, the weight of his upper body pressed her lower. Her arms around him drew him along, as if he'd needed that aid to find her in the dark. He ran his hand along her hip, then lower, to the hem of her short denim skirt. Her legs were bare, soft, warm. He spread his hand to take in the maximum sensation. She moved against him, under him, and the rein he'd been holding tight for so long loosened even more.

He brought the skirt up with his hand, extending the pleasure by going slow, so slow. Sliding his fingers around to the incredible soft vulnerability of her inner thigh. She made a sound in her throat and tightened her fingers in his hair. She wanted him. Jenny... Jenny wanted him.

For weeks he'd held on to the impossibility of it, used that to hold off from her, to keep that line between them. But in the capsule of passion formed by their bodies, no line existed, nothing to hold off his own desires.

He wanted her. Any way he could have her. Now. Right here...

Here.

He shoved himself upright and swore. And swore again to himself when she sat up, eyes wide and confused.

"A pickup, for God's sake."

"What?"

"Noth..." No, wait, he'd spell it out, and her own reaction would help restore the distance he couldn't maintain right now. Holding her by the shoulders, he brought them face-to-face. "I damn near took you in that chair the other night. And now I almost did it here, in the front seat of a pickup. But I am not quite far enough gone yet to make love to you in a truck."

"I've never made love in a truck." And damned if she didn't sound intrigued. "Not even in a car. I wasn't that kind of girl in high school, and then, Edward didn't consider it dignified. I've always sort of wondered..."

"No."

"Here I am a thirty-one-year-old woman who's been married and divorced, had two kids, but I never had what's sort of a rite of passage in our society—"

"No."

Her voice dipped again. "I can't blame you. Someone who's had two kids... I mean, there're a lot of women around younger and prettier. Certainly firmer, so—"

"He really did a number on you, didn't he?"

Her eyes widened. From his question or his demanding tone he didn't know.

"I don't—"

"Don't you know how desirable you are, Jenny Peters? Don't you honestly know how you could have me sweating just by walking across the kitchen wiping your hands on a towel?"

She didn't have to answer. He saw she didn't know. She wondered, she hoped. But Guinevere Peters didn't know it down deep in her soul, where she needed that certainty.

And he couldn't do a damn thing except show her.

Chapter Nine

He jerked open the truck door and wrapped a hand around her wrist. She hesitated, but didn't resist, sliding across the seat behind him. The movement opened her blouse and he swallowed as the weak light pearled her throat and the soft top curve of her breasts above the plain bra.

"Where are we going?" She didn't sound scared, but her earlier uncertainty had company.

"My cabin. It's right here."

She asked no more, but held on to his hand as he led the way along the dark, narrow path through the young pines that hid the cabin from the road. He opened the door and stepped back to let her pass.

"You don't lock it?"

He watched her move into the single room, knowing she was making conversation out of nervousness.

"No. No sense locking out good folks who might need it for an emergency, because if the other kind wants to get in, they will."

He lit the lantern, then held it high to provide light as she ran her hand over the rounded surface of the log wall, looked through the open door to the closet-size bathroom, fingered the material of the curtain over the only window, set the old rocker in gentle motion with a touch to its back, then put a palm to the smooth rock of the fireplace. He watched her every touch.

"What a great fireplace."

"Thanks. I built it. Built the whole place." His nod took in what she'd examined, plus the bedstead with its three-quarters-size mattress and old blankets, but Jenny didn't look in that direction.

"You did? It's wonderful. It must have taken a lot of patience, and skill."

"I can be patient. And skillful. When that's called for."

Her gaze never left the design of rock, but the heightened color in her cheeks told that she'd understood his meaning. Figuring her out—here shy, there bold, now assured, then uncertain—was as much a puzzle as fitting together the individual rocks to form a cohesive unit that would stand, and serve.

"You must have terrific fires," she said brightly.

"You want me to lay a fire?"

"It is rather cool in here..."

She didn't seem aware that her blouse still gaped open, allowing the lantern light to cast a fascinating shadow show—and he wasn't about to remind her.

"Jenny..." He put the lantern on the end of the mantel and closed the space to her. He didn't touch her but waited for her eyes to come to his face. "Jenny, I'll light a fire if that's what you want. But what I want is to make love to you. To lay you on that bed and fight the cold with another heat." He stepped closer. "You wanted to talk about this, and that's what I have to say."

She put her hand, just her fingertips really, against his cheek. Her fingers felt cold, but he resisted the urge to take her hand between both of his and warm it.

He laid his hands on her shoulders, close to her throat, and slipped them under the loosened collar. His thumbs followed the line that defined her collarbone, sweeping out toward the point of her shoulders, then back to meet in the center. He slid his thumbs up her throat to hook under her chin, though it needed no help from him to tip back so her eyes met his before he spoke.

"I want to be inside you."

Her eyes stayed locked with his when his thumbs dropped back to the delicate indentation at the base of her throat, rested there a moment to absorb the beat of her pulse, before sweeping wide again. This time he spread his hands to catch the material of her blouse and the narrow straps of her bra, drawing them aside as he cupped her shoulders, then slid down her arms, baring her shoulders and the flaring curve of the top of her breasts.

She had dropped her hand to her side, standing utterly still except for the pulse at the base of her throat and the movement of her watchful eyes, but now she slipped one arm free and reached for his hat. She hesitated long enough for him to wonder what she intended, but he realized he didn't care, not with her palm brushing against his temple and her thumb stroking his forehead.

In one quick move, she pushed the brim so the hat tumbled off the back of his head and to the floor.

"Do you want me to pick it up?" Only Jenny could manage to sound both polite and defiant.

"Leave it." How could he think about hats when her gesture had stroked his chest with fire from the rub of her breasts?

He jerked his shirt out of his jeans and pulled at the remaining buttons, strong thread more than his finesse preventing any from popping off. She stood still until he started to shrug the shirt off, then she took hold of the material, meaning to assist him, but nearly stopping his action dead with the jolt of her fleeting touches.

Finally free of the shirt, he tossed it in the general vicinity of his hat. "Leave that, too," he said hoarsely, reaching for her.

Her skirt shouldn't have been that complicated. Some sort of hook at the side of the waist, then a simple zipper. But he had to do it all by feel, because he was kissing her collarbone, and down to that smooth, soft rise of her breasts. And his fingers' coordination suffered a setback every time she stroked her palms across his shoulders, into his hair, then down his back. Her hands stroked lower, dipping under the back waist of his jeans and shot his coordination to hell.

But by that time he'd finished the mechanics and only had to start the skirt down her hips. It fell to the floor on its own. The blouse and bra had worked lower, but still covered too much of her breasts for his taste. One button held the blouse closed at her waist. Below, she wore high-cut panties that looked to be the same material as her bra.

"Want me to pick it up?"

"No." She gave a slight gasp as he pressed her back again, and her legs met the bed. "Leave it."

She stepped out of one shoe, but before she could slip off the other, he bore her down to the mattress, taking her mouth with hot, wet kisses.

He went to stand, but his legs felt as if they'd escaped his command. To mask his unsteadiness, he rested a knee on the mattress and removed Jenny's shoe. Then he toed off his boots, swearing at their humanlike recalcitrance. He eased back down beside her, his body blocking most of the light so it took a moment for his eyes to adjust to the shadows and see that she smiled faintly.

He ran a finger along the line of her smile.

"What's that for?"

"Don't you think it's a little late to try to scare me into leaving with your bad language, Tucker?"

Leaving. The word jarred him, lying here on his side beside her, looking down at her. He focused on another instead. "Are you scared, Jenny?"

Her smiled faded. "Yes."

"Do you want to stop?"

"No."

Now he smiled. It was so much like her. A little uncertain, totally honest, determined to go ahead.

"It's up to you, Jenny. Next move's yours."

Her glare caught him off guard. "Gates, if you say *you're the boss...*" Her mock indignation didn't wash away all the nervousness, but it hid some.

He chuckled and held out his free arm in surrender. Then he let it drop so his hand cradled her hip. "I'm not saying a word. I'm just waiting."

Though waiting might kill him right here and now.

She ran her hand down his chest. The feather-light caress would have tickled, if it hadn't burned. When her fingers encountered his belt buckle, she hesitated.

Jenny stared at that piece of metal, not frightened, not even nervous precisely, but a little awed. Jenny Peters, always so cautious. Jenny Peters, who had never made love with anyone except her husband. Jenny Peters, who had never even initiated a kiss except with her husband, and not often then. Jenny Peters was about to make love with a man she'd known barely a month.

She traced the raised pattern on the buckle with her forefinger.

Jenny Peters was going to make love with Tucker Gates. Something she'd been trying not to think about, but finding it impossible not to dream about.

"Open it. Open the buckle."

The rasp of his voice mesmerized her. She followed his direction without hesitation—because what it instructed was exactly what she wanted to do.

She concentrated on the cool intricacies of the metal, the warm suppleness of the leather, focused on manipulating them to her will, shut out the sound of her own shallow breathing. And when she mastered the buckle, she did not hesitate. She opened the snap and started easing down the zipper, her fingers warmed by the heat of his body.

Tucker didn't say anything, he didn't move her hands to hurry her. He simply grasped the waist of his jeans and the briefs she'd glimpsed and skimmed them down, over his legs and off. With the jeans in one hand, he dug in the pocket and pulled out a packet, which he laid on the corner of the mattress.

Before Jenny could absorb the import of that or the fact of his nakedness, much less get nervous, he had pressed her back with a kiss that robbed her of breath but gifted her with a thousand other pleasures.

She was aware of him removing the rest of her clothes, she had to be, because she heard her own voice advise, "In the front. Hooks . . . in front," when he fumbled for the clasp of her bra. But the individual motions flowed into a river of sensation.

His hands on her. Her hands on him.

It sounded so simple, and it was. And nothing had ever equaled it. Nothing.

Except what he drew out of her, from deep inside her and brought to the surface where his hands caressed it and stroked it and loved it. She felt herself shimmering, glowing, and tried to tell him.

But the words came out mundane, inane.

"I love your hair." Syllables escaped in halting gasps as he kissed and nibbled at her navel. She tangled her fingers into his hair as he continued working his way back up her body along a path of indulgent kisses.

"It's long."

She smiled. Not at the protest, but because his words were as inane and mundane, his voice as strained as hers.

He turned his head and caught her little finger between his lips, laving it with his tongue. She stroked the curve of his ear, the smoothness behind his lobe, the prickle on his jaw. She molded her palm against his cheek, exerting slight pressure to bring his face up. Their eyes met for a long, charged moment.

Releasing her finger, he raised himself over her on braced arms. He bent his elbows, dipping to put his mouth over her nipple, tugging gently. Then he pushed upright.

Without breaking the look, he shifted his weight to one arm and reached to the top corner of the bed for the packet. He knelt there, unabashedly preparing to make love to her, and she watched him, another trickle of amazement at herself slipping through her.

He bent and kissed her. A kiss with a bit of a question in it. She opened her mouth, touching his tongue with hers, welcoming it.

Still kissing her, he shifted so both his legs were between hers, and she opened to him. He released her mouth and raised his head to meet her eyes as he entered her. He moved slowly, so slowly. She felt the effort it cost him in the taut muscles under her roving hands.

"Jenny—"

But he couldn't know the effort it cost her. She needed him. Now. Totally. Urging him forward with her hands, she tilted her hips.

"Yes, Tucker..."

"Jenny... If you—yes. Like that..."

Movement expressed emotion, carried it, amplified it. She couldn't separate them. Didn't want to analyze, only to experience. And to share.

Reality centered on the roll and contraction of his muscles under her hands, against her body, inside her, as they sought something beyond reality, where there were no lines. Only this...

"Tucker...?"

She reached it, caught it, held it to her for a sliver of eternity where they tumbled together.

Tucker bowed over her and thrust a final time, his face stark, before he collapsed onto her. She held him. Each breath he drew compressed her with a sweet weight. Hands spread wide across his shoulder blades, she measured each sharp exhalation. Until they evened and slowed.

He rolled away. When he jackknifed upright to grasp the covers from the bottom of the bed, she pulled up the scratchy blanket he handed her. She watched his back, wondering if he would get up and leave her.

He could get up, gain some distance. Tucker considered it. Maybe he didn't have the strength. Or the energy. He dropped back to the mattress beside her.

A bed this size didn't leave much room. They lay side by side, skin meeting skin wherever the blanket wasn't.

"You okay?" Tension clutched at him, because he wasn't sure. Not of her, not of himself. And most of all not of what they'd just done.

"I'm fine."

She sounded as tight as he felt. He spat out a mental expletive. He never should have touched her.

"You don't sound it." God, he sounded grim, even to his own ears.

"I am, really. I'm just tired." She hesitated and he braced. "I guess you could say I'm Tuckered out."

Laughter exploded from him, gusting with nerves as well as amusement.

"Jokes? You're making jokes?" He rolled her over, sliding his hands to her waist, tickling. "Think you're pretty funny?"

When he heard her laughter, he knew he wasn't the only one who'd felt tension.

He couldn't pinpoint when the passion returned—or maybe it had been there all along, under the laughter. But in a shorter time than he would have believed possible, he was stroking her skin, needing to draw from her the soft cries she'd made before, instead of laughter.

The need clawed at him, he didn't like it but couldn't ignore it. Damn, he didn't like it, he thought, even as he fumbled to take another foil packet from his discarded jeans.

When he turned back to her, bearing her down to the mattress, Jenny kissed him as passionately as before, but he thought he'd caught a shadow of the uncertainty in her eyes.

Abruptly, he rolled on his back, carrying her with him. Her eyes widened as he brought her to position over him. The uncertainty was gone, replaced by surprise, a hint of curiosity, and bright, burning desire. *Jenny. Jenny...*

He might have said the words aloud as he thrust up and she met him.

He stroked her back, and she listened to his voice telling how he'd found this little parcel of land tucked up next to the Double Bar X and bought it eight years ago, building the cabin over the next few years.

"We should get back. It'll be morning soon," he said after a silence.

She sighed deeply, filled with too many emotions to hold them all in. "It's been quite a day. You know, I became a sister today—or yesterday, probably, by now."

"So that's what made you so touchy this morning. I've heard that sibling rivalry can be a powerful thing. Especially for someone who's been an only child all this time, had all the attention . . ."

"You better not be saying I was a spoiled only child, Tucker Gates. And, no, I don't feel any sibling rivalry with my baby brother...my brother. You have no idea how I used to wish and dream that I would have little brothers and sisters, someone to fuss over, take care of and watch over."

"It's overrated."

She propped herself on an elbow to see his face. "You have younger brothers and sisters? I thought you were an only child, though I couldn't say why, you never said—"

"I don't have brothers or sisters. I didn't say that. I said having someone you had to take care of is overrated. Gets old real fast. Makes you old real fast."

She could ask, and he might answer. But he might not. Instead, she stroked across his chest, down his ribs, and back. Long, slow, regular strokes. After a while, his eyes drifted closed. It took longer for a deep sigh to escape him. She felt the give in his muscles.

"I had a father." His eyes opened to stare at the ceiling. "Carter—my father—might not have done any better if my mother hadn't died when I was real young, but he sure wasn't cut out to be a single parent. Probably wasn't cut out to be a father at all. He told me once, deep in the Jim Beam, that he'd lost at baby roulette—I was the bullet—so he had to marry my mother.

"He was a good hand, though, really knew ranching and we found a pretty good place, almost settled, you know?" The hint of wistfulness caught at her heart. "But Carter always did have a liking for booze and the wrong woman. The wrong woman got him fired, and then the booze took hold. After that, we went from job to job, sticking for a few months if I could keep a tight enough rein on him, otherwise we'd be gone in a few weeks."

He caught her hand, moved it to the slice of mattress between them, then released it immediately. "Somebody to take care of? I sure as hell had that."

She knew there was more, and she might not have another chance to learn it from this man who held so much in. But tears fought to escape, and she knew with absolute certainty that if she cried over his story, she would not only lose any gate to his past, but to his present.

He sat up, sliding back to rest against the log wall. Fighting the urge to touch him, to try to draw him back to her physically, if no other way, she sat, too, covering herself with a blanket. He still hadn't looked at her.

"So, when it comes to all that family stuff, no thanks. I've done my time."

"It doesn't have to be that way."

"Doesn't it? Look at you—you had a mother who tried to make you into a puppet, a husband who took up where she left off and a father who ignored you. Why in God's name would you be so high on family? Far as I can tell, they haven't done you any favors.''

He didn't mention Greg and Debbie, but she thought she heard criticism of them, too, and she stiffened.

''I've also had a father who's turned around the past few years and his wife who's become my friend. My family's given me a lot. Yes, sometimes headaches, but also Greg's smile when he took his first step, Debbie's eyes the first time she saw a bird fly. They've given me their wonder and their curiosity and their accomplishments when I'd forgotten I could have any of my own.''

Now he looked at her, and the bleakness in his dark eyes brought the burn of tears nearer the surface.

''You go ahead and believe that. That's fine for you. For me, I say no thanks. I don't want anything to do with it. I've never tried to fool anyone about that. That sort of life's not in my future. That's why Rebecca and I parted ways last fall. She wanted what I can't give—to anybody.''

Jenny had felt Tucker's resistance to being involved with the family, but she'd also seen the way he dealt with her children, especially Greg, and she'd experienced his patience in drawing out the story of her past and her concerns of the present. Perhaps she'd let herself hope.... But he'd just made his position clear.

If it sounded like rejection, felt like rejection and tasted like rejection there was no sense in pretending otherwise.

''I think your reasons are dead wrong, Tucker. But I'm glad you've said all this because we do agree on the end result. I'm not interested in getting involved with anyone, either. My children need a lot of attention now and I'm still learning my way with being independent, so the last thing I would want to do is get involved with anyone.''

* * *

Fine. It had been just what he wanted to hear. It couldn't have been better.

Well, maybe it would have been better if she hadn't spoken the words sitting naked next to him, her hip brushing his, her hand holding the blanket to her breasts, her hair tousled and her skin flushed from the rub of his whiskers. Maybe he would have concentrated completely on the words then, instead of thinking about pulling the covers away.

But she'd said the words, and that's what counted.

She hadn't read too much into the fact that a chemical interaction politely termed hormones had driven the two of them into bed together to do things that he damn well wasn't going to think about ever again because his body didn't understand that it had been a one-shot deal.

But he knew it was.

Not that it was bad that it had happened. It was good that it had happened. Because now the hormones wouldn't have the same hold on him.

And it seemed to work that way with Jenny. After an awkward parting that night, she'd seemed calm the next day, content to be cordial, to damn near be his buddy.

He hated it.

He was sick of greeting her as if he didn't remember what she sounded like when he'd brought her to the edge, or what she looked like when she'd pushed him over it. Didn't she feel it when their hands brushed passing salt or mustard around the table? Hell, they didn't even have to touch. Being careful not to touch as they checked Boomerang's leg did enough. Or the day he'd sat beside her in her new four-wheel drive because they both had to go to Cody, and Deaver had pointed out the inefficiency of separate trips. Or when they met in the compact quarters of the back hall.

He'd survived five days of it, though for the last three, he'd found it smarter to reset fence posts at a good distance from the house.

Deaver stopped him as he loaded a thermos and brown paper bag in the truck.

"Not coming for lunch again today, huh?"

"Doesn't make sense to get all the way out there just to come back."

"Uh-huh." The two syllables spoke more of Deaver's skepticism than agreement. "Never known you to be so intent on getting the far fence sections set. We got some closer in we'll be using sooner than those."

Tucker shrugged. "These need to get done, too. Rest of you can take care of the closer sections between other jobs. These are better done full-day."

Deaver shook his head. "I didn't come down with the rain yesterday, you know. You're tied in knots over that woman, and you're hiding away."

"I'm not going to talk about this, Deaver."

He swung into the driver's seat.

But Deaver was going to talk. He was also going to stand in the way so Tucker couldn't close the door and therefore couldn't leave until Deaver let him.

"You're a piece of wet rawhide tied tight and left to dry. Something's got to give, and I'm telling you right now, it ought to be you."

"You don't know what you're talking about. I've seen what happens. I've learned that damn lesson. You want Greg Peters to end up like Sammy? You want—"

"It's not the same—"

"The hell it's not!" Tucker's roar stirred some birds in the tree he'd parked under, but Deaver went still. "I won't do that to him. I won't do it to me. And, God help me, I won't do it to Jenny. I can't do it to Jenny."

Chapter Ten

One skill she'd retained from the old Jenny days was to present a calm exterior, while inside her feelings swirled around like feathers in a hurricane.

But it was harder than she remembered.

She'd gained time by informing Debbie and Greg that she would drive them to school when that coincided with her schedule—otherwise, they were to take the bus. They had surprisingly little to say about it, and she reminded herself of the value of facing issues, at the same time ignoring Tucker's voice whispering "I told you so" in her mind.

But time did not equal peace. The afternoon rides on Flash had provided her only respites. That was why she'd pushed farther, gone longer than she might have otherwise.

She'd learned the satisfaction of being open about her emotions, of letting people know how she felt. And she couldn't remember feeling anything as strong as this; though she didn't know exactly *what* she felt at any particular moment, it always was strong.

As strong as the physical reaction she'd had that night in Tucker's cabin. Nearly a decade married and twice a mother, and she hadn't known what making love could be.

Flash's head came up, and he nickered.

Jenny looked around quickly, for the first time realizing clouds had poured over the mountains, blocking out much of the sun. The memory of Tucker's warnings repeated in her head. She'd wound up the mountainside for quite a stretch through the trees, then had come down into an unfamiliar area of the ranch. At least she thought she was still on Double Bar X land. Could she have crossed a boundary without being aware of it?

No, she hadn't left the ranch, because that was Tucker over by a fence, working shirtless in one of the few remaining patches of afternoon warmth.

Just the sight of him brought a physical reaction. But it was more than a physical reaction that prompted her to stop Flash. She quieted the horse as she watched Tucker.

He slipped a chain around the metal post, then hooked a yard-long piece of metal into a box that rested at the base of the post. Using the long piece of metal as a handle, he pumped it, raising the post a few inches. Repositioning the chain, he repeated the action in rhythmic efficiency.

Watching a physical job well done brought a pleasure she hadn't appreciated before. She pushed aside the question of how much of her appreciation had to do with the worker.

Not until he looked up and saw her did she realize she hadn't made the decision whether or not to go down to him. But she wouldn't turn away now. She hoped the gathered clouds did not constitute an omen.

He straightened, waiting for her, not welcoming. He looked away only once, to his shirt, suspended from a post six yards away.

"Jenny," he greeted her evenly when she came close enough. "Didn't know you rode this area."

"I haven't before." She hesitated a moment, then dismounted. It seemed silly to remain mounted, looming over him. But he didn't look especially pleased to have her at ground level. "What are you doing?"

"Resetting posts."

He clearly wanted to leave it there, almost as clearly as he wished she'd leave. She looked at him, waiting. Even Flash shifted weight as if impatient.

"They work down over the seasons," he offered at last.

"And that's bad?" A solitary drop landed on her arm.

"They get so low they wouldn't keep a rabbit in, much less a cow. Sometimes heavy snow piles up against the wires, dragging them down."

"And you have to do this every spring?" Maybe through the casual exchange of question and answer they could rebuild some measure of ease.

"Some."

"How much?"

Another drop. Then a third.

"Depends on how hard the winter is. Some years more than others."

Drops turned to a rush.

"Get in the truck."

Tucker took Flash's reins and looped them around a secure section of fence, then paid no more attention to her, gathering his tools with efficient speed. Without a word, she headed to the truck about seventy yards away. But then she jogged back, carrying a sheet of plastic she'd found in the back of the pickup.

"What are you doing?" he demanded. "Get in the truck."

"But Flash—"

"Won't melt. He'll turn his rear end to the rain and stand it out."

"I won't melt, either, and it's a good saddle." She shook out the sheet and flopped one side over Flash's back.

"God, you're stubborn." He took the other side of the sheet and finished spreading it. "Now, get going."

She started off first, but he outsprinted her and jerked open the driver's door. "Get in!"

She scrambled past the steering wheel and across the seat to leave room for Tucker. Both windows were open; the wind had driven rain in the driver's seat, but the passenger side remained dry.

"Towel in back," he said, pulling the door closed behind him.

Jenny started twisting around to reach over the seat back for the length of green terry cloth, but froze when Tucker arched off the seat with an outraged *"Ahhhh!"*

The puddle on the seat had just soaked through Tucker's jeans and into his consciousness. Trying to keep out of contact with the water, he rolled up the window.

"Move over," she said with a chuckle, sliding over on her knees as she grabbed the towel. "It's dry here."

As she turned back with the towel she gave in to temptation, using a fingertip to push a wet lock of hair behind his ear. He froze for an instant, then leaned away from her.

"Don't."

She dropped to a sitting position, her back against the passenger door. "I'm sorry. It was a simple gesture of affection. I wasn't trying... I didn't mean to, uh, to make you uncomfortable."

"Use the towel, Jenny."

She scraped her hair back and wiped her face, accepting the momentary sanctuary, then down her throat. Water sculpted her blouse to her body. The towel didn't make a dent in it. She pulled it loose; it molded right back to her torso.

"Here." She tossed the towel, now damp but better than nothing, to Tucker as she slewed around in the seat to put as much of her back to him as possible. But she could still see him rubbing the towel in his hair and against his bare chest. And she could feel the moist warmth coming off his body beside her.

He tossed the towel over his shoulder into the well behind the seat.

"Affection isn't what I feel when you touch me, Jenny. I thought I'd made that damn clear."

She looked at him, trying to decipher his tone. "You don't sound very happy about it. And besides, why can't you have both... affection and... and the other feelings?"

Tucker dropped his head to the seat back. "When you look like this, affection comes in a damn poor second to what you call *other feelings.* We're in a truck, with it pouring down rain. And I am not in the mood for a cold shower. Even though that's exactly what I need. Because doing what I feel like when you touch me wouldn't change anything."

She absorbed that speech, then took a deep breath.

"I wanted you to make love to me in the truck that night. I—"

"Jenny—"

"No, I'm going to say this. You don't want to say things, but I do. I need to, because I never used to think I had the right to say what I felt. But now I do, so I'm telling you, I'd never known that kind of passion in my life, and I wanted it. I... I wanted you. I wanted you very much." It surprised her how much even now. "I've never thought of myself as a very passionate person."

Tucker rolled his head on the edge of the seat back to look at her. She knew that, though she didn't meet his eyes. Wanting to say something didn't necessarily make it any easier, especially with his dark eyes studying her. "My mother never thought strong feelings about anything were very ladylike, and Edward said I wasn't—passionate, I mean . . . and certainly with him I didn't—"

"I don't want to hear about Edward."

At that she did look up. "I'm sorry, I didn't—"

"No more apologizing, remember, Jenny?" From gentle, his tone turned brisk. "Besides, sounds to me like Edward's the sorry one. Anybody who'd say you weren't passionate has got to be loco."

He took her hand, clenched in a tense fist and slowly opened the fingers with one hand until they fanned out over his other palm, while she watched, trying to remember to breathe, fascinated by the exquisite care his big, rough hands could administer. He ran the pad of his index finger around the tips of her fingers.

"I was real grateful you'd worn down those long nails you had when you arrived here to something not so lethal. Otherwise, I could have been marked for life."

She jerked her head up to meet his teasing eyes. "I scratched you? Oh, God, I'm so—" She cut it off herself.

"I heal quick." In a blink, the light in his eyes turned hot and intense. "And I didn't feel a thing I didn't enjoy."

His hand closed around hers. They leaned into each other, slow and cautious, watchful. Their lips met, parted, came back together. Slow and cautious evaporated.

He held her head between his palms, slowly raising his gaze from her mouth to her eyes. "It's not going to solve anything, you know."

He released her but made no effort to move away. Neither did she.

"I know. I don't think this... this attraction between us—"

"This passion?" he teased softly. She hadn't seen this side of him before.

"This passion," she accepted. "I don't think it's meant to solve things. It just *is*. Maybe if we don't expect more of it..."

The teasing gone, he studied her. "Maybe." He dropped his head to kiss her. When he looked up again, she could see the fire in her blood reflected in his eyes. "And I wouldn't want to deny you a rite of passage, now would I?"

Marveling—not at her boldness, but at the fact that it didn't feel bold at all, just right—she leaned over to drop a kiss on his shoulder, then lower to flick his brown nipple with her tongue. "I hope you wouldn't want to deny me that."

"I wouldn't want to deny you anything."

Jenny heard a tension under those words, saw a darkness deeper than the color of his eyes. How could she battle that in him? How could she free him from whatever he was fighting when she didn't even know what it was?

Tucker shifted closer, at the same time lifting her legs across his. He leaned over and flipped open the glove compartment. Her eyes widened as he took hold of a condom packet.

"Some risks aren't worth taking," he informed her roughly. He put the packet on the dashboard, closed the glove compartment and sat back, as if waiting for comment.

Remembering his reference to his father's story of "baby roulette," she knew he thought of pregnancy before disease. But she couldn't really argue with either.

She kissed his chin and felt his thighs relax under hers. Putting her arms around him, she met his mouth, open and hot, and felt other parts of him tighten.

She came out of the kiss to an unexpected sensation.

"What are you doing?"

"Taking your boots off. This won't work with your boots on."

The practicalities struck her for the first time, not in any way cooling her desire, but making her wonder. "I'm not sure it's going to work at all," she said doubtfully.

"It'll work," he vowed, taking time out to kiss her thoroughly.

When he started pulling down her jeans, another doubt hit her.

"I've been riding."

He didn't look up from his task. "I put that together as soon as I saw you on Flash."

"I must smell like a horse."

Now he did look up. He stroked the length of her leg.

"No. You smell like Jenny. Always." He kissed her abdomen, open-mouthed, then licked the spot his mouth had just warmed, a caress that arched her toward the source of her pleasure, toward him.

She could ask no greater assurance. Yet he gave it, with slow, deliberate caresses that she returned in full measure as they opened buttons, removed clothes, cooperating in the confines of the truck as the rain beyond the window continued and the heat between them built. The pace was not as leisurely now, as the need built.

Jenny held him close, welcoming the weight of his body against her. The rough surface of the seat scratched her back and rumpled clothes not completely removed pressed into her skin, and none of it mattered, none of it compared to the shiver of lightning inside every time he touched her.

"Can you get your leg around here?"

"I don't—"

Tucker wrapped his hand around her ankle and started her leg in the direction he wanted. "Yes, like that...just like that."

"But how will you be able to... Oh...oh!"

"Just like that, Jenny...Jenny, just like that..."

Rain over, they took the sheet of plastic off Flash and brought him up to the pickup.

Tucker told her to get in, then handed the reins in through the window to her. "I'll go real slow, but if something spooks him and he starts to bolt, let go."

He wished he had the common sense to take his own advice. He would have let go back in the cabin or maybe that first time in the office when she'd realized they were smiling at each other and she shied away from him.

He should have let her go.

He couldn't be someone he wasn't for her. He couldn't unlearn his life for her.

The fact that she turned to him as he brought the truck to a stop outside the barn, eyes wide and gray, and said, "It's all right, Tucker. I don't want you to think I expect anything of you. It's like we said before, neither one of us wants to get involved. It'll be okay," did nothing to ease his feelings.

It wasn't okay. As much as he wanted her, he couldn't make love with Jenny Peters anymore, not without risking more than he had to give.

Tucker took Greg with him the next day to work on the fence posts.

By the end of the day, he had a headache no aspirin would dissolve and a nagging suspicion that Greg Peters had started constructing a pedestal under Tucker's reluctant feet.

But balanced against the danger of encountering Jenny alone, he figured he had to take the risk, so he invited Greg to come along Sunday, too. The way the boy jumped at the offer tightened the clamp behind Tucker's eyes.

He was relieved when Greg, apparently bored, wandered away after an hour to poke around the irrigation ditch where the fence cornered. Then he felt guilty.

Tomorrow, Tucker promised himself, he'd figure another way to deal with this, and he'd start building more distance between himself and Greg.

A mocking voice noted that with the distance he needed between himself and two-thirds of the Peters family, he might as well move out of state. He did his best to ignore it.

Greg returned excitedly bearing an Indian arrowhead he'd found caught in brush by the edge of the water. Tucker paused to examine it and to speculate that it might have come down from the mountains in the spring melt, into a stream that fed the irrigation ditch, then caught in the brush when the water level dropped.

"Water's shaped this land all along." As Tucker returned to work, he touched on the geology that showed the area had once been underwater and mentioned how irrigation techniques had opened the area around Powell to homesteading. It wasn't often he had somebody to talk to while he worked; it had been particularly silent these recent, isolated days.

"How do you know all that?"

Greg sat tailor-style a couple feet away, elbows on knees, and chin supported in his palms, as he watched.

The question brought Tucker up short. Last thing he intended was impressing the boy. "Pick things up here and there." Then, despite himself, he tacked on a pointed addition. "Listened in school and did my homework."

Greg made a face, but no other response, and Tucker decided to let his inadvertent venture into instructing die out in silence. He moved on to the next post, and Greg followed.

"I can help you," Greg offered after a while.

"No need."

"I watched yesterday and I've seen how it works and—"

"I said, no need." Tucker spoke more harshly than he'd intended, but he'd just spotted the dust trail of an approaching vehicle.

Greg sank into silence while Tucker kept one eye on the arrival as he finished that post. Jenny's four-wheel drive came to a stop beside his truck, which occupied the only shade around, and she got out.

He tamped dirt around the reset post, which was already plenty firm. But moving on to the next post would move him that much closer to Jenny.

It didn't matter. She came to where he kept packing dirt, until he felt like a fool ignoring her.

He straightened. "What is it?"

"You took both sets of keys to the storage shed with you. Deaver sent me after a key because he needs the dynamite to get that stump out."

He shook his head, starting toward the next post now that it meant putting some space between them. "Only have mine." He pointed to the clutter of keys splayed on his jacket on the ground nearby.

"The other set's in your truck glove compartment. I saw them there Friday."

The heated blast of memory bubbled in his blood and tightened his gut. He turned away. "I'll get them."

He started for the truck and Jenny came with him, saying nothing. The move made sense—she could take the keys from him and just leave. She didn't walk too close, but would any distance be enough for him not to imagine he caught her scent and not to want to slide his hands over her until his very skin absorbed that essence of her?

He yanked the passenger door open as if the breeze it created could blow her away from him, far away.

He was digging for the keys, the ring caught on a pencil wedged tight at an angle, when her voice came to him.

"When did Greg learn how to do that?"

"Do what?" he demanded. There, he had the pencil loose. Another second and . . .

"Lift the posts like that. With the jack. Isn't that what it's call—"

Tucker jerked his head back and saw through the windshield that Greg had the jack positioned on the post and was ready to try the handle. Tucker threw down the keys, not caring where they landed, roared a "No" and sprinted toward the boy.

"What's wrong?"

He was aware of Jenny's startled question. He was aware of Greg's fear-widened eyes, even felt a flash of something, knowing he'd caused that look. But mostly he was aware of the boy taking a hasty step back from the handle. The kind of handle he'd seen jerk up and break the jaw of a man who hadn't used it properly. The kind he'd heard had hit a kid in the head, causing brain damage.

"What's the matter? I just wanted to—"

Tucker pulled Greg away. "Don't you ever touch a piece of equipment on this place unless I tell you you can, do you understand?"

"But I wanted to help and—"

"Do you understand?"

"—I watched all day yesterday and I'm sure I can do it. I just wanted to try."

Tucker knew Jenny had joined them, but the adrenaline still pumped too hot to moderate his reaction.

"You just wanted to try? How about just trying to get a cracked skull?" The image drove his voice low and menacing. "You don't ever use a tool without my say-so, is that clear?"

"Yes." It wavered, but was audible.

"Go get in my car, Greg," Jenny gave the quiet order.

Tucker hadn't finished. "I want to make damn sure you understand—"

"He said he did." Jenny stepped between him and the boy. "Go on, Greg, get in the car."

Greg gave Tucker a quick look, then obeyed his mother. If the slump of the retreating boy's shoulders hadn't told of his misery, the glimpse Tucker had gotten of his face would have. The kid was about to cry.

Tucker threw the handle down on the ground. It bounced once and clanged noisily against the bowl of the shovel.

"There was no reason for that."

"If I damaged Double Bar X property, I'll pay for it."

"That's not what I meant, and you know it. There is no reason for you to take out what's wrong between us on my son." She spoke in a voice he didn't recognize but had been expecting. A haughty, cold tone. It vanished with her next words, and he didn't know if he felt relieved or robbed of a safeguard. "You know how he looks up to you. All you had to do was say a word or raise an eyebrow. You didn't have to humiliate him that way. Especially in front of me."

"Lady, you're the one who said you didn't want me interfering between you and your precious son."

"There's a big difference between not interfering and being cruel to a child who looks up to you. Who only wants to please you and—"

"I don't want the kid to please me. How many times do I have to say that?"

"You don't want a lot of things." Her patience had slipped. "But sometimes you get them, and then you just have to make the most of them. You don't want any part of this family, but that's no reason to be cruel. I'll accept your callousness toward me but not toward my son."

"Callous? Cruel?" His tone mocked her. "That's putting it pretty high, don't you think?"

She stared back at him. "No, I don't."

"Then why don't you get out of here, away from my callous and cruel ways?"

Still meeting his look, she nodded once. "I'm going." Then, before he could wonder if she meant back to where she came from, much less work out if that would be a victory or a defeat for him, she added with emphasis, "Back to the *house*. I think you better find somewhere else to eat dinner tonight and give us all a chance to cool off."

"You know, Tucker might have had some cause for flying off the handle that way."

A glint in Deaver's eyes told Jenny he'd used the pun deliberately, but she was in no mood for his dry humor.

Dinner was over, but she hadn't cooled off. Not even with the brisk evening breeze here on the porch where Deaver had sauntered out and sat beside her, infinitely casual. He hadn't fooled her. He had something to say.

"There is no excuse for berating a child. For making that child feel worthless." She knew what it felt like, though her mother had been much more subtle, and she didn't want to think of her child feeling that way.

"Maybe not, maybe not. But being scared spitless can make a man forget his tongue."

"What are you talking about?"

"You know, those jack handles can fly loose. Not all that rare, either, not in the hands of those that aren't accustomed to them. That's a lot of steel to hit a young fella like Greg in the face. Has quite a wallop." He scratched the back of his neck. "Quite a wallop. Kind that can do damage."

She sat staring at the southern horizon, viewing Tucker's outburst in a different light.

"He could have just told Greg not to use it. He didn't have to shout at him that way. He didn't have to be so cutting."

"Well, I don't exactly know the rights of what happened, but from reading between the lines of the story Greg's telling, I suspect Tucker said Greg shouldn't touch the thing. I'm not saying Tucker shouldn't have realized that's exactly what would set a boy like Greg to wanting to do it, to show he could. But Tucker's been, uh, mighty distracted of late."

Jenny met his look directly, refusing to pretend she didn't know what he meant. The old reprobate's eyes glinted with mischief.

"Mighty distracted," he repeated. Then the glint died and he added seriously, "There's something else."

"What else?"

"There's history." He stared at the darkening sky as if he could see the past in it. "Tucker's history."

"You mean that he and his father moved around a lot?"

Deaver's attention came back to her. "Told you that, did he?"

"He . . . uh, he mentioned it."

But she wouldn't expose even to Deaver the other revelations he'd made, pitifully few though they were. Those were Tucker's vulnerabilities, and she would protect them no matter what. Nor would she try to put into clumsy words the delicate sketch of understanding for his pain that his words and her knowledge of him had begun to form. Because that was part of caring deeply for this difficult man, and that was *her* vulnerability.

"Did he mention what started Carter Gates drifting from place to place?"

"No." Not directly, though she'd gathered it had to do with a woman.

"Carter never had the best sense where it came to women. That's right, I knew Carter Gates. Even saw him and Tucker's ma married." He shook his head. "That's just what I'm talking about. Any fool could see she wasn't cut out for that life, but that's another story. Amy'd been dead a couple years and Tucker was about eight, nine when I hooked up with Carter again. He had a real good spot as manager for the Bristhursts. Steady work, little house to live in with Tucker. Then one summer, the owner's daughter came home from college back East. She was pretty enough and spoiled as all get-out. And Carter... well, like I said, if woman-sense was rain, he'd a been a drought. The father found out they were tangled up, and being an old-fashioned type, didn't hold much with that concept of all folks being equal, so he didn't like it a bit, and the girl, she went from clinging to Carter to pointing a finger at him in a blink of an eye. And before you knew it, Carter and Tucker were out."

"And Tucker knew why?" He must have. It explained so much about his attitude toward owners.

Deaver nodded. "Carter was never too careful what he said in front of the boy. After that, he had trouble finding anything steady and he went into real heavy drinking. I can't imagine him watching his mouth then. Sometimes the boy had to live with a great-aunt because Carter just couldn't

support them—a good enough woman but not real understanding of a growing boy. Don't think Tucker finished out
a year in the same school where he started it."

Which explained his empathy for Greg and Debbie at being the new kids.

"Carter straightened out after a while, but the drinking
did something to his insides. We'd hired at the same place
when he died. I went and got Tucker from this ranch he was
working while he took courses up to Montana, like Karl's
doing here. We buried Carter in the family plot near Cheyenne. By that time, the great-aunt was long gone, and Carter'd been away so long nobody knew him. It was just me
and Tucker—eighteen and already a good sight older than
the father he was putting in the ground."

Jenny could feel the air cooling rapidly now, chilling her
arms and neck, but it could have been snowing and she
wouldn't have walked away from Deaver's tale.

"Worked out that I found some work up the same place
as Tucker." She almost smiled at the casual just-so-
happened tone. "So I was there when . . ."

The chill congealed into a shiver. Without knowing what
he was about to say, she dreaded hearing this . . . and knew
she had to. She put her hand on his forearm.

"What happened, Deaver? I need to know."

He turned, examining her face despite the darkness,
searching for things that could glow even in shadows.

"I suppose you do," he said. He put his tough, gnarled
hand over hers. "There was a boy at this place, son of the
owners. Sammy. Gawky, skinny kid with freckles. Not a
mean-hearted kid, not down deep, but wild. His folks were
always having trouble with him. Sheriff came out more than
once, and Sammy was only twelve or so. But he took to
Tucker. Watched him all the time. Tickled the owners pink
because Sammy did better following Tucker. Tucker had his

own troubles, but he was good to the boy, showing him how to do things, patient with him when Sammy got fidgety."

An image of Tucker speaking low and quiet to Greg and Debbie, unruffled but insistent, came, and she could easily envision how good he was with this other boy.

"But like I said, Tucker had troubles of his own. Had a couple go-rounds with whiskey that had me wondering..."

He let it hang so long that Jenny prompted softly, "Wondering if he was like his father?"

Deaver shook his head. "I shouldn't have. Even as a boy he had steel in him Carter didn't. Maybe too much. He took too much on his shoulders, as a boy and later, with Sammy."

"What happened, Deaver?"

For a long moment, she thought he wouldn't answer, then he cleared his throat and started. "It was in August. A real hot day, a scorcher, and we'd had a few in a row. Sun burning down all day, not enough cloud to shade a fly. More like the California desert than Montana that week. We knew about frostbite, not about heat exposure. And not what it could do when a skinny twelve-year-old kid downs a good part of a quart of whiskey, then passes out in the closed cab of a pickup sitting in the sun."

"Oh, my God."

"He was dead when we found him. We all knew it, but Tucker wouldn't listen. He drove like a maniac to the clinic only to have doctors tell him what we'd said. Only they added technical terms about alcohol poisoning compounded by heat exposure. Sheriff ruled it an accident. Sammy's parents knew it was and said as much to Tucker. But he wouldn't listen. He wouldn't listen to anybody."

"But why?"

"It was his whiskey Sammy took, and it was him Sammy imitated. He couldn't ever forgive himself for that, for get-

ting drunk himself a couple times and letting the boy see it.
He said he knew the boy looked up to him, so it was his
fault. He couldn't ever forgive himself for that.'' Deaver
shook his head. ''He couldn't ever forgive himself.''

So he'd found the Double Bar X, where he'd had no
owners on hand to hurt him the way the Bristhurst girl had
once hurt him and his father, and no impressionable
youngsters that he might put at risk by being even an unwilling role model.

Until she'd shown up, with Debbie and Greg. A double
source of danger in his eyes.

She wiped away tears. Yes, she understood Tucker Gates
much better now, and she ached for him. But that might not
change anything, because if he didn't open himself up
enough to risk connecting with people, he'd never learn that
not every woman would betray him, and that he wouldn't let
down any child who looked up to him.

Chapter Eleven

"I want to talk to you, Greg."

Tucker had stayed away not only from dinner but through the night, then gone straight back to finish that section of fence. So this afternoon provided his first chance to seek out Greg.

The boy looked up, startled, then glanced around quickly as if searching an escape. Tucker felt about two inches tall.

With the feed bin behind him and Tucker in front of him leaving no way out, Greg reverted to bluster. "I suppose you want to yell at me some more."

"Not particularly."

The bluster ebbed, allowing puzzlement in. "Then what do you want?"

"First, I want to say I'm sorry. Not for what I said and not for shouting at you to drop the handle, because you could have gotten hurt. But I am sorry I kept yelling at you."

"Oh." The puzzlement deepened.

"The other thing I want to say is you are not to do anything like that again. You don't know your way around tools or the machinery or animals, yet." The final word came as a surprise to Tucker, one he didn't intend to stop to examine. "You're not familiar with the ways of a ranch and—"

"And I'm a city kid." Greg's interruption had the bitterness of a remembered taunt.

"Yeah, you are. But that doesn't mean anything. Everybody's got to be taught things like that. Some learn earlier, that's all. Because they're around people doing those things—their mothers and fathers. You learned other things, things city kids know from watching their parents."

Greg's skeptical look challenged him to name one.

Tucker searched his memory. "Like tennis. You know how to play tennis."

Greg nodded, and Tucker started to let out a sigh of relief. It died midbreath.

"Yeah, but my parents didn't teach me that. Dad got the name of the coach his boss liked and had Mom sign me up for lessons. And he sent me to camp for baseball and soccer. He has a career, so he can't take time for things like that. He's too busy to teach me things. You probably are, too."

Edward Peters had a lot to answer for.

Tucker waited until Greg met his eyes to answer. "I can teach you, but it's not like tennis or baseball. It's not a game on a ranch. It's work. I'm not saying you can't have fun, but if you learn how to do something, pretty soon you'll be expected to do it. And you have to be responsible enough to follow through. People rely on you, the animals need you to do your work so they'll stay alive. So before you say you want me to teach you something, you think about the responsibility that goes with it."

Greg said nothing. Tucker decided to make sure they were both clear.

"Okay?"

"Okay."

"Good. And in the meantime, I'm going to repeat what I told you out there yesterday—though this time I'm not going to be shouting." His mouth quirked up, and after a moment of blank surprise, Greg's mouth lifted slightly, too. Then Tucker went serious. "Most any tool can be dangerous for someone who doesn't know how to use it. Things you wouldn't think could be dangerous. So you are not to try anything, not to touch anything unless you have an okay from Deaver or me. You understand?"

"Yes . . . sir."

As they walked back to the house—Greg for supper and a good sleep in his own bed, Tucker to grab a shower and head for another sleepless night in the cabin—Tucker wondered at that belated, unsolicited addition of "sir." And he wondered at the powerful urge to put his arm around the boy's shoulders and bring him closer to his side.

Tucker spent the next seventy-two hours as a stranger to satisfaction. He was either around Jenny and thinking he shouldn't be or—banishing himself to distant work, town meals and lonely nights in the cabin—he was craving her.

Tonight, he'd lingered in Cody for dinner and stuck around a bar on Sheridan Street that would have its share of tourists in another month but for now boasted only locals telling stories he'd heard a dozen times. He'd considered staying in the cabin again, but decided he'd already done his penance for the night. Besides, driving in, he'd noted the house was dark except the back hall light and one low lamp by the phone Jenny always left on.

Easing down the hall between the kitchen and his room, trying not to think about Jenny upstairs, breathing steady and deep as she slept, a sound spun him around, and he stared right at her.

"What the hell are you . . ."

He didn't finish. He could see. She clutched a purple blouse to her chest as if it were a magic shield, standing there at the door of the little laundry room with the dryer still open behind her and a hanger ready on its top. She wore a bathrobe, a no-nonsense terry one in a peach color darker than the white that showed at her throat and lighter than the color in her cheeks. The bathrobe came to her knees and showed bare skin below, including her feet.

He brought his eyes from those bare feet, toes curled slightly into the nap of the rug in front of her new appliances, up her body to her eyes.

Abruptly, she pivoted and nudged the dryer door closed. It bounced open and she gave it a firmer touch.

Without looking at him, she said, "I didn't hear the truck. I didn't hear anything until you came in," letting him know she would have skedaddled if she'd heard him. Why should that bother him when he'd done his best to stay out of her path? "The dryer must have been running."

"What are you still doing up?"

"Debbie wants to wear this shirt to school tomorrow. She has to give a presentation, and she says it's been good luck for her." She snapped the shirt, airing out creases her grip might have put in. "Liz gave it to her."

"She could have gotten it done earlier."

"She forgot until bedtime."

"So you stay up half the night getting it ready for her?"

She gave him a quick frown before inserting the hanger and buttoning the shirt's placket. "Don't start, Tucker. And when it comes to staying up half the night, you're a great one to talk. At least I'm not sitting on a stool in some bar killing my brain cells."

He smiled without much humor. "A booth, and it was more like anesthetizing them." And even that had worn off. "You look tired, Jenny."

Her back to him, she paused in the act of hanging the blouse for two heartbeats, then reached the last two inches to hook it over the rod, and smoothed down the fabric so it hung straight. With as much care, she turned to face him.

"So do you, Tucker."

"I am. I haven't been getting much rest." He met her eyes. "I miss you, Jenny."

Jenny would have laughed if it hadn't made her want to cry.

He made it sound as if he'd confessed one of those sins he'd told her about at the beginning, trying to scare her off. But she thought she knew him better now; he was trying to scare himself off.

Deliberately, she stepped closer and brushed the stubbled line of his jaw with the back of her fingers, then placed her palm on his cheek, the slash of his cheekbone a familiar ridge under her fingertips.

"I miss you, too, Tucker."

His hands wrapped around her arms, just above her elbows. He neither pulled her closer nor pushed her away, but kept them both anchored where they stood.

Slowly, he squeezed his eyes closed and dropped his head back slightly, as if imploring the heavens he wouldn't look at for strength. "Jenny, I can't—"

"Then don't," she whispered, absorbing as much of the sensation of touching him as she could through her palm.

He moved fast, the speed and the tightness of his hold driving the air from her as he wrapped one arm diagonally across her back and the other around her shoulders. His kiss was blatant, immediately demanding. She curled her arms around his neck and hung on.

But if she'd expected the storm to pass, she was wrong. Instead, it infected her. He wasn't rough, but he wasn't subtle.

He cupped her breast through the bulk of the robe, rubbing and stroking, while he used his other hand on her buttocks to bring their lower bodies close. She moved against him, the imprint of his arousal apparent even through the layers of cloth.

Jerking open the tie belt of her robe, he gave a grunt of satisfaction that gave way to a growl of frustration as he took in the row of small buttons from throat to waist on her nightshirt. It would have been comical, if she hadn't been just as frustrated.

She started unbuttoning herself, then paused. Looking up to meet his eyes, she continued, slow, deliberate. Making him accept the gift she gave.

He swallowed, and the tuck appeared between his brows, but he didn't ease his hold on her, and he didn't look away.

When she'd finished, clear to the waist, he kissed her. Gently, but oh so hungry. She stood quietly as he placed the back of his fingers at the base of her throat, then gradually followed the open line of her nightshirt. He watched his hand's progress, past her collarbone, down the valley of her breasts, between her ribs and to her waist. And she watched him.

Spreading his hand inside the cloth at the side of her waist, he drew her toward him again. His other hand gathered in the material of her robe and nightshirt, sliding down her hip until he reached bare skin there, too.

She met his kiss but kept her hands pressed on his chest to maintain some space between them—enough space for her to start attacking the buttons on his shirt. He make a sound deep in his throat at the first contact of her fingers with his skin, and she broke away from his mouth to press her lips to the spot low on his throat where it originated.

He dropped his head back like a man whose patience had just broken.

It had.

"I'm taking you to bed, Jenny. Now."

She didn't argue.

He hooked an arm around her waist, at times lifting her feet from the floor as he headed down the short hall to his room. Inside, she half sat on the edge of the low dresser just inside as he closed and locked the door. She hadn't let go of him all this time. When he turned to face her, she slid her hands down his chest, pausing to open two more buttons, then not wanting to pause anymore. He wore no belt to frustrate her tonight. She unsnapped his jeans, her sigh of release synchronizing with his indrawn breath.

He stepped between her knees, spreading them to accommodate his hips.

"Jenny...let me..." The thought seemed to scatter as her touch reached bare skin. "Let me take you to bed."

She knew how a touch—his touch—could drive thoughts away as easily as dust before the wind. His hands on her shoulders as he drew back robe and nightshirt together. His lips at the juncture of shoulder and throat. His whiskered jaw prickling at her temple as he murmured his intentions into her hair.

"That's so..." She tilted her head back and welcomed his deep, hot kiss. "...so far away."

He nipped at her earlobe as he leaned over her, freeing her arms from sleeves. The robe dropped to the dresser top around her hips. The nightshirt he pulled over her head and flung somewhere behind her. "Truck's farther."

She chuckled, fascinated and aroused by the way the movement rubbed her breasts against his bare chest. His shirt was gone. Had she done that?

"You once said a chair..."

"Bed," he insisted.

She had ways to argue with him that didn't involve words. She pushed down his jeans to allow her more access.

"Jenny..."

"Here, Tucker. I want you now." She arched toward him, at the same time gently cupping him. "Here."

The first touch of him against her heated flesh drew a gasp from her. "Tucker." She opened to him, knowing the possible consequences, fully willing to bear his child.

He stood absolutely still, and she saw sweat bead along his upper lip and on his forehead. His eyes held torment, and she thought he, too, considered the possibility of creating a baby. And she wondered if, for the first time, his reaction to that possibility wasn't automatic.

Then, with an oath, he broke the contact, backing away a spare inch and dragging his jeans up enough that he could reach into the pocket for the condom packet. She watched him, accepting his decision, as he performed the task despite hands not entirely steady.

He met her eyes. Without breaking the look, he gripped her hips, angling her to accept him. She wrapped her arms and legs around him. And they joined.

Jenny wanted to keep her eyes open, wanted to record every expression, every look, every movement. But it wasn't possible. Because she couldn't hold herself even that infinitesimal distance away from her response to Tucker.

She could only give. And take. Sensation. Scent. Sound. Satisfaction... Ah, satisfaction that drained even the memory of want. Satisfaction that echoed from his hoarse cry of completion. Satisfaction that welled with tenderness for this man, for herself, and for what happened between them.

Tucker leaned heavily against her. But somehow they'd found a balance that allowed her to hold his greater weight without being borne down herself. She stroked his back in absent, lazy rhythms.

"Damn, Jenny... what you do to me."

His voice was so low, she didn't think she was meant to hear the words, but she did, and she held them to her heart.

Her skin was beginning to cool before he straightened away from her, the balance abruptly disrupted. He looked at her steadily, a thorough examination that started with her eyes, took in the rest of her, until returning to her eyes.

Embarrassment skirted at the edge of her emotions, not quite strong enough to break in.

But when he stepped back, it elbowed closer, along with the awareness of the physical reminders of what they had done, and where. She twisted around in search of her robe; the nightshirt was nowhere in sight.

"Don't move."

She froze at his command, turning back almost reluctantly. As if he'd been waiting for her to face him again, he deliberately toed off his boots, then shucked off his jeans and briefs that had been pushed out of the way when dignity had come in a poor second to the need to come together. Had he sensed her embarrassment and wanted to soothe it by letting her see his own vulnerable position?

If only he would do that in other ways, by telling her the secrets that shut him off from the world, from her.

"Are you okay, Jenny? Did I hurt you?"

The last question was raw, as he stepped back between her legs, both of them now naked.

"No, you didn't hurt me, Tucker." She touched his cheek and smiled up at him. After a long moment, his frown eased, and he smiled slightly.

"You think you could put up with something as tame as a bed now?"

"Well," she drawled, playing up to his mood, "that is pretty tame, but I suppose..."

"No, don't get down."

He stopped her by guiding her arms around his neck, her legs back around his waist, then sliding his hand under her bottom. "This time, Jenny, I'm making sure to take you to bed."

He laid her on the mattress, carefully positioning her head on the pillow that smelled faintly of him. From the drawer he pulled a handful of foil packets, and tossed them on the nightstand.

When he joined her, they lay on their sides, face to face. He pushed her hair back, then stroked the exposed line of her shoulder.

"Tell me what I've missed. Tell me what's been happening here."

His voice held a real hunger that tightened her throat. How lonely he must be on the other side of the line he tried so hard to live behind. Their desire for each other had been the one thing that had drawn him across it. If she couldn't break it down completely, she could use moments like this to show him what he could have if he would erase that line.

"Well, Rambo's training is coming along. Although he hasn't quite mastered the difference between newspapers and other paper. Last night, Greg left some of his homework on the floor by his bed and today he had to tell the teacher that the dog hadn't eaten his homework, but had destroyed it through the other end of the digestive process."

Tucker's face relaxed into a smile, and she went on with details of the daily life he'd exiled himself from.

Woven among her anecdotes was the acknowledgment of changes. Debbie and Greg had a few light chores, shared some of the responsibilities for Rambo and took the bus most days. They'd also each had a friend over to play after school and to stay for dinner in the past week. Tucker didn't ask and she didn't say what role his words had had in this, but she realized with something like awe that it didn't really matter. Not to him, and not to her. The changes benefited Debbie and Greg—what did it matter where they came from?

Also woven among her words was a communication of touches. With palm or fingertips or the back of his fingers, he caressed her. Her shoulders, her arms, the inside of her elbow, her hip, her ribs, her throat. And she returned the touches, no single gesture advancing their intimacy but the sum revealing and responding.

He kissed her throat, then her shoulder. "Now tell me about you, Jenny. Tell me about your reading. Tell me about the museum."

She tried. But this came harder. Perhaps because it was foreign to speak of her accomplishments. But more, she thought, because her attention focused tighter and tighter on the pleasure of his touches and of touching him.

"Did you learn about the preferred time for immunizations?" he asked, then slid his leg between hers, pressing against her.

She managed to answer, jumbled, but almost reasonable. He showed no inclination to criticize, especially when she arched closer to him, brushing her breasts against his chest and sliding higher on his leg.

He started to roll to his back, an arm around her to take her with. But she resisted to hold her position.

"Jenny?"

She ran her hand down his muscled back to his buttocks, then pressed, urging him toward her. He held for a moment, then complied. Matched along their lengths, they kissed, exploring equally, parting only at the insistence of demanding lungs.

Tucker twisted his head to look at the nightstand behind him, then turned back to Jenny. "I don't want to move. Can you reach a condom?"

She stretched over him, his hand spread across her back technically steadying her, but also intensifying the most unsettling sensations.

"Got one." She eased back and held it out to him.

"You put it on." Her protest started automatically. Tucker stilled it with a kiss and repeated, "You put it on."

She did. With little skill and no efficiency, but with pleasure at touching him this way and, yes, a bit of satisfaction that her touches brought that intense, fiery look to his eyes.

Making a sound low in his throat, he drew her top leg high over his hip, then held there an instant as they looked at each other.

Jenny's heart changed rhythm, slipped from the almost frantic pulse of excitement, to a deeper, more powerful beat. She saw in his eyes an uncertainty, almost a fear, and the possibility he would withdraw flashed into her mind.

Then he came forward, pushing into her, opening her and joining with her. Beginning the dance only they could do together. They never looked away from each other.

Tucker lay on his back, holding Jenny as morning edged nearer. They'd collapsed with her half-draped over him, facedown. That's how they remained, though she'd turned her face into his neck so he felt the warm pulse of her breath against his skin and matched it as he stroked her hair.

He'd never known such physical satisfaction, such total ease in his body. And so much torment in his soul.

Coming together outside. Coming apart inside.

He wanted this. God, he wanted it so much. All of it. All the daily intimacy promised by the sharing they'd just done. Not the powerful lovemaking alone. But the everyday words and the shared looks.

Wanted it, and knew he couldn't have it.

"Jenny, I can't do this."

She chuckled into his shoulder. "I'd have to disagree about that, cowboy." She looked up, her teasing smile freezing as she caught his expression. "What do you mean?"

"This—us. You and me. The boss and hired hand—"

"That's ridic—"

He put a finger over her mouth. "It's not. It's real. The line between owners and employees is real, and it's there for a reason. It protects the people on both sides of the line."

"That's from a century ago, Tucker. The world isn't like that anymore. People are just people—"

He shook his head doggedly. "You can try to talk it away, but it's there, Jenny. I've seen it and I've felt it. It's there, and I've seen it hurt people."

"How have you felt it, Tucker? How have you seen it hurt people?"

He ignored her questions. "I told you once that ravishing women in their houses, especially with their kids around wasn't my style. I promised you, you wouldn't have to worry about that. But I can't keep my promises about that—not to you and not to myself. God, I can hardly stop from taking you on a wing chair or the damn dryer. And I didn't stop myself when it came to the pickup and the bureau. I can't do that to you anymore."

"You weren't alone, Tucker. I was there, too, and I could have stopped it. I didn't because I wanted to be with you. I wanted to make love—"

"And eventually you'll want more, and you should have it. A family. Everything. You deserve it. You deserve the best there is, Jenny. I can't give it to you."

Jenny grabbed on to calm, holding it desperately. This was it, the fight she'd seen coming a long time. The fight for his heart. The fight she had to win.

"What can't you give me, Tucker?" she asked softly.

"I know who I am, Jenny. I don't have any illusions about that. I've known this about myself a long time." The sound he made could have been intended as a laugh. "Maybe it's hereditary. My father sure wasn't much for family. He wasn't a bad man, but he shouldn't have been a father and God knows, he shouldn't have brought up a kid alone."

"But that's not you, Tucker."

He didn't seem to hear. "I care about you, Jenny. Maybe I . . . But there's not just you to consider."

"You mean Greg and Debbie."

"Yes."

"But you like them. . . ."

"Of course I like them. That's not the point."

"Then what is?"

"You're their mother. You're responsible for them. Being with you means being part of that. Sharing it. Being their . . . sharing that responsibility."

He couldn't even bring himself to say, *being their father.* Heartache sharpened her voice. "And you don't want that?"

"Hell, no, I don't want it. I'm just like my old man. I don't know the first thing about being a father. I don't—"

"Yes, you do. You know the very first thing, the most important thing—being honest with them. Letting them know what you want from them, what you expect from them. When they don't do it, you come down on them. But when they do do it, you praise them. You're fair, and you're consistent. They know where they stand with you."

She smoothed back his hair from his forehead with her palm, hoping to lift the shadows from his eyes. But the shadows came from inside.

She couldn't give up, though. She had to keep trying. "And you know something else important about being a father, Tucker. You know that those children are separate, individual people. Not yours to mold or maneuver, but people in their own right."

She saw the answer in his eyes before she finished.

He shook his head. "I'm not the kind to be a father, Jenny. Having some kid looking up to me, thinking if he follows me, he'll be doing what's right, thinking if he follows me, he'll..."

Tell me, Tucker. Please. Tell me, so we can face this together.

If he'd tell her, she could fight it. But he had to face it enough on his own to tell her, or nothing she said would ever matter to him. He had himself so closed off, so locked up that what she said just rolled off him. But if he took the risk, if he opened himself up...

"There's a stock sale, big sale in Billings tomorrow. It's early, so I'll go up tonight. See what there is."

"See what there is? What do you mean?"

Sitting up, he didn't look at her. "There's usually ranchers looking for people there. Or they know about something."

"Something?" She sat up, too, tightening the covers around her. "What are you talking about?"

"Jobs. I should be able to get another job. I think my leaving the Double Bar X would be best for everybody."

The past two days had been the worst of her life. Jenny hoped she'd never face any to top them. She felt so helpless—once a staple of her life, but a feeling she'd fought hard to overcome. An unfamiliar feeling since she'd come to the Double Bar X, and most unwelcome.

Tucker wouldn't be swayed. She'd tried. All her belief that he had to open up first hadn't stopped her from trying to persuade him. In the end, frustration had chilled and sharpened her voice.

"So, you'll go someplace and work for somebody else and dream about your own place and then you think everything will be all right. But it won't. Because you're still drawing those lines between people. Stupid, arbitrary lines that won't protect you from what you're running from."

"You don't know what the hell you're talking about. How could you? *Guinevere Ferrington Peters.* You don't know," he'd finally snapped at her.

Then he left his bed, and her, to put in a full day's work on the ranch before throwing some things in a bag and heading for Billings at about five-thirty. She watched him leave from her bedroom window.

She suspected he'd said something to Deaver from the way the older man looked at her, sympathetic and disappointed. Manny, Karl and the kids picked up the atmosphere. Dinner the night Tucker left was quiet. The next morning's breakfast worse, and by lunch no one said much at all.

Manny offered to fix dinner the second night, and she accepted. So she wasn't in the kitchen when Tucker came in.

At her bedroom window again, she saw the top of his hat as he walked into the house. *He's tired.* Then she berated herself—as if she could read his emotional state from the tilt of his hat and the set of his shoulders.

I will not fall apart over this.

She sat on the edge of the bed and realized that was the truth. She wouldn't fall apart. She'd earned her strength, and it wouldn't desert her.

But it did make her sad. So sad, that she couldn't reach Tucker, that he wouldn't let himself be reached. It was such a waste . . . he would be so lonely. . . .

That's when the tears came.

Everyone else was seated for dinner when she went down. Tucker glanced at her, then immediately away. It was probably too brief a look to see beyond the repairs she'd performed with cold water and makeup. But it was long enough for her to see shadows under his eyes, the downward slant of his mouth.

"Tucker's got something to tell us and he wouldn't say anything until you came down," Greg announced.

"I'm here now," she said as calmly as she could.

"What're you going to tell us, Tucker?" Greg demanded.

Tucker rested his forearms against the edge of the table and cupped one hand over the other, but said nothing.

"Best get it said, boy." Deaver's words sounded more of fatalism than support.

"I got an offer to manage a spread up in Montana."

Nobody said anything. Nobody moved.

"Big spread," Tucker went on, as if compelled to fill the silence. "Owned by a Hollywood producer who's decided he wants to return it to a working ranch. Seems he had a vegetarian girlfriend who didn't want cattle, but they broke up, and now this guy's gung ho. I can set it up the way I want. Lots of freedom."

And an absentee owner, Jenny thought with pain.

"You're leaving?" Greg's cry was of stark betrayal.

"I won't go until I'm sure you can find the right person to run the Double Bar. I wouldn't do that to you."

His reassurances meant nothing to the boy. What did Greg care about the running of the ranch? For that matter, what did she care compared to the issue of Tucker leaving? The Double Bar lost its heart without Tucker.

"Are you taking Deaver?" Debbie demanded.

Tucker didn't smile, didn't come close, but some of the grimness lifted from his face.

"That's up to Deaver."

Attention shifted to the older man. He returned the looks under bushy red and gray eyebrows dropped low in a frown. "I'll have to think on that. But I wouldn't go until *I'm* satisfied things are settled here."

His emphasis indicated he was a much tougher judge of such things than Tucker.

"Who cares about that?" Greg's voice rose. "You're just a bunch of hired hands, anyway. We're the owners. We're in charge. Go ahead—leave. All of you. We don't need any of you. We don't need you!" He scraped his chair back, fumbling to get out of it.

"Greg—"

"Greg—"

He heeded neither Jenny nor Tucker.

"You're just a quitter!"

He knocked the chair sideways to get free of it—only Karl's quick grab saving it from going over—and ran out of the room, Rambo chasing after him.

Greg's steps pounded up the staircase, followed by a slamming door. Then there was silence. Across the table, Tucker met her eyes.

Did he see in her eyes an echo of her son's charge?

Tucker sat in the office, the door closed, the lights off, and looked out the window. The acres he knew better than any other human being reached to the black bulk of the mountains that held up the western sky. Closer, his eyes took in vague, shadowed forms, but he didn't need light to see the bunkhouse, the barn, the garage, the calving shed and the other buildings. He could find his way to the storage shed blind, could work the tricky lock on the machine shop in his sleep, could predict the weather by how much the door to the tack room stuck.

It had been so easy to find the job that would take him away from all of it, so incredibly easy.

He supposed he should feel good about that. Should be real flattered by the things that producer fellow's agent at the sale had to say. But right now the clearer memory was turning through the Double Bar X's gates, coming down the driveway to his first view of the house, the buildings. His world. And that figure at the second-floor bedroom window.

He hadn't expected telling them would be easy, but he hadn't expected the pain, either. It didn't let up. And it wouldn't until he left. He hoped to God it would then.

But before he could find out, he had to line up someone to take over. The right kind of person. There'd been that Jackson guy he'd talked to in Billings, but he hadn't been good enough. How was he going to get through this until he did find somebody good enough?

He knew he needed to do this for everybody's good—for Jenny, for the kids, for himself—but, God . . .

Tucker Gates swiveled his chair, turning his back on the window.

He knew what he had to do.

Jenny pulled the afghan tighter around her drawn-up knees, setting the rocker in her bedroom in gentle motion.

Tucker couldn't leave.

He belonged to the Double Bar X, he *was* the Double Bar X. He loved it so much. He wanted to own it, to stay here forever. He'd spent ten happy years here until they'd crashed into his life.

But he wouldn't stay with them here. No matter how wrongheaded she thought his feelings, she couldn't change that. He'd made that clear.

And how could she stay here without him? How could she look at the mountains without feeling that first kiss? Look at the pasture without thinking of his love of the land? Sit in the office without remembering his passion for the ranch—and her?

She knew what she had to do.

"...So the best thing is for us to head back to Chicago."

Jenny had called them into the parlor before breakfast and made a long, reasoned speech about cultural opportunities, being close to their father, her father, Liz, the new baby, chances to further their academics and the strong grounding they had from this time in Wyoming and how they'd take it with them wherever they went. No matter how far away from the Double Bar X.

"But you love it here, Mom. Why do you want to leave? That doesn't make sense."

Jenny had to swallow the lump of emotion at her daughter's focus on her reaction. Yes, they had all changed at the Double Bar X. "I've told you why, Debbie."

"But if it's because we didn't want to come, that's better now and—"

"We'll be better, Mom, honest," Greg interjected. "We're learning about the ranch and stuff and I won't do anything stupid to make Tucker mad. I won't, I promise—you tell him that. Maybe he won't go."

They were making this difficult. Much too difficult.

"I don't want to leave. I want to stay here," said Debbie, stubbornness in her voice. "Greg hasn't liked it, but that doesn't mean—"

"I do, too. I do like it. I don't want to go, either, so just shut up, Debbie."

His sister gave him a long, considering look. "You don't want to go?"

"No."

They both turned to Jenny.

"We like it. We have friends. School's okay. We have horses and the calves and Deaver and Manny and Karl—"

"And Tucker," Greg muttered, "even if he is leaving."

"We don't want to go," Debbie concluded.

"I'm glad you've both come to like it here." Her throat tightened. She'd wanted so much for them to like it. "And we can arrange to come back for vacations." And arrange for Tucker to be away at those times. "But it's time for us to go..." She couldn't say *home*. The Double Bar X was home now. "...back."

"We thought you were crazy to bring us out here, but we got to like it, and now you want to take us away. But you love it and we don't want to—"

"Why should we—"

"That's enough!" Debbie and Greg gaped. Jenny had never shouted at her children. "We're going to leave. We have to. And I don't want to hear any more about it."

She didn't. In fact, she didn't hear any more from the children before they left for school. Or when they returned. Only discarded school clothes and books in their rooms gave evidence of their presence.

When it came time for dinner, there was no sign of them at all.

That's when she worried.

Chapter Twelve

The minute he opened the door, Tucker knew something was wrong.

Something beyond the wrong he'd spent the day trying to drive out of his mind by punishing his muscles. Deaver, Manny and even young Karl had made a point of telling him he was a fool. But he could have ignored that. No, he'd tackled the fence in the northwest corner to stay as far away as he could from Jenny, who had said nothing.

But she hadn't left him alone. Not for a second.

Grimly, he acknowledged the Double Bar X didn't have enough fence to escape his own thoughts. On top of that, chores closer to home had backed up. Time to stop avoiding things. But that didn't mean taking on more pain than he had to. So, he'd arrived late for dinner, so everybody would have started eating already, and he could cut the time with the Peters family to a minimum.

But when he walked in, nobody was eating.

Jenny, in the act of hanging up the phone, spun to the doorway and turned away immediately. But not before he'd seen her hope crash. He took an involuntary step toward her.

"What's wrong?"

She kept her back to him, so he looked to the others. Deaver, Manny and Karl had also looked up at his entrance but now glanced toward Jenny's back, then away, indicating it was up to Jenny to tell him.

"Deaver and Karl, if you'd please go ahead with...uh, with what we talked about. Manny, could you please give Tucker his dinner before you go? I'll keep calling."

"What's going on here?" Nobody paid any attention to Tucker's demand. Karl walked past him without a look, while Manny went to the oven for a filled plate he set at Tucker's usual place, then he, too, left. "Deaver, what is this?"

Deaver paused at the door. "It's Double Bar X business. Not your concern anymore." Then he left.

Jenny depressed and released the switch on the wall phone to disconnect without having talked to anyone. Consulting a list on the counter, she started dialing again. In two strides he reached the phone and held down the switch.

"What the hell is going on, Jenny?"

"It's all right, Tucker. Go ahead and eat your dinner. We're taking care of it."

"Taking care of..." It slammed into him like being thrown from a bucking horse. "The kids. Debbie and Greg—where are they?"

Fear flashed across her eyes, then she looked away. "I don't know. They didn't come in for dinner."

"Did they get off the school bus? Who saw them last? What were they—"

"Tucker. We're taking care of it. They were here after school, changed their clothes, then Karl saw them taking off across the pasture behind the barn on foot. They had Rambo with them."

"It's dark now. They could have gotten lost."

"I know," she said. Despite her outward calm, he felt like a brute for reminding her. "We're trying to take this in logical order. I checked the house, now Deaver, Karl and Manny are checking the barns and sheds while I call their friends from school, just in case. Mrs. Downs is coming over to stay here in case they come back, or someone calls. And we'll spread out to look farther out, if we have to."

"I'm coming."

"No, Tucker, you stay here and eat your dinner. Really, there's no need—"

"I'm coming."

"Tucker, there's no need and . . . and it's really not your concern."

He stared at her, a fierce hand squeezing breath out of his lungs.

Not his concern. God, he hadn't wanted it to be. He'd done his damnedest to keep it from being his concern. And what good had it done? None.

Because he would have traded everything he had to guarantee those kids' safety and to shelter Jenny from the fear she tried so hard to mask.

Jenny was trying to give him what he'd asked, and all he could think of was how he hated being excluded from this family. They'd invited him in during the good times, and he'd been too scared of the past to try it. But now, facing one of the bad times, he knew he had no choice. Maybe he never had.

It sure as hell would make no difference how far away he ran—to the far corner of the Double Bar X, to the far cor-

ner of Montana or to some far corner of the world. They
were in his heart. They'd always go with him. No matter
where he went on this earth, and likely beyond, he'd have
this concern and affection for Debbie and Greg . . . and this
heart-swelling love for their mother.

But knowing that and absorbing it were two different
things. That would come later, when he had time to consider this, time to sort things out with Jenny. After they had
the kids back, safe.

Finding Greg and Debbie was the first issue to sort out.

"You don't want me to go?"

"I didn't—"

"You afraid I'll take over and push you aside like Edward would?"

This denial came slower. "I didn't say—"

"You didn't have to say it. I saw that look when you were
waiting for me to march over you. I wouldn't do that to you,
Jenny, not now. I'm not saying there wouldn't be times
when I'd try, but not now."

"I wouldn't have let you, anyhow."

It was his fighter back, and he was damn glad to see her—
it chased some of the fear from her eyes. He almost grinned.
"I know you wouldn't have. That's why I didn't try. But you
can't stop me from going out looking for those kids, Jenny.
If not with you, I'll go alone. I know this place and—"

"With me, Tucker. I want you with me, please."

He wanted to take her in his arms, to shelter her. But that
wasn't what she needed now. He nodded and gave her what
she did need.

"Okay. You finish calling. Have you eaten anything?"

"I'm not hungry, really."

"Too bad." He got the other plate from the oven and set
it in front of her. "You need fuel."

He finished off his dinner and, between futile calls, he nagged her into eating about a third of hers. When Karl, Manny and Deaver reported back without having found the kids in any of the outbuildings, he fought the urge to take over, instead leaving to gather what he thought they'd need—warm clothes, a couple blankets, flashlights, extra batteries, a thermos for coffee, food, rope, an electric lantern and a first-aid kit he tried to keep out of Jenny's sight.

He returned to find only Jenny in the kitchen.

"Where to first, then?"

"I was trying to think of other places they might go for shelter, if they got stuck out there in the dark. Where they didn't know how to get back."

"What makes you think they'll look for shelter?" With city kids, it might be best to search the open areas.

Jenny looked up, surprise clear in her face. "Because you told them to."

"Me?"

"Yes. I heard you a couple times and the kids told me. About how exposure can be a risk even in summer."

He stared. "You think they listened to me?" It came out gruffer than he intended.

"I know they did." She said it with such conviction. "They repeated all the details of looking for a windbreak, remembering the mountains lie to the west, being careful of ditches or streams by listening for the sound of water and the way the banks are built up."

"They told you that?" Debbie and Greg had looked dead bored when he'd talked about those things.

"Yes. I was thinking about those things, putting them together and... Maybe the cabin..."

He shook his head. "They don't know about it. Nobody knows about it. Not even Manny and Karl. Nobody except Deaver. And you."

He didn't try to stop the memories from showing in his eyes as they met hers. She broke the look and moved away, busying herself with filling the thermos with coffee. But he'd seen her reaction. And it might be unfair to want her to feel that way when he'd told her over and over that their roads could only go different directions, but, God, it struck something deep and lonely in him to know she did.

He picked up the conversation with no more reference to the cabin. "But I did tell them about some old line shacks out on the edges of our land when I was telling them how they worked the place in the old days. If they got the idea the shacks are more elaborate than they are . . ."

That's where they headed.

"They're okay, Jenny."

His voice came out of the dark, solid and steady even with the reverberations his pickup absorbed from the rough dirt track that took them away from another line shack, another crumbling structure inhabited by nothing more than a few wild animals. To get to this last one, they'd driven almost all the way, but for the first two they'd had to park the truck and do the last part on foot in the dark.

They'd been back to the house once, checking to see if there were any messages, any sign, any miracle that brought Debbie and Greg to their beds, asleep and safe.

Nothing.

So they'd returned to checking more distant possibilities while Manny, Karl and Deaver fanned out to cover the area nearer the house. At least they'd all reported in that they'd checked the most dangerous areas—streams, irrigation ditches, an old well and some other areas the men hadn't itemized for her—and found no sign of the children. That eased some of the worst concern.

"I know they are. I think I'd feel it if they weren't. Maybe that's just wishful thinking, but I really do. Once Greg was with his friend's family and they had a car accident—I got all edgy even before the hospital called and said he'd broken his arm. I don't feel that way now."

But maybe her maternal radar worked only on broken limbs, or on car accidents or in Illinois. Maybe the open spaces of Wyoming threw it off. Maybe...maybe she was getting overtired and not thinking straight.

She shivered.

"Want a blanket?"

"No. I'm fine, thanks."

"How about some coffee?"

"Oh, sure." She unscrewed the thermos and poured. "Here."

He smiled, a movement of shadows. "I meant for you, but I won't turn it down—after you've had some."

She took a sip, recognized the benefit of the warmth and caffeine and drank more before refilling the cup for Tucker.

"I just can't figure out where they could have gotten to."

The windshield was gray with the first light of morning.

Tucker brought the truck to a stop in the yard outside the house and turned off the ignition. Through the big kitchen window, they could see Manny moving around and Karl with his head pillowed on his arms on the table. No question they hadn't found Debbie and Grog.

By tacit agreement or shared inertia, Jenny and Tucker sat silently in the truck, recruiting their energy and thoughts. After a night of racing thoughts, Jenny's mind felt empty of anything except inarticulate prayers.

"Jenny, I think there's something we have to consider, here. A possibility."

"No!" A single, strangled syllable of protest and denial.

Tucker pulled her across the seat into his arms, an awkward embrace, but so welcome. The stubble of his overnight beard caught in her hair and prickled her temple. She welcomed the sensation. She'd had the comfort of his presence, but not his touch through this long, long night.

"No, not that. I'm sorry, Jenny, I wasn't thinking. I should have said it another way. I mean they might be hiding on purpose. That they're not being found because they don't intend to let themselves be found."

"But..." *But why?* she'd intended to ask. Before it was out, though, she had an answer.

"Was anything bothering them? I mean today—yesterday—in particular. The atmosphere around here hasn't been the best lately, and they knew that." Tucker clearly had reached the stage of exhaustion that required talking to think. "But seems like there'd have to be something more, some spur that would get them moving toward doing something like this, only—"

"There was."

"What?"

"There was a spur." She thunked her fingertips against her breastbone. "Me."

"What do you mean, *you?*"

"I told them this morning—yesterday morning—that we were going to leave the Double Bar X. They weren't happy about it."

"Why on God's earth did you tell them that?"

"Because we *are* going to leave. It's senseless for you to leave. It would be wrong to let you take that job in Montana. This is your home. You belong here. So we'll leave, and then you can get back to your peaceful life."

"Of all the stupid—"

"I've told you, Tucker Gates, don't call me stupid." She started to pull away, but he wouldn't release her.

He held up a hand. "Sorry. That was partially aimed at myself. But there's no reason for you to be leaving. You belong here, too, you and the kids."

"I won't let you leave the place you love because you're not comfortable with us here, so—"

"Maybe that's changing."

"What?" She stilled, afraid to move, almost afraid to breathe in case that shattered the fragile bubble of what he was saying, what she *hoped* he was saying. "What's changing?"

"My being uncomfortable with having the Peters family around here. Maybe it's getting so I'd only be comfortable if you *are* around here."

She leaned back for a full view of his eyes, losing some of their dark mysteries in the growing light. "Maybe?"

He met her look. Gently, he pushed a lock of hair that had snagged on his whiskered chin off her cheek. "I have things to say to you, Jenny. But this isn't the time. And before I say them, I have some hard things to tell you that might change how you feel about all this. About me."

"It won't change how I feel, Tucker."

"You can't know that until you hear what I have to say."

"I know."

"You can't. It's more compl... What is he doing?"

Jenny followed the line of Tucker's focus. Deaver had come out of the bunkhouse, carrying a paper bag with faint grease marks, the kind bags get from doughnuts or Manny's sourdough muffins. As Deaver turned to look toward the house, she could see that under his other arm he held a bulky bundle of clothing.

Her heartbeat doubled. Wasn't that Greg's winter jacket? And the blue, surely that matched Debbie's.

Jenny leaned over to honk the horn. Before she reached it, Tucker's hand clamped around her wrist.

"Wait."

She looked from Tucker's narrowed eyes to the familiar faded ginger and gray head of Deaver Smith. Deaver stepped off the porch and headed around behind the bunkhouse, coming out the far side.

"Let's see what he does."

"See what he does, why? We should..." She sucked in a breath, looked from Deaver's retreating form to Tucker and back. Deaver's maneuver had kept him from being spotted from the big kitchen window. He got in his truck and headed down the driveway, with neither Manny nor Karl showing any sign of having heard him. "You don't think...?"

"I don't know."

"He wouldn't do that. He wouldn't do that to me, to all of us. Let us be so worried. He wouldn't. Would he?"

"I don't know."

"But why would he do that? Why would he help them?"

Tucker met her look, his eyes expressive. "Because he's a stubborn old man who's spent the past fifteen years sure he knew the right way for me to run my life."

"I'll kill him."

Tucker turned the ignition key and started after Deaver at a safe distance.

"You'll have to beat me to him."

Through the solid cabin door Jenny could just make out the rumble of Deaver's voice. No sign—or sound—indicated if Debbie and Greg were inside with him. She looked at Tucker, who shrugged slightly and turned the knob.

Debbie, facing the door, spotted them first. She froze in the act of zipping her winter jacket, leaving visible layers of T-shirt, shirt and two sweaters. Rambo, nestled in the rumpled covers of the bed, slept peacefully. Beyond his sister,

Greg struggled to insert an equally layered arm into his jacket while Deaver emptied the paper bag, pulling out muffins, paper towels and sealed plastic containers of juice.

"...And I don't want to hear any complaining about no butter or such. You'll eat it, and you'll be thankful."

Deaver's grumble continued. But Greg, caught by his sister's stillness, turned to follow the direction of her look.

"Mom. Tucker." He strangled the names, trying to swallow at the same time.

Jenny wanted to wrap her arms around them so tight that the pressure of their bodies would convince her they were real, and whole. She wanted to shake them so hard that the explanation for putting her through such hell would come tumbling out. She wanted to sit down and reason out why they each looked from her to Tucker as if seeking the answer to some important riddle.

She stood motionless.

In no hurry, Deaver turned in their direction. A glance seemed to satisfy him.

"Good. Glad to see you two. Plenty of muffins, but you'll have to share a juice."

"You're glad?" Jenny sputtered.

"Of course I am. Why wouldn't I be..." He broke off and glowered, first at Jenny, then at Tucker. "You think I had anything to do with them sneaking away like that? No sir." Now he directed the glare at Greg, then Debbie. "I vote for tanning their hides but good."

Greg appeared disconcerted, but Debbie didn't blink. In fact, she finished zipping her jacket, then helped her brother with his.

That simple gesture raised another question in Jenny's mind. But she needed to unravel the first puzzle before they went any further—with all the mysteries and possibilities of the past twelve hours, she longed to have at least one settled to her satisfaction. "But you were bringing things to them—the coats and muffins."

"Well, when I stopped to think it through 'bout an hour ago, I started realizing they'd taken off without telling anybody where they were heading because they meant to disappear. Then I figured there weren't many places they could have gone, but Tucker's cabin was one and since I'd been on the lookout for smoke and hadn't seen any—"

"I was right!" Debbie aimed her triumph at Greg. "I told you we couldn't have a fire!"

Maybe some things hadn't changed, Jenny thought.

Deaver was undeterred. "—I figured they'd be cold and most likely hungry if I was right. But I didn't want to get anybody's hopes up if I wasn't, so I figured I'd come look myself first."

"How'd they know about my cabin?"

Deaver shook his head, not in denial of Tucker's implied accusation, but in wonder at himself. "I showed it to Debbie one day we were out this direction. Mentioned how you have to go halfway round the world to get here by road, but it's not far by horse or by foot."

"It is too far," grumbled Greg. "It took us forever to get here."

"You were just scared 'cause it was getting dark."

"I was not!" The alliance had developed cracks. "And it was cold when we got here."

"You hogged all the covers."

"I did not!"

"I also mentioned," Deaver went on with grim emphasis to Debbie, "that it was private, no trespassing allowed."

She shuffled her feet, but met his look. "You said it was always open for emergencies. This was an emergency."

"There was no emergency you didn't create yourself, Deborah Barton Peters," Jenny reminded, finally advancing into the small room. Tucker closed the door and stayed by it. "You and your brother are—"

"Hold on there a second," advised Deaver. "I think I'm beginning to understand."

Jenny wished she did. "Understand what?"

"Some colts—stubborn ones, mule-headed ones—you gotta blindfold before you can put the saddle on them first time."

"What are you talking about?"

"I know," volunteered Debbie.

Jenny gave her daughter a quelling look that had no apparent effect and turned around to Tucker. "What is he talking about?"

"Old ways of breaking a young colt to saddle," Tucker answered slowly, the double groove cutting deep between his eyebrows.

Jenny waited for further explanation, but he was looking at her children. She did the same, demanding, "What does that have to do with running away, hiding out here all night, scaring us all to death?"

"You wouldn't listen to us when we said we didn't want to go back to Chicago," Debbie said. "We had to make you listen."

"And you thought this would make me change my mind? You know that isn't how things work. We're going back to the house and after we all get some sleep, I will decide on the appropriate punishment for this."

"We'll take our punishment," said Greg, a nine-year-old gunslinger declaring his readiness to die in the shoot-out at noon.

Debbie stepped to his side, earlier disputes about distance, fires and covers apparently forgotten. "We knew you'd punish us, but we figured it's worth it."

"*What's* worth it? What did you hope to accomplish?" Jenny asked, more in despair than hoping for a rational answer.

Tucker, perhaps responding to that despair, took two long strides to her side. For an instant, she thought he might put his arm around her or at least take her hand. But he simply stood beside her.

"Exactly what they did accomplish," rumbled Deaver. "To give you two something else to focus on so you'd stop shying away from each other. To make the two of you see you're being drifty." He glared at Tucker. "Especially you. So you'd open your eyes and see the saddle was already settled on your back. No amount of bucking's going to change that. And deep down, you don't want to change it."

The silence that followed was heavy with uncertainty. Jenny tried hard not to look at Tucker, but nobody else showed that reluctance. The other sets of eyes in the room stared hard at him, and her.

"Are we still going to leave, Mom?" Debbie's voice quavered, and tears spilled from her large, serious eyes.

Jenny steeled herself against folding her daughter in her arms. This was too complicated to let a ten-year-old's tears decide, even her ten-year-old's rare tears.

She cut a look at Tucker and felt something give in her heart. He stared at Debbie, thunderstruck, miserable, a strong man shaken to his foundation by Debbie's tears. And he hadn't even received the second half of her children's one-two punch.

That came when Greg, chin belligerently raised, but eyes suspiciously shiny, demanded, "Are you still leaving, Tucker?"

Tucker looked from one child to the other, and Jenny knew he loved them. If only he knew it, too.

His eyes came to her, and she had the impression he held on to that look like a lifeline. She returned it openly, steadily, hiding nothing. It was her lifeline, too.

"Your mother and I have to do some talking," he answered, not taking his eyes off Jenny.

"Then go do it and quit circling around it like a no-brain hen."

Deaver's words seemed to galvanize Tucker. Sparing a glare at the older man, he took Jenny's hand and started her toward the door.

"What? Now?"

"Yes," he answered on the far side of the door, which closed behind them with enough emphasis to have been the work of three sets of hands. "Now."

He didn't slacken speed until he escorted her into the truck. That's where he seemed to run out of steam, though. With action he was fine. Words came harder.

"There are things about me, Jenny... Things you don't know. I wish I could change them, I wish I could take back the past. But I can't, and when you know about them, you might—"

"I love you, Tucker."

He sucked in a breath and let it out slow. "You might change your mind. I could be the last guy you'd want around your kids. When it comes to being a role model for a kid, I'm the worst kind of failure, Jenny. The worst. I..." He clenched his hands around the steering wheel. "I'm responsible for a boy's death. A boy not much older than Debbie or Greg."

He waited, as if he saw that as the end of the story, as if he expected her to get out and walk away from him.

"Tell me, Tucker."

His facts matched the ones Deaver had told, but they rested amid layers of self-blame.

"Tucker, you can't keep punishing yourself for something that was no fault of yours."

"I should have known better. I should have—"

"Been perfect. I guess we all should be. But we aren't. You didn't entice that boy into drinking whiskey. You couldn't know that he'd steal your bottle. And you couldn't know he would pass out in the hot truck and how that would interact with the alcohol."

"I shouldn't have been drinking. I knew the kid watched me, admired me. Admired." He made the word a bitter accusation. "Yeah, some great role model I am."

"You are. You're a wonderful role model. I told you before, Tucker. You're honest, you look at people one by one. You respect people." She traced the twin creases between his brows, then the grooves at either side of his mouth. "You believe in the people you care about more than they believe in themselves. That's a tremendous gift. I've seen it with Greg and Debbie and Karl and Deaver. And I've seen it with me. You accepted my strength when I wasn't sure I had any." She kissed the corner of his mouth. "I can think of no one I would rather have my children grow up to be like than you, Tucker."

His eyes bored into hers, searching for doubts. "You're willing to take the risk?"

He held her away from him, studying her eyes. But she didn't mind, because that way she saw the beginning of belief enter his. She didn't fool herself. This was only a start. He'd spent too long behind those lines of his not to need time to adjust, to accept.

No, he was not an easy man, and the one Tucker Gates would always be the hardest on was himself.

But she would help.

"There's no risk with entrusting my family to you, Tucker. There never has been. The better question is if you're willing to take the risk of being a family man."

"I love you, Jenny. You, and the kids. I could leave this place, but I couldn't ever leave you all behind. What I feel would go with me wherever I went, wherever you are." He brushed his lips across her forehead. "I'd rather have you all here, where I can keep an eye on you."

"And vice versa."

A slow smile fanned the grooves around his mouth. "Very much vice versa."

He put his arm around her, bending his head to meet her open lips, with faint, promising touches of their tongues giving way to a deeper kiss. Then another.

"And you won't mind sleeping with the boss on a regular basis?"

"You mean if the boss is my wife and the basis is real regular?"

"That sounds wonderful."

He grinned at her. "Doesn't sound bad, does it? But I've got an even better idea."

"Better?"

The grin widened at her dubious tone. "How about sleeping with my wife and partner on a regular basis?"

"Partner?"

"I want to buy in on the Double Bar X. Half share."

"But that's not necessary, you'd still run—"

"It's necessary to me."

No, Tucker Gates wouldn't ever be an easy man. But he could be gentle, and he would be *her* man. Always.

"I'd be proud to have you as my partner, Tucker."

He started to enfold her in his arms. Trying to hold off her laughter and her desire as well as him, she pressed a hand against his chest and straightened her arm.

"Wait just a minute. I've got a condition, too."

"Condition? That wasn't a condition, it was just good sense. What are you shaking your head at?"

"Don't try to distract me with your arguments. Are you willing to accept my condition or not?"

"Do I get to hear this condition first?" She shook her head again. "No, I didn't think so." And for all their teasing, she knew this took some real courage on his part. Hers, too—what if he said no?

"Okay, I accept your condition. Now what is it?"

"That you show me how it's possible to make love in that wing chair. You said you almost made love to me in that chair the night you showed me the finances, and I keep looking at it and trying to figure it out...."

He whooped a shout of laughter that drew three figures out of the cabin as if they had been waiting for just such a signal. But before they arrived at the truck, he had time to make a promise, "It would be my pleasure to show you how it works."

And later that night, with the Double Bar X firmly settled as the Gates family's spread, the house quiet and the office door locked, it was very much their pleasure.

* * * * *